tragic

CHERRY GROVE SERIES, BOOK ONE

COLE LEPLEY

Cole Lepley

Tragic
Copyright © 2019 Cole Lepley

PLAYLIST

"Dead"- Madison Beer
"Somebody Else"- The 1975
"Outta My Head" – Khalid (w/John Mayer)
"Better"- Khalid
"Too Young" – Sabrina Carpenter
"Got You On My Mind" – NF
"Exchange" – Bryson Tiller
"Pretty Little Fears" – 6Lack
"Bad Idea" – Ariana Grande
"Someone You Loved" – Lewis Capaldi
"Pieces(Hushed)" – Andrew Belle
"Senorita" – Shawn Mendes and Camila Cabello
"Only" - NF

WORTH IT

Elliot

$\mathcal{I}$n three days, I turn eighteen.

I've been staring at the blades of the fan spinning on my bedroom ceiling for hours now. My mind has been racing about the future and it has me worried I'm making a mistake. I'm not sure why my impending adulthood is causing me to reconsider all of my life's choices, but it is. I turn my head and lock my gaze on exhibit A.

Judah is still sleeping beside me, his lips slightly parted with soft snores. We've been together for almost four years now, but our relationship is about to change. It's not that we've fallen out of love with each other, or even that we had a serious fight. The only thing that will be different is the distance between us. Seven hours to be exact.

I watch Judah sleep for a moment before turning on my side and moving his arm to rest on my hip. There isn't one feature of his face that I would change. From his short, dark brown hair, sculpted jaw line, and all the way down his six-foot two frame. If I could just do something about his attitude, he'd be perfect.

My hand runs through the soft stubble on his cheek, causing him to stir . After mumbling something incoherent for a moment, his honey brown eyes peek up at me. "It's too early, babe."

I lean forward with a smile and place a quick kiss on the other side of his face. "I know," I say, sitting up in the bed. "I wanted to let you know I'm going for a run."

Judah laughs and then turns his head away to cough. He sounds as rough as he looks. I'm surprised he can even speak at this point. Last night he was completely wasted—and acting like a total dick. One last party with our friends all together before half of us move on to college and the rest start senior year. To be honest, it felt like an end to a lot of things, and I'm not sure how I feel about that.

My feet hit the plush carpet, and I stand up from the bed. He stretches out, groaning as the full effects of his hangover more than likely hit him.

After pulling on a pair of track pants and tank top, I turn back to him. "You don't have to get up. I'll be back soon."

He flashes the same sexy smirk that gets me every time. "Don't be too long. I'm only home for a couple more days."

That statement makes my heart sink a little deeper in my chest. When Judah graduated at the beginning of the summer that should've been the end of us. I think there are rules about that sort of thing when it comes to high school sweethearts. But instead of breaking up, we both agreed to an open relationship when we're apart. That may seem cut and dry, but we never talked about what would happen if one of us fell in love. Is there an out clause if we do, or is this all just temporary?

So many questions are already forming in my mind, and he hasn't even left yet.

He doesn't wait for my reply before rolling over and falling back to sleep. With a sigh, I head to the adjoining bathroom to perform my daily routine before going down to the kitchen. It's barely seven in the morning, but I always get up early to run with my older brother Oliver.

The house is extremely quiet, so I try to make as little noise as possible while I begin to prepare breakfast. As an athlete, I'm not one of those girls who starves themselves to maintain a banging body. With a strict exercise routine, and being blessed with damn good genetics, I'd say most girls would kill for my figure.

As I'm reaching into the refrigerator for some eggs, I hear footsteps stomp along the hardwood floors. Ollie must be awake already.

"I'll run at least seven miles today. I know I drank a lot last night and I don't need a lecture from you," I say, not looking up. Having your brother as your track coach and personal trainer does have its drawbacks.

"It's not Oliver," Hunter remarks, his voice rough.

I stifle a laugh when I see my brother's best friend stumbling around the corner. Apparently, we all went a little hard last night.

His messy blond hair is sticking up on one side and his pale blue eyes are bloodshot. He clears his throat and leans along the large granite island in the center of the room.

"Ollie's still entertaining his company from last night, so you're stuck with me this morning."

My eyes roll to the heavens. Oliver Monroe is the embodiment of the salacious playboy. He believes that every inch of ground he walks on should be worshiped by everyone that crosses his path. If you don't believe that, you could just ask

3

him—he'll tell you. That being said, I love him and wouldn't trade him for anything. Our parents are so busy operating the ski resort we own across town that he practically raised me. That could have a lot to do with the thought process on my current situation. I can't name a single girl that would be okay with an open relationship. Especially with a quarterback that has a reputation for roaming hands.

The irritation is no doubt written all over my face. "Who's this one?" I ask in a short tone, as I turn to open the refrigerator. I pull out two bottles of water and hand one to him.

He gives me a grateful smile and takes a large swig before answering. "Molly. He had her chasing him around most of the night, so I saw it coming."

I turn away from him to make my eggs when he continues. "I slept on the couch in the guest house. Big mistake."

With a laugh, I glance over my shoulder. "Aw, you got a front row seat to the show?"

Hunter grabs an apple from the wire basket sitting on the counter, and I'm captivated as he takes a bite, juice dripping down his lips. When his tongue swipes out to catch it, I avert my eyes quickly. Hunter has always been extremely attractive to me, but I'm guessing the lack of love I'm currently feeling is starting to skew that into something weird. He's like a second brother to me—nothing more.

His deep chuckle snaps me out of it, and I reach for a saucepan. I place it on the stove and crack several eggs in before turning around to see the devastation on his face. "Yeah," he says, swallowing another bite. "I didn't fucking sleep at all."

"I can run by myself, you know. You don't need to go with me."

He smiles. "I don't mind, Elle. I like running with you."

The sincerity in his tone makes me smile back. Sometimes it's nice to have someone you can rely on.

$\sim$

*M*y lungs burn like they're on fire, and each one of my legs feel as if they weigh a thousand pounds. This doesn't stop me. Hunter is gaining on me, which only makes me push harder. If I were being honest, he's probably letting me win.

"Come on, Elle. Just a little further," Hunter pants from behind me. He barely grits the words out, so the exhaustion is taking a toll on him as well. *Good.* This is the longest we've ever run together, and if he really is letting me win, I'd hate to think I'm making it easy on him.

I steal a glance back and catch a glimpse of the sweat trickling down his sculpted, tanned torso. Quickly, I face forward, but not before seeing the hint of a smile his face. He's definitely letting me win.

Pushing through the pain, I almost collapse on the wooden rungs of the fence at the end of the road. My chest heaves in and out when I lean over, sweat pouring down the back of my neck and soaking through my sports bra. His hand clutches my shoulder, and I almost cringe away. Being this sweaty cannot be sexy—not that I care or anything.

"That was perfect, Elle. Your fastest time yet."

I nod. My mouth is so dry I'm not sure words will come out. He smiles again and hands me his water bottle.

After taking a much needed drink, I reach back and pull together the matted brown curls that have fallen from my ponytail and refasten them on top of my head. His eyes wander up my body when I stretch upward. His attention has my lips curling into another smile. I too, enjoy being wanted.

"Elliot?"

My eyes snap back to Hunter, and he laughs a little. "You cool? You seem off today."

5

I shake my head, and despite my best attempts, a few long tendrils fall from my intricate bun. "I was just thinking is all."

He rolls his hand in a *keep going* motion. "About what?"

My response is hesitant and I'm not sure why. "Summer coming to an end. Starting senior year—without Judah."

He wipes his forehead with the back of his hand and squints into the sunlight. "What's up with you two anyway? He seemed extra douchey last night."

I lean back against the fence, and I try my best to remain casual. It's too soon to be acting so needy. Judah hasn't even left yet.

"He's just trying to live it up the best he can before he goes to Ithaca next week."

"Ah, yes—Cornell. He'll be seven hours away at college. How are you going to deal with that?"

I shrug. "We have an understanding."

Hunter shoots me a skeptical look before handing the water bottle back. "Which is?"

"Don't ask, don't tell."

He laughs loudly. "Are you fucking kidding me? That's insane."

"It's makes perfect sense actually. I'm staying here for at least another year, and after that I've made it pretty clear I'm going to WVU. No reason to torture ourselves with that long-distance bullshit if we don't have to."

"And both of you are completely cool with that?"

Again, I only nod in response.

Hunter shakes his head, clearly not sold on any part of it. "That's straight up asking for trouble. One of you—*most likely him*—is going to take full advantage of that arrangement and fuck everything beyond repair." When my eyes widen, he laughs again. "You should break up now."

"If it's meant to be then it will, and if not?" I give half a shrug. "There's somebody better out there that I haven't met yet."

6

He raises an eyebrow. "Do you honestly mean that? I know you guys haven't been totally solid over the years, but you've been together a long time. This is a drastic change."

I narrow my eyes at him and push off from the fence. My stomach doesn't flip the way it did earlier when I thought about Judah being with someone else. Maybe I've come to expect it from him—or maybe I don't really care anymore. "I'm fine with it," I say.

Hunter laughs again stretching his hamstrings back with his hand and leaning forward slightly. I watch the beads of sweat trickle from his almost too long blond hair, before he reaches back and grabs the other leg.

I cross my arms. "Why are you so concerned with what I'm doing?"

Hunter scoffs. "It's ridiculous. If Judah wants to be an ass and fuck sorority girls behind your back, he should do it alone." His eyes suddenly turn darker and the muscle in jaw starts to tick. "You shouldn't let him treat you like that, Elle."

His light, blue eyes, so unlike my hazel ones, pierce me with intensity. The more penetrating his look becomes, the harder it gets to turn away from them. I give him a playful shove in an attempt to diffuse the tension I created.

"I said it's fine." He doesn't budge, so I keep going. "I'm starting school next week anyway. He's only staying for my birthday and then he's leaving for Cornell for a least a few months. His football schedule alone is packed."

"And you think that'll be enough to keep him distracted?"

His words are starting to make me angry. He's being awfully judgmental for someone who lives with a girl he barely considers his girlfriend. Honestly, I've never seen Hunter be serious with anyone period. It must be a bond he shares with my brother. There's four years between us, but I swear sometimes I think I'm more mature than he is.

I huff a humorless laugh. "I guess we'll see."

When I move toward the road again, he steps in my path.

His hand falls to my waist and I look up at him. "I'm not trying to be a dick, Elle. I'm just looking out for you." He kisses my forehead and then takes a step back. He puts one of his earbuds back in and shakes his head in disappointment. "You deserve so much better than that."

I don't even have a chance to open my mouth before he starts jogging toward the road. Hunter's always been protective of me, so I get where he's coming from. I'm not sure why this kind of behavior is acceptable to me, but it just is. I've never had a good reason to question my worth before, but Hunter's words resonate in me.

I stretch my legs quickly and take off down the path after him. When I reach the bend, Hunter is jogging leisurely along the side of the road. He waits for me to catch up and this time he doesn't race me. We run side by side the entire three miles back to the house.

My heart pounds in my chest when we finally reach the driveway. No matter how much I try to calm it, for the first time, I think it's about to break.

2

BETTER OFF

Hunter

*E*lliot Monroe is off-limits to me. I say this like a mantra while she lounges causally across the pool from me. She takes her time rubbing tanning oil down those long, sexy legs of hers, too. I'm not watching or anything. I would never do that.

Fog is starting to form in the corners of my sunglasses, so I push them further up on my nose. I lean back in the lounge chair and rest my elbow on the armrest. The beer clenched in my hand is getting warmer by the second, so I take a long drink. She looks over at me and smiles. I swallow hard and tip my bottle to her. If I'm not mistaken, I think I saw a blush on those cheeks. Maybe it's wishful thinking, but—damn, she's been looking good lately. I take that back. She's always looked good, like really smoking hot—but she's Ollie's little sister.

He's been my best friend, my ride or fucking die, for the past six years. I moved here sophomore year of high school from Texas after my parents got divorced. My relationship with my mom hasn't been the same since, so I've basically been surfing couches the entire time.

Ollie's been trying to take me in like a lost puppy ever since. I think he's lonely here in this insanely large house all by himself. His parents are almost never here and Elliot— well, Elliot's always gone, too. Or at least she was. Now that her and Judah have this bullshit agreement going on, she's been spending the majority of her time running or moping around the pool.

This is very odd for her. She's the type of girl who was constantly surrounded by friends and attention since she was old enough to bat those hazel eyes at someone. She may be a girl, but she has the swagger of a seasoned player. She flirts just by walking into a room—and pretends not to notice.

She notices alright.

She fucking loves it.

That's not the only problem. She's my best friend, too. I've been sitting up late nights with her, missing frat parties and every other fun thing college guys do, to listen to her complain about some thankless jock. I'm not complaining or anything. Being there for Elliot isn't some annoying task I've been forced to do—it's something I need to do. I care about his girls in ways I can't describe. She's so much more on the inside than she portrays on the outside, and I think I'm one of the only ones who get to see it.

I fucking love *that*.

There's nothing sexier than a fine ass girl who's also cool to hang out with. I could talk to her endlessly and never get bored. I can't count how many nights I've fallen asleep to the sound of her just breathing because she fell asleep first. If I'm being honest, that's probably the biggest reason I can never have Elliot. I genuinely respect her. So much so that keeping her from getting too close is probably the best thing I could ever do for her.

She deserves better than me—and a million fucking times better than Judah Holloway. That kid's the biggest fucking tool I've ever met. He's the walking definition of the hometown hero, quarterback peaking in high school. That's a lie actually. He's going to Cornell University to study architecture like his father. If being a football legend wasn't enough, he's also smart.

Not smart enough to keep her happy though.

"Get up, man," Ollie says from behind me.

I turn my head to see Oliver standing with his hands on his hips, a frustrated expression on his face. Oh yeah—*tennis.*

I tilt back the rest of my beer in once fast gulp and set my empty bottle on the cement patio before pushing up from the chair. "You took forever to get ready. What the fuck were you doing?"

He smiles while he stands there looking like a tennis instructor at the Country Club. I bet he ironed that shirt and everything. Scratch that—I bet he made someone iron that shirt for him.

Oliver nods toward the tennis court on the end of the property. "We're losing daylight. I haven't worked out since yesterday and I feel like fucking shit."

With a laugh, I follow him down the stone sidewalk. Ollie's fiercely competitive. If it's a sport—Ollie plays it. On and off the court.

The game starts off fairly calm, but quickly escalates into a battle. He throws the ball up in the air and cracks it in my direction at lightning speed. It flies past my face so fast, I feel the wind off of it.

"Jesus, Hunter. You're supposed to hit it back to me." He

bends down and takes a drink from his water bottle. "What's with you, man? You've been acting like a little bitch this whole week."

After chasing the ball and retrieving it, I return to the net and glare at him. "Nothing's the matter with me."

Oliver rolls his eyes and points his racket at me. "This is about a girl."

I shake my head in protest. "No, it's not."

"Yes, it is. I know you, asshole. You get all strung up when you fall in love. Which is quicker than most girls do, I might add."

"Are you saying I'm some kind of pussy?"

He smirks. "Your words, dude." When my nostrils flare, he laughs. "I'm sorry, man. Is this about Regan?"

"No," I say quickly.

"You two good?"

I shrug and my eyes drift back to the pool for a moment. When I look to Oliver again, he has a skeptical expression. I need to lie. "She's fine. I'm not sure where it's going, but I guess we're okay."

He gives me an incredulous look. "You moved in with her —after only a couple of months. Sounds pretty serious to me."

It's not actually. Sure, I like her—but it's not that deep for either of us. She needed help with rent, and I'm tired of the subtle comments my mom was making about me moving home after college. Her new boyfriend and I have never gotten along, and I'm pretty sure she's still harboring some resentment about my father. Well, that's something I'll never apologize for.

"I don't have a choice," I say finally. "Rent is expensive in town, and I'm only going to be a part time substitute up at Eastern."

"That's it?" he says, still slightly confused. Ollie would never understand what it's like to work for something. His family is stupid rich. He refuses to work with his dad in the family business and works at our old high school as a physical education teacher and girl's track coach. I'll give you one guess how he came up with that career choice.

"Okay, I may have something that will cheer you up?"

I bounce the ball with my racket. "Let's hear it."

"I might have a job for you at Central."

Now he's got my attention. "Yeah?"

"Well, you remember Mr. Young, right?"

"The English teacher with the handlebar mustache?"

He snaps his fingers. "Yep, that's the one. Aside from being really fucking weird, he just had some kind of mental breakdown. He threw a desk at a kid and everything."

I can't help but laugh. "Seriously?"

A wistful smile crosses his face. He loves a dramatic exit. "Yeah. I wish I could have seen it. I bet it was amazing."

I cock my head. "As amusing as that is, how is it supposed to make me feel better?"

"You really are dense. I can get you that job. Full time, benefits, the American dream and all that bullshit." He raises his arms triumphantly and grins.

That sounds great and all, but we only graduated a couple years ago. I never saw myself ending up back at my old school. I always wanted to do more with my teaching degree. I shrug. "I don't know. I was thinking about maybe going to grad school so I can be a college professor."

He scoffs and sets up to serve the ball again. "Fuck going back to school." He smirks at me. "Come work with me. You can be my assistant coach."

I laugh. "Why don't you just coach football?"

The question brings his racket to a halt mid-air. My eyes mindlessly drift to the scar on his knee, and I regret bringing it up. I feel like a dick. After tearing his ACL senior year, Ollie lost his ride to LSU. I'm pretty sure we accommodated for that loss during our own four years at WVU, but I think he's still bitter about what could have been. Cherry Grove is a small town in West Virginia—most people don't consider themselves to be a success if they stay here.

His arrogant smile falls, and he shrugs. "The team's going to be shit without Judah anyway. Why bother?"

Instead of laughing at his quick cover-up, the mention of that asshole's name brings my blood pressure to the point of boiling almost instantly. I grit my teeth. "Did you hear about the stunt that douchebag is pulling on your sister."

All remaining humor leaves his face. His jaw pops, and his over-protective, big brother mode kicks in. "No," he says coldly. "What did he do?"

I laugh once and drape my arms over the net between us. "He convinced her to have an open relationship while they're at school."

Oliver's brows knit together for a moment. He's probably thinking. It may take a moment for him to ravel this together.

I wait patiently for a few more seconds until he laughs causally. "So?"

Now I'm getting pissed. "So? He's going to fuck other girls at school. You know that, right?"

He bounces the ball on the court with his racket while he speaks. "She can do that, too. They both win."

I push off the net forcefully and throw my arms out. "How can you say that? You couldn't possibly want that for her."

Oliver scoffs, brushing me off. "Calm down, dude. She's too young to be serious anyway. She has one year of high school and four years of college to focus on." He bounces the ball up and catches it in his palm and then gives me a pointed look. "Elliot doesn't need to get serious with anyone."

My stomach muscles tense. That sounded more like a threat than anything. The last thing I want is to make Oliver think I want her for myself. That being said—he should know this is wrong. Not only that, but he shouldn't accept something like that for someone he loves so much.

Oliver blows out a long breath and then smiles. "Look, I'm sorry. I get that you're concerned for her, but you don't need to be." He takes a step back and pats his chest. "That's what she has me for."

I laugh for real this time. "You're not exactly the greatest role model."

He shoots me a look like my comment was absurd. "What's that supposed to mean?"

I don't say what I'm really thinking because I know Ollie. He's fucking serious right now. There isn't one person on this Earth that could possibly tell him different either. He thinks his behavior—*and attitude toward life in general*—is completely acceptable. That's the irony in all of this. Coming from Oliver—it kind of is.

"Nothing, man," I say with a laugh. The tension on his face subsides, and I take a breath. It doesn't take much to calm him down. "I'm just worried is all."

He nods. "I get that, but she's tough. She knows what she wants, and if Judah acts like an asshole, she'll break up with him. She always did before. What could possibly change now?"

That's what worries me. What's it going to take for her to see he sucks as a human being? Almost four whole years of breaking up and getting back together only to fall into the exact same pattern as before. That's kind of tragic if you ask me.

Oliver twirls his racket around obliviously, and I sigh. There's no point in arguing with him. He always finds a way to twist any situation to make himself sound right. Most of the time it actually works—but not this time.

"Fine. She's a big girl, and she can do what she wants."

"Exactly," he says with a grin. He nods to the house and

then bends his elbow to rest the racket on his shoulder. "I need a drink and then we're going out."

I groan. "Are you serious? I'm still hungover from last night."

"Me too, but it's the only way to make it feel better." He gives me a knowing smile. "You know I'm right."

I chuckle under my breath and start walking toward the sidewalk that leads up to the house. "Yeah, Ollie," I say over my shoulder. "You're always right."

A part of me wants to scream that he's delusional in thinking that she's okay. I know her well enough to know that she's really not. I'm not sure why I feel the need to protect her so much, but I do. There's something about her so precious to me, and I want it to remain pure.

No matter what I have to do.

3

CROSS MY HEART

Elliot

"This is a big deal, Elle. You're the reigning queen," Cameron Grey remarks from beside me. She doesn't look up from her lounge chair as she meticulously paints her toenails a hideous shade of red. She's been my best friend since grade school, but clearly hasn't adapted my sense of style.

I push my over-sized sunglasses on top of my head and glare over at her. "It's not a big deal." My shoulders shrug. "Besides, I don't care anymore really."

Cameron dips her brush back in the polish for a moment and then smiles to herself. "Did Judah say you weren't allowed or something because he won't be here?"

Laughter bursts from my chest. I can't believe she seriously just said that. "Are you kidding me? Judah doesn't tell me what to do."

She laughs. "Are you going to let him join a fraternity?"

This conversation is really starting to give me a headache. All I wanted to do was soak up some of the last few remaining rays of summer before Judah came over tonight. I wasn't prepared to defend what's left of my relationship.

I reach for my water bottle and take a long drink before answering. My fingers continue to twist the cap back and forth. "He can do whatever he wants. We're taking a break while he's at school."

Cameron pauses mid-stroke. "Why in the hell would you do that?" Her head pops up and she quickly sets her nail polish aside before swinging her legs around to face me in her chair. "You mean to tell me that he's allowed to cheat when he's at Cornell?"

I shake my head. "It's not like that. We're just being causal about it until we decide if it works or not."

"That makes literally no sense."

She looks horrified, and it almost makes me laugh—not that I would. A part of me knows this isn't funny, and honestly, I'm not even sure I'm completely okay with it. Judah and I have been fighting over college ever since the start of last year. I knew he was always going to go to Cornell. It's not only about football for him, it's tradition.

Since Ollie decided not to work with my parents at the resort after graduation, I have big shoes to fill. My dad, Mason, is harder on my brother than he is on me. I think he expects more from him and that's why they butt heads all of the time. It's either that or the fact that they're so much alike. They both try so hard to act like they have no idea how similar they are. Personally—I think it's hilarious.

Cameron is still anxiously awaiting a reply from me, and I don't really have one for her. The arrangement Judah and I have makes sense to me, but when I try to explain it to someone their initial reaction is always to think I'm crazy.

I take a deep breath. "Look, I know it's sounds unconventional, but you and I both know Judah can't be alone. I'd rather not have to worry about it while he's so far away from me."

She brushes her long, red hair over her shoulder and shakes her head. "But won't you still worry about it? I mean, just because you're taking some messed up break from being faithful to each other doesn't mean that you can just turn your feelings off like that." She snaps her fingers pointedly, her expression surprisingly serious.

When I remain stoic, her eyes widen, and I sputter a laugh instead. "What do you want me to tell you? We both agreed to this, and I need to see what it feels like to be without him. He's the only guy I've ever been with, and things weren't that great."

"That's ridiculous. You two are high school royalty. Everyone worships you guys."

"Yeah," I say dryly, locking eyes with her. "And high school's over."

"Not for us," she says in a small voice. I think she might actually be sad this is our last year. She scoots her chair closer to mine. "Is he even coming home to take you to Fall Festival?"

I shrug. "I don't know. I didn't ask him—I'm sure he's probably busy."

Cameron looks pensive for a moment and then she flashes a demure smile. "Okay, fine." She quickly reaches over and grabs my phone from my hand. Her hair flicks me in the face as she turns away from me.

"Hey!" I protest, reaching for it.

She types off a message as if her life depends on it and hands it back to me with a smug smile. "There. It's done."

I give her a quizzical look. "What's done?" I glance down

at my phone and read her message. I'm horrified when I get a reply from Judah.

For sure I'll take you. See you tonight babe x

"You whore!"

Cameron laughs to herself as she readjusts her chair. "Don't be so dramatic, Elle," she says mockingly.

"Great, Cam. Now he thinks I'm needy." I stand up and pull a towel around my waist before shooting her a look of irritation. "He didn't even leave yet and now it's like I'm asking him to come back. He'll think I'm weak."

Cameron gives me an incredulous look. "Elle, you are a girl, remember? You're allowed to have actual feelings. You don't always have to act like your hot brother."

I remain offended until she gets to the part about Ollie. My face scrunches up at the thought of my best friend and my brother. Just wrong.

"Ew," I say rather dramatically. She laughs, but I keep going. "Don't talk about my brother like that." I motion over my shoulder. "I'm going to get a drink. You want something?"

She shakes her head and immediately becomes engrossed in her own phone. Good. I hope she keeps her hands off of mine. The last thing I need is for Judah to think I'll be lost without him. I'm sure I'll be just fine.

At this point I need something stronger than water to get me through this day. I walk briskly over to the house and head straight for my dad's stash of booze in the butler's pantry. They're pretty much never home, and I'm almost certain Ollie is the only one who actually drinks it.

I'm standing in the hallway, tilting back a bottle of Crown, when Hunter struts around the corner. His expression is mildly amused, and he's wearing a polo shirt and khaki pants. Not exactly his typical attire.

I raise an eyebrow and lower the bottle from my lips. "Why do you look like you got a job at State Farm?"

He laughs, and his eyes light up. "What? Ollie and I were golfing at the Lodge."

I nod, taking another drink. My face scrunches up when the harsh liquor burns its way down my throat. He steps closer to me and reaches for the bottle. I hand it to him and sputter a cough. "Rough day."

"Obviously," he says before taking a drink of his own. He places the bottle back on the shelf behind me and then leans on the wall. He tilts his head to me. "What happened?"

"Nothing," I say quickly, stepping around him. He follows me of course, and I sigh when I enter the kitchen. There's a note on the counter from my mom explaining about dinner in the fridge. Unless it's a holiday, we usually don't sit down and have nightly meals together.

Hunter remains skeptical, doing that intense thing with his eyes again. I've never been able to lie to him. I sigh once more and pull the towel tighter around my waist. "Tonight, I turn eighteen."

He smiles. "Yeah, Elle. That's a big deal."

"Is it?" I say, laughing bitterly. I shoulder past him. "It doesn't feel like it to me."

He continues to shadow me, his footsteps echoing on the hardwood. I pause at the sink and place both hands on the edge, not turning around. "It's like I'm too young to feel this way." I turn to face him and cross my arms. "I already feel over all the drama and bullshit that being young entails, and I still have another year of high school. I'm not even really that sad Judah won't be here this year. How fucked up is that?" I laugh again. "Yesterday I was almost crying because I was scared to be without him and now—now I'm just numb."

I like the fact that he waits patiently for me to finish my theatrical spiel before he speaks. He gives me a polite smile, leaning on the counter next to me. "Elle, I've told you a million times—you're better than that douchebag. He was lucky to get almost four years with you and now's your chance to really find yourself this year on your own." He leans in and shakes me by my shoulders gently until I finally smile. "This is a good thing, girl."

"Maybe," I say, averting my eyes from his.

He takes a step closer and tilts his head down to me, so I have to look at him again. When he has my attention, he smiles and brushes a loose curl behind my ear. "I'll take that as a sign you'll at least try, and if it makes you sad, you know I'll always be here to talk to, right?"

I nod as a lump suddenly forms in my throat. Why can't all guys be as sweet as Hunter? He's been there for me at the drop of hat since I met him and has never made me feel like a burden to him. He genuinely cares about my feelings, and I'm pretty sure there are few people I can actually say that about. Being popular doesn't necessarily mean you are loved by all who surround you. It's quite the opposite actually. There's always sharks circling in the water just waiting for a scandal to brew.

Thankfully, I've been relatively safe in that department. Aside from the back and forth with me and Judah, I've never really done anything scandalous to tarnish my reputation. I left the building of our empire solely up to my brother. I would have to do something pretty drastic to top Ollie.

Hunter hugs me to his chest, and I sigh and bring my arms around him. I take comfort in his embrace for a moment, but then I remember I'm standing here with only a small towel over my bikini. I've worn my fair share of revealing outfits, but there's something about the way his hands feel rubbing the bare skin of my back right now. It sends shivers down to my toes, and there isn't anything intimate about what we're doing. I've hugged him a million times—fell asleep on him even, and never gave it a second thought.

Now? Now I'm kinda wishing he'd take that polo shirt off and show me what's been driving those balls all day.

My cheeks flush at the thought when he pulls back from me. God, I really am starting to sound like Ollie more and more every day. If only my typical girl emotions would stop creeping in and making me question basically everything right now. I'm filled with conflicting feelings, and I've never felt so lost.

Hunter nudges my shoulder when I remain quiet. He gives me a tentative smile this time when I look over at him. "Have fun tonight, okay? Don't think about it too hard and just enjoy your birthday with him."

Even though it surprises me that he's actually insisting I enjoy Judah's company after blatantly protesting our relationship, it makes me smile that he's saying it because he thinks it will make me happy.

I don't know the last time I felt like someone did that for me without the promise of getting something out of it in return. It makes me wonder what it would be like if I had that all of the time.

I guess it is my birthday—and I do get one wish.

~

*J*udah brings me to our favorite restaurant in town for dinner. By typical standards it would be considered more of a dive than anything, but I love it. I love the old red booths and smell of stale grease and apple pie. It's an odd combination, but weirdly comforting.

Only I'm not feeling comfortable right now. I've barely taken two bites of my burger and Judah is already shoving the last bite into his mouth. He takes a large sip of soda and then nods to my plate. "What's up?"

"Nothing," I say casually. I pick up my now lukewarm

burger and take a small bite for show. He leans back in the worn vinyl seat and raises an eyebrow.

"You're weird. What's wrong?"

When I shake my head, he leans forward and interrupts me. "I'm serious, babe. Don't tell me you're fine when clearly, you're not. You think I don't know you by now?"

He grins at me, but instead of feeling relief, my stomach flips. If he really knew me, he would know we're clearly holding onto something that's undoubtedly going to end. Most likely erupting in flames by the end of the month tops.

"I'm seriously fine," I say, flashing my brightest smile. My face falls too quickly, and he mirrors my expression.

With a deep sigh, he leans in further and pulls one of my hands across the table. After pressing it to his lips, he lets our hands rest between us. His thumb starts to move slowly across the back of my hand. "This summer went too fast, Elle. I'm upset about leaving, too."

His warm, brown eyes hold the kind of sadness I thought I felt in my heart. Yes, my heart is the part of me that's hurting, but it's not broken—it's twisted. I'm having more and more second thoughts every time I think about it. Maybe I do need to see what it's like without him. It would be nice to see what it feels like to be treated well for a change.

Even so, I still love Judah, and I'll miss him terribly. "Me, too," I whisper.

He stretches all the way across the table this time and kisses me hard. His lips linger on mine and the plates clatter beneath his weight. I'm pretty sure he put his hand in my burger. I kiss him back and wrap my arms around his neck the best I can to deepen our kiss. As our tongues start to melt together a spatter of applause begins to break out. Oh yeah—we're not alone.

I pull back as the heat rises in my cheeks. Judah of course just grins and falls back into his side of the booth. I reach over and shove him, and he laughs. He fake rubs his shoulder like I actually hurt him. "What? They enjoyed the show."

I try not to, but start laughing anyway. This is who we are. A giant ball of sexual chemistry, mixed with severely inflated egos, and a sprinkle of pride. Well, probably more than a sprinkle.

I'll never know what it feels like to have a deep, meaningful relationship if I hold onto this. I know our separation will do more good than harm. Hunter asked me to try, and I think I'll keep that promise.

4

HOUSE GUEST

Hunter

Ollie and I have been going hard the past few weeks. I think he's trying to bank it all up before school starts in a couple days. Being a teacher and a rational adult is hard for him. Alcohol and pussy seem to get him through his struggle.

It's not helping me very much. I've barely spoken to Regan in four days and haven't been home for longer than a few minutes in over a week. Our relationship is casual, but even I know this is a problem. That thought is immediately confirmed when I step inside the small apartment we share. My luggage is stacked by the door with my mail neatly piled on top. I drop my keys to the side table with a clang.

"Regan?"

I take a few steps into the living room as she is walking out from the bedroom down the short hallway. Her blonde hair is twisted into a messy bun, and she has a look of irritation on her face. She stops a few feet from me and crosses her arms. "Here for a change of clothes?"

When I open my mouth to respond, she beats me to it and motions to the front door. "I figured I'd help you out."

I sigh. "I'm sorry I've been shitty at communicating lately, but—"

She scoffs loudly. "Shitty at communicating. Is that what you call it?" Her blue eyes narrow. "You've been gone since last Sunday."

"I was with Ollie."

"Well, I think you should *stay* with Ollie," she counters.

I release a long breath and run a hand through my hair. "Wow. Okay, you're pissed."

"I'm not pissed, Hunter. I'm over it. You were all about it when we first started dating, but the moment it started to turn into something real you've been distancing yourself from me." She laughs bitterly, stepping around me. "You don't even bother to come home anymore."

Home. To be honest it never felt like a home with her. I barely know her. We rushed into this because we were both searching for something that neither one of us could provide the other. Regan longs for security and someone to take care of her, and I—well, I'm not sure what I'm searching for, but this isn't it.

"I'm sorry," I say again. It seems stupid, but I don't know what else *to* say. I don't want to lie to the girl or drag something out that was never going to be anything. All of those things considered, it still puts me in a predicament. I'm basically homeless now. *Fucking amazing.*

She's staring at me, and she must see the panic on my face because she sighs. "Look, you can stay here until you find a place. I'm not going to be a total bitch even though you kind of deserve it."

"I really am sorry," I say sincerely. I take a step toward her and surprisingly she doesn't pull back from me. She lets me hug her, and I start to feel a little bit better. "I'll be out as soon as I can."

~

Oliver convinced me to stay with him while I figure out my new living situation. He excitedly offered up the guest house and refused to take no for an answer. We've also been day drinking since about ten in the morning. By the time I start moving my belongings in from my truck, it's already getting dark outside.

It's basically an entire house if you ask me. It has a large master bedroom with an attached bathroom that has the biggest Jacuzzi tub I've ever seen. I've spent quite a few memorable nights in there. I cringe a little at the memory. I hope they clean it regularly.

The front door opens, and I turn around to see Elliot carrying an armful of sheets. She hands them to me with a smile. "Ollie's been in here—a lot."

I shake my head. "Say no more."

She flops down on the over-sized couch and tilts her head to me. "So, what do you want to do tonight?"

I raise an eyebrow. "What do you mean?"

She rolls her eyes. "I'll ignore the fact that you just insinuated you don't want to hang out with me." She walks over and playfully slaps me in the chest with the back of her hand. "You're obviously heartbroken so I'm here to cheer you up."

I laugh. "Do I look upset to you?"

She purses her lips and does a small lap around me. "Hmm. I'm not sure. You could be hiding your sorrow well."

I set the sheets down and grab her shoulders so she has to face me. "Elliot, I'm fine. This wasn't much of a surprise."

Her face falls and she wraps her arms around my neck, catching me off guard. "You poor thing. You're in denial."

My laughter shakes us both as she squeezes me tighter. Her concern for me is adorable, but completely unwarranted. "Elle, you can hang out if it would make you feel better."

She pulls back and claps her hands together in excitement. "I thought you'd say that." She bounces quickly back to her bag and pulls out an assortment of candy and popcorn. She gives a wicked grin. "I also queued up some scary movies on Netflix."

It's my turn to grin. "So—you want to Netflix and chill with me?"

She tosses a throw pillow at my head. "Don't be a perv, Hunter. I'm here for support and not the kind you're thinking of."

I hold my hands up with another chuckle. "Okay, I'm sorry."

She smiles. "Good, because I really want to see the new Rob Zombie movie and I'm too scared to watch it by myself."

I chew on the inside of my cheek so I don't respond. If she wants to cuddle in the dark with me, all she has to do is ask. Pushing that thought aside, I nod toward the bedroom and proceed to walk in and start changing Oliver's sex sheets from the bed. Elliot follows behind me and lingers in the doorway.

"You okay?" I ask over my shoulder. Her forehead scrunches up like she's confused, so I keep going. "About Judah? He left yesterday."

"Yeah, that," she says. There's a briskness to her tone, and I can't tell if it's bitter or sad. "He texted me when he got there, and I haven't really said anything back since. I think it's best if we don't talk much."

I fluff the new sheet on the bed and then glance back to her again. "Out of sight, out mind, eh?"

Elliot laughs once. "Something like that." She walks over and straightens the corner of the sheet across from me. "He'll be back for Fall Festival in about a month, so I guess we'll see how I feel until then."

I watch her motionlessly as she smooths the edges and stands to face me. By all accounts, she still looks flawless—but I can see through it. This is harder for her than she wants to admit, and I don't think it's entirely because of him. Elliot isn't used to being alone. My biggest is fear is that she'll jump into something just as shallow and damaging as she had before.

She walks over and places her hand on my shoulder, comforting *me* this time. "Are you sure you're okay?"

"Yeah, I'll be fine," I say softly. She bites her lip and I can't help myself. The air in this room is far too heavy and she is far too sweet. "There is one thing."

She runs her hand through her hair and smiles. "Anything."

I want to tell her that she should never say something like to me. My mind goes into a montage of dirty things. I brush it off with a smirk and lean into her.

"I'm kind of afraid of the dark—maybe you should stay." I press my lips together to keep my laughter inside and she punches me in the arm.

"I'll buy you a night light."

I shrug. "It was worth a try."

Instead of pretending to be fake-offended, her expression turns somewhat sad again. "You know what?" she almost whispers.

I brush the hair from her face and give a small smile. "What, sweetheart?"

Her eyes drift to the floor and she picks at the strings of

her hoodie, not meeting my eyes for a moment. When she looks at up at me, her gaze is hesitant.

"I'm actually the one that could use the company tonight." She smiles again, but I swear I can see a tear forming in the corner of her eye. "I'm just really glad you're here."

Before she can say anything else, I pull her against my chest and hug her tight. I kiss her temple and then rest my chin on the top of her head. I can't describe how it feels to have her in my arms like this. I like it. I like having her close to me, and I can't deny the new onset of fluttering in my chest. I'm all kinds of fucked up over this for so many reasons—but I don't want it to stop just yet.

"I'm glad I'm here, too."

PROMISES ARE THE SWEETEST LIES

Elliot

A stabbing in my back wakes me up out of a rather peaceful sleep. I tilt my gaze to Hunter curled up behind me. Mystery solved. My eyes drift to the television asking if we are still there. Netflix is such an asshole.

I give Hunter a nudge, and he lazily opens his eyes. I press my ass back against him, and he lets out a grunt. It takes a few moments for him to realize what he's doing to me. He inches away from me. "Sorry about that. Mornings and all."

I giggle. "Sure, it is."

I stand up from the couch and stretch my arms above my head. "Sorry I passed out."

He grins up at me. "I didn't mind."

With another laugh, I give a pointed look to his crotch. "Obviously."

He continues to eye me from his position on the couch, and I get that strange feeling in the pit of my stomach again. I try to brush it off while I search for my shoes. "Oliver is going to be pissed. He's making me run sprints this morning."

"He's such a slave driver. Why don't you just stay here, and we'll polish off the rest of season two?" He pulls the blanket back and waggles his eyebrows. "You know you want to know what happens after Blair graduates."

"If I crawl back under that blanket with you, I'll really be late."

He shrugs. "It's better than running sprints."

I laugh while I struggle to tie my left sneaker. "Maybe some other time." I give him a wink over my shoulder, and his grin widens right before I walk out of the door.

I close the door behind me and make my way across the patio where I'm intercepted by a brooding Oliver. He crosses his arms after glancing at his watch. "You're late."

"I know. I'm sorry."

He cocks his head, looking over my shoulder and then back to me. "And what were you doing in the guest house?"

I scoff. "Me and Hunter were watching horror movies, and I fell asleep."

He raises an eyebrow. "Is that all?"

I punch him in the arm, and I step past him. "Of course, douchebag. He's like my brother." That's a total lie. I've thought about Hunter a million different ways over the past week and none of them were fraternal.

I make my way quickly up to my room to change into my track pants and a tank top. My phone buzzes from my bedside table. I didn't even realize I'd left it here. I pick it up and see four missed texts from Judah. Not really what I want to deal with right now, so I click them off and scroll to my favorite playlist. I'll let the music drown out the excessive thoughts in my head—especially the ones I shouldn't be having.

~

*O*liver pushes me hard, and I actually enjoy it. He thinks he's being a dick by screaming at me to run faster, but it fuels me. I take pleasure in the fact that I'm able to surpass people's expectations. I hate to lose.

After two hours of the most grueling sprints and cardio, we finally take a break. We sit side by side on the bleachers, drinking water, in silence.

I glance over at Oliver and he really looks like he wants to say something. "Come out with it, Ollie. I know there's something super important swirling around in that brain of yours."

He folds his hands in lap and sighs. "I don't want you with Hunter."

I lean back and give him a stunned look. "Whoa. Where's this coming from?"

He rolls his eyes. "I'm not stupid. I see how you two are together." He pauses and looks over at me. "I know you, Elle. You'll break his heart and I won't have a best friend anymore."

"That's awfully judgmental of you."

"Really? I've seen you bring a six-foot-tall quarterback to his knees and not even flinch." I narrow my eyes at him, and he holds his hands up in defense. "Hey, I have no right to say anything. I'm the same way when it comes to relationships. I just don't want you to do it to him, okay?"

I shake my head. "Ollie, I would never—Hunter is important to me. I genuinely like him, and there are very few people I can say that about."

Oliver laughs. "Just make sure that *like* you feel doesn't

lead to anything more." He pauses for a moment as if he doesn't want to say anymore—but then he does. "It will destroy him."

I laugh again. "Hunter? He's pretty much a carbon copy of you. He barely has feelings himself."

Oliver lowers his voice. "You don't know everything about him, Elle. And he would kill me for talking to you about this."

A part of me wants to immediately call bullshit. I knew Ollie would have a problem with me dating any of his friends, especially Hunter. The look on his face, however, gives me pause.

"Why? What's his deal?"

Oliver closes his eyes and tents his hands around his mouth, blowing out a breath through his nose. "Elle, the games you and Judah play—he would never go for that shit."

My face scrunches up in disgust. "Games? What in the hell are you talking about?"

He turns to me on the bleachers and gives me a look like I'm an idiot. That makes me angrier. "The back and forth, making each other jealous with other people when you don't get your way. Hunter doesn't play games and he's too old for you."

I cross my arms indignantly. "Four years is not a big deal. Are you saying I'm immature?"

He laughs. "You're barely eighteen, and he's a teacher. You're on two totally different playing fields. He may only be a couple years older than you, but trust me—it would end in disaster."

I stand up from the bleachers. "Well, good thing Hunter and I are just friends. You have nothing to worry about."

"Elle," Oliver says in warning.

I cross my fingers over my heart. "Promise. Just friends, okay?"

He nods once. I'm not sure he believes me, and more importantly, I'm not sure I believe myself.

~

The steam from the shower is still clouding the mirror as I pull on a pair of black lacy panties and matching bra. Not that I have anyone to impress with them, I just always like to look cute. I have the door open slightly so the steam can escape while I do my make-up.

I prop one leg up on the counter and begin to apply floral scented lotion from my upper thigh down to my calf when the door opens wider.

Hunter does a double take and immediately covers his eyes. "Oh, I'm sorry. I was looking for towels."

This causes me to smile. "What are you so embarrassed for?"

"Um, you're practically naked."

I pull my leg down and pry his hand from his eyes. "I'm wearing more than a bikini would cover."

He looks me up and down and visibly swallows. "Nope. This is much different."

My smile morphs into something more sinister. "Then maybe you should take your shirt off and we'd be even."

He laughs once. "Elliot, what are you trying to do?"

I cross my arms. "It's only fair. You get to see me. I should get the same in return."

"You've seen me without a shirt on a million times."

Feeling suddenly bold, I stand my ground. "It shouldn't be a problem then."

Amusement flashes in his eyes before he reaches back and pulls his T-shirt over his head. He squares his shoulders in front of me, and I take in his perfectly toned six-pack. I bite my lip, and he lets out some sort of strangled grunt like the one from earlier.

"There," he says, holding his hands out to his sides. "You happy?"

The muscles in his abdomen flex and cause my stomach to clench. I cock my head to the side. "Take off your pants too."

His pale, blue eyes widen. "Are you serious?"

I shrug. "Do you see me wearing pants?"

He runs his hand roughly down his face and speaks through his hands. "Elle, I'm not sure we should be doing this."

I step closer. "Why not?"

His gaze meets mine, and my insides instantly turn liquid. "It's a bad idea."

My hands travel to the buckle of his belt. I slowly release it from the loops and let it fall to the floor with a clang. I lean in close to his ear. "The best ones always are."

My hands are still hovering over the top button of his pants when I feel him harden beneath them. I reach my hand inside and run it along the length of him and he hisses through his teeth.

"Elle—"

I ignore him and then bring my hand back up to release the button, causing his jeans to fall to his knees. He quickly kicks them aside, and I smile. "There, now we're even."

His eyes turn darker as we stand close together, half-naked in my bathroom. He tilts his head to me. "Is this what you wanted, Elle? Are you satisfied now?"

The rough tone to his voice makes my stomach flip. Am I satisfied? —absolutely not, but I literally just promised Ollie I wouldn't do this. No matter how tempting it is to push things further with Hunter, I respect his wishes. Surely, he has a good reason for wanting to keep us apart.

I give a small shrug and step past him. "For now."

I catch a look of pleasure on his face before he's completely out of view. The confidence in my voice surprises even me. I hurry into my bedroom and lock the door behind me. I'm not sure what would happen if he followed me in here, but I know it would also be a bad idea.

The screen of my phone lights up from my dresser, and I walk over to see who called. Five new texts from Judah. I skim them briefly, but don't respond. It really pisses me off he's this attentive now that we're no longer exclusive. I can't see wasting my entire senior year on someone who will probably cheat on me at the next sorority mixer.

With a sigh, I toss my phone to my bed and go in search of some clothes. I pull on a pair of cotton shorts and a tank top before stepping out onto my balcony. It goes a few minutes before I see Hunter walk across the patio to the guest house.

He put his clothes back on, but there is something hesitant about the way he moves. It's almost as if he wants to turn around—and then he does. He stops just before the door and turns back to the main house. Our eyes lock in the moonlit darkness, and I'm paralyzed. A part of me wants to run down there and tackle him into the guest house, ripping off all of his clothes in the process. The more rational part of my brain knows that will only lead to more trouble, and I want a fresh start this year.

Slowly, the corners of his lips turn up, and he shakes his head. Neither one of us says anything as he turns back around and steps inside the door. I stand there motionless and alone, holding onto a promise I'm not sure I'll be able to keep.

6

BEAUTIFUL

Hunter

I couldn't sleep last night. Thoughts of Elliot standing on her balcony clouded my mind. Even from a distance, I could see it in her eyes. The dynamic between us has shifted, and I'm not sure what to do. On one hand, Elliot is incredibly beautiful, and smart, and basically perfect—but she's also Ollie's little sister. Although we've never had *that* conversation, I'm pretty sure he would have a problem with me dating her. He flipped his shit when he found out we were running together. I can only imagine what his reaction would be if we fucked around.

Despite my reservations, I promised Elliot I would take her shopping for new shoes today. I think it's just an excuse to have a chauffeur take her shopping. I've seen how many pairs of tennis shoes she has.

I'm currently seated outside an obnoxious store, next to a mannequin dressed in a pair of swim trunks, while music blasts in my ear. The things I do for this girl. Twenty long minutes later she emerges with a smile while toting two more bags.

"Find anything good?" I ask, standing to stretch out my legs.

She scoffs. "Of course. I just need to make one last quick stop and then we can get lunch."

I internally cringe. She says this after every store we go into.

As we begin to make our way toward the escalator, I take the new set of bags from her hand and add them to the others I'm already carrying. She smiles up at me.

"I'm so happy I brought you. You're a very useful shopping partner."

Adjusting my grip on the over-stuffed paper bags, I smile back. "You know how you could show your appreciation?"

"How's that?" she asks while staring into the window of another store.

I laugh, nudging her arm. "You could feed me. We've been at this for hours. I'm starving." When she turns to finally give me her attention, I give her a pathetic face back and she laughs too.

Elliot pinches my cheek. "Aw, you poor baby. It's so exhausting walking around a mall all day." She pulls her hand back and runs it through her hair, a smirk playing on her lips. "No wonder I always run faster than you."

Throwing my head back, I let out a chuckle. "Yeah right. I let you win because I feel bad for you. Losing all the time wouldn't be good for your self-esteem."

Her eyebrow arches. "Is that so?" She moves in front of

me, looking directly into my eyes. "Care to make a friendly wager?"

"What did you have in mind?"

The smile on her face turns almost sinister. "When we go for our run later, if I win, you have to sit with me and watch a Gossip Girl marathon on Netflix tonight."

"What about if I win?"

She purses her lips for a moment and then shrugs. "Then we can just watch whatever dumb show you want to."

Although watching that show kind of sounds like torture, I'm stuck on the fact that she's already planning on hanging out with me tonight. Ever since I moved into the guest house, she's been finding more and more reasons to spend time with me. Not that I'm complaining, but the more time alone I have with Elliot, the more I feel like we're about to cross a line we shouldn't be.

Again, against my better judgment, I smile back at her. "Okay, you're on."

She claps her hands together excitedly. "You're so gonna lose." With a wink she practically skips into another store, and this time, I can't hide my smile. She's too fucking cute.

$\sim$

*T*he real reason I let Elliot win is because I get to run behind her. It's not as fun right now though because she has us running up some sort of mountain. She claims it's to get a better incline. I'm about to pass out.

Her long ponytail whips back and she shuffles on her feet and runs backwards, facing me. "Come on, we're almost to the top."

She's barely winded, and my lungs feel like they're on fire. This girl may literally kill me.

"What do I get if I make it to the top?"

She smirks as her only response and then turns back

41

around. I push through the cramp forming in my leg and pass her just before we crest the peak.

I raise my hands in victory. "Ah, that feels good. Can't win them all, Elle."

She bends at the waist and rests her hands on her knees. "You're savage."

I walk around the top of the clearing and take in the view. It's mostly obscured by towering pine trees, but there are several large rocks lining a very steep cliff. "This is cool."

She stands upright and smooths out her ponytail. "Yeah, it's quiet. Not a lot of people come up this trail."

My eyes travel down her fitted black track pants and cropped tank top. "Is that so?"

The look she gives me in return takes the air right out of my lungs again. There's something casually seductive about her eyes. She can smolder you with her stare without even trying. It must be something she was born with, because a look like that can't be taught.

She steps around me and crosses her arms, looking out over the edge. "I love coming up here. Sometimes when I run, I feel like I'm never getting anywhere. No matter how far I go, it's an empty victory." She takes a breath. "But up here, I can breathe."

I know the feeling all too well. Until I got out of my relationship with Regan, I never realized how mundane my life was becoming. I was turning into a person I never thought I would be. It's like I was settling for something easy and comfortable so I wouldn't have the urge to lose control. The fear of losing something you can't live without is what drives most people to madness. I can attest to that.

I move to stand beside her. "Is Judah still giving you shit?"

She sighs, glancing over at me briefly. "It seems like he's trying, but I don't know. We've been together for such a long time, but something feels off about us. Having him gone is really bringing a lot of clarity."

"So, maybe you made the right decision then?"

Her shoulders shrug slightly, but she doesn't look at me this time. "Do you think you did?" When I don't answer right away, she looks over at me. "With Regan, I mean. Do you miss her?"

I shove my hands in the pockets of my track pants. "Um, sure I guess I do a little. I knew she wasn't the one for me though." I meet her eyes again. "It would be cruel of me to hold on to something I knew I didn't want to have."

She smiles, dipping her head slightly. "Well, I think the next girl will be lucky to have you. Any girl would be."

The emotion her words stir inside of me is startling. Every moment I spend with her builds onto the next until I have a series of memories stacked up to play in my head on repeat. How this girl can't see that she's worth so much more than she lets herself have is beyond me.

I throw my arm over her shoulder, hugging her. She wraps her arms around my waist in return. "Same goes for you, Elle."

Placing a kiss in her hair, I rest my chin on the top of her head. I already feel lucky, and she's the reason.

~

*W*e make it back to the house a little after dark, and Oliver is seated at the breakfast bar eyeing us with suspicion. "Where were you two all day?"

Elliot walks past him and grabs a water from the fridge. "We went shopping and then went for a run." She pauses and leans back against the counter. "The better question is, where are you going? You smell like you just stepped out of an Armani ad."

Oliver smirks. "Just dinner. With Jill."

Elliot arches an eyebrow. "Don't you mean Molly?"

Now Oliver looks confused. He scratches his head. "Who's Molly?"

I almost laugh. The revolving door of girls he has around must be hard to keep track of. Poor, Ollie.

Elliot rolls her eyes. "Never mind. Have fun on your date."

Oliver scoffs. "Not a date, just dinner." He fumbles with the buttons on his shirt and Elliot bursts into laughter.

"I'm going to take a shower." She pats him on the back as she walks down the hall. Before she's out of view she turns back and shoots me a wink before disappearing up the stairs.

Oliver returns his attention back to me. "Don't be stupid," he says in a low voice.

"What are you talking about?"

He narrows his eyes at me, and I flinch.

"Okay, you need to elaborate a little further."

Oliver rolls his eyes. "I'm not an idiot. You've been spending an awful lot of time together."

I shake my head. "No, Elle and I are just friends. She's having a rough time right now, and I'm just trying to make her feel better."

"That better be all it is," he grits out.

I hold my hands up in defense. "Ollie, I swear to you. Nothing is going on."

"Don't lie to me motherfucker, I mean it." His typically calm expression is replaced by one bordering on menacing. It surprises me.

I work to keep my voice even. "I promise."

He gives me a stiff nod and grabs his keys off the counter. "I probably won't be back until late, but let's meet up tomorrow after your interview. I want to hear all about it while I kick your ass at racquetball."

"Sounds good, man. Have fun."

He laughs as he makes his way out of the door. I wait until his taillights are no longer visible before taking the stairs to Elliot's room. She's seated on her bed with her damp curls flowing around her. I knock on the open door, and lean against the frame.

"You still up for hanging out or are you too tired?"

She smiles at me, standing up. "No, I was just sitting here wondering what boring, guy show you're going to make me watch."

It's my turn to give her a wicked grin. "I guess you'll have to wait and see."

~

*T*wo hours later, I throw my hands up in disgust. "How can you be in love with this? Their relationship is total bullshit."

Elliot scoffs from her spot beside me on the couch. Her hair is wild in a messy bun, and her face is free of make-up. I've never seen her look so beautiful.

She motions dramatically to the screen. "Seriously? Chuck and Blair are the greatest couple that ever lived. Their love will carry through to generations."

I can't help myself, tilting my head back and laughing loudly. When I stop to look over at her, her expression remains serious. "Oh my God, you actually mean that. They do terrible things to each other all the while claiming everlasting devotion." I lean back into the cushion and laugh again. "It's the most toxic thing I've ever seen."

Elliot smiles wistfully, tucking her legs underneath her. "I think it's beautiful."

I want to tell her that I think she's beautiful, but I don't. Instead, I reach my hand in the popcorn bowl between us, take a handful, and then throw it at her face. "You're deluded. That's why girls today have such a poor sense of what a relationship is supposed to be like. Their minds are poisoned by crap like this."

She brushes away several stray kernels with a laugh.

45

"You're such a guy. If you watch this long enough, I bet you'll change your mind. Girls want a guy that drives them insane with rage, but makes their heart beat faster all at the same time." She moves her hand across her midsection. "That feeling in your stomach where you think you might throw up, but you also feel kind of amazing. That's when you know."

Her viewpoint intrigues me, so I press further. "When you know what?"

She shrugs. "That you found the one you can't live without."

My stare falls to her lips for a moment before drifting back up to her eyes again. "How do you know what it feels like if you never felt it before?"

Her chest rises and falls before she turns away from me and back to the screen. "I'm still waiting," she says causally.

Even though I know she's trying to come off aloof about this, I can tell that it bothers her. She's spent her whole life trying to please everyone around her, but never really took the time to make herself happy. I'm glad she's here with me. At least I know she's somewhere her presence is cherished and not made into the object of someone's desire. A prize that they never really deserved to win. If I'm really being honest, I'm glad she's here for me too. For the first time, I don't feel so alone.

7

PRETTY LITTLE FEARS

Elliot

*a*s I walk through the halls on my first day of senior year I feel a certain confidence in my step. To be honest, I pretty much always feel that way, but this year is different. I don't have Judah draped all over me all the time and I don't have to be constantly worrying if he's going to fly off the handle about someone looking at me for too long. One of the many flaws that Judah possesses is an extremely jealous temper. Major turn-off for me.

I stop at my usual locker and am immediately caught off guard by the note attached to it. I pull it off without reading it and type in my combination. Before I can stop them, dozens of roses come spilling out at me.

Cameron leans against the locker beside me, snickering to herself.

"Oh my God," I cry, bending down to retrieve the unwanted floral display.

She snatches the note from my hand, and I glare up at her. She clears her throat dramatically. "To Elle. Have a great first day. I love you—Judah." She holds her hand to her chest when she finishes.

"This is not cute, Cam," I grumble.

Cameron looks confused. "Um, yes, it is. I would die if my boyfriend showered me with flowers on my first day of class." She waves the card at me with a smirk and speaks in a sing-song voice. "And he went to the 'good' florist."

"He's not my boyfriend," I deadpan.

She crosses her arms and huffs. "You're being stupid. Just tell him that you love him, and you'll go to Cornell next year. He obviously loves you."

"This means nothing, he's just scared I'll find someone else." Frustration surges through me as I stand with an armful of red and pink roses. I almost have them all shoved in my locker when I hear a whistle from behind me. *Ollie.*

"Holy shit, Elle. Are those from Judah?" Oliver remarks.

"Yes," I say, exasperated.

He laughs. "I thought you guys were seeing other people."

"We are. He's being an idiot." I slam my locker shut and turn to face him. "What time is practice?"

"It's at four. Don't be late." He smirks to himself and then walks away toward his office.

Cameron fans herself with her hand. "Your brother is so hot. Too bad he's a teacher. I would totally…"

"Cam! Eww. Don't talk about Ollie like that."

She smiles. "Okay, sorry. But you have to admit it would be kind of hot to get it on with a teacher."

My stomach dips at her words. Hunter is a teacher. Thank God he doesn't have a job here. I don't know what I'd

48

do if I had to suffer through the temptation at home *and* at school.

With a sigh, I give her a shove toward our Ethics class. "Let's go. It's the first day and I don't want to be late."

❧

I tap my pen against my desk impatiently while I wait for my last class to let out. I've been on the fence about skipping practice today and getting drunk instead. Call it teenage rebellion if you want, but the stunt Judah pulled with the flowers is still pissing me off. Besides, Ollie is a dick for having practice on the first day of school anyway.

Dylan Andrews pokes me in the shoulder from the seat behind me. I turn my head slightly.

"What are you doing tonight, Elliot? I only have practice until six."

I turn around a little more and he flashes his crooked smile at me. He's adorable in that tasseled dark hair, blue eyes kind of way. There's also the fact that he's the new quarterback since Judah graduated. Even though he's one of Judah's closest friends, Dylan and I have history. We dated for two weeks junior year after I caught Judah texting Kelsey Thomas. He always tries to swoop back in every time Judah and I fight.

I twirl a strand of hair around my finger and pretend to look disinterested. "Hmm, I'm not sure."

"You still seeing Judah?"

I stifle a laugh. He's so predictable. That being said, if I'm really going to move on from Judah, seeing someone else is the perfect way to start. My mind then drifts to Hunter. Even though I try to hide it when I'm around him now, my feelings for him are moving in a direction very far from friendship. The only problem is, he doesn't seem to feel the same way.

Aside from snuggling and casual flirting, he hasn't made a single move further. So that only leaves me with one option —make him see what he's missing.

I shake my head, and Dylan's smile widens enough to expose the dimple in his right cheek. *Yeah, he's cute.*

I tilt my head to him. "We're exploring our options this year."

"Nice." He bites his bottom lip and leans forward toward me. "Maybe I can be one of those options?"

With a coy smile, I shrug. "We'll see."

The bell rings abruptly and we both stand. The corners of his mouth turn up, and he looks me up and down. "Do you want a ride home?"

I smile. "No. I have practice." I turn on my heel and leave him standing with his mouth half open as I quickly make my exit.

As I'm rounding the corner, I come to sudden stop when I collide with a very firm chest. My eyes travel up to an amused-looking Hunter, and he's wearing a tie. Why does he look so sexy wearing a tie?

What the fuck? School is supposed to be the one place I don't have to face the constant temptation he represents.

"What are you doing here?" I whisper.

He opens his mouth to answer me, but then Mr. Bellamy, the principal, comes up behind him. "Oh, Elliot. You know Hunter Graham, right? He graduated with your brother Oliver."

I offer my sweetest smile. "Of course. Good to see you."

Hunter grins. "You as well."

Mr. Bellamy also smiles, which isn't making any of this less awkward. "I think he'll make a good addition to our staff."

I choke on the breath of air I was trying to inhale. "Staff?"

"Yes, he'll be taking over for Mr. Young in the English department."

"How nice," I grit out, forcing another smile.

Mr. Bellamy pats him on the back on the way past. "See you Monday."

"Looking forward to it, sir," Hunter calls back. He tilts his head down at me with another mischievous grin.

"What are you smiling about?"

He tucks his hands causally in his pockets, the smirk permanently etched on his face at this point. "Nothing."

This makes me angrier, so I lower my voice. "When were you going to tell me about this?"

Hunter looks confused. "I'm telling you right now, I guess. I thought you'd be happy for me."

I clench my jaw and mask my hurt with irritation. "Well, I take honors English, so I guess I won't be seeing you."

His eyes light up. "That's my first class."

"What?!"

He laughs. "I'm sorry. I wanted to talk to you about it first, but they offered me the job on the spot, and you know how desperate I am."

How desperate *he* is? He's the one who's left me sick with desire for the last two weeks. I take a step back. He cannot be serious right now. Obviously I've been making up this whole attraction between us up in my head. I feel like an idiot—then I see Dylan still lingering at his locker down the hallway.

A wicked smile crosses my face. "See you Monday, Mr. Graham."

I turn around and walk directly to Dylan and run my hand along the letters on his jacket. "You still want to give me a ride home?"

"You know it."

He shoves the rest of his books in his locker and slings his arm around me as we start to walk toward the exit. I steal a glance over my shoulder at Hunter. Still standing in the spot

I left him in, all amusement dissolved from his face. Me: 1 Hunter: 0

≈

*I*t turns out that Dylan's an excellent kisser. That's one quality I must have forgotten about him. He's not the brightest bulb, but kissing is a good enough attribute to make up for it. And it's time that I accepted if I want to kiss someone, it's *not* going to be Hunter.

Dylan had been texting me all evening. When he showed up after practice—I just happened to be in my bikini. The vicinity of the hot tub to the guest house is approximately twenty feet. That made it the perfect place to start our evening.

His tongue dives further into my mouth and his hands begin to wander to my waist. I consider stopping him, but what's the fun in that?

"Elliot!" Oliver's voice booms loudly across the pool at me, and I jump.

"You scared the shit out of me," I say, clutching my chest.

"Where were you today? You missed practice."

I pull Dylan back toward me. "I was busy." I continue where we left off, and a growl comes from Oliver.

"If you miss again, I'm not going to let you compete this week."

I don't take my lips from Dylan's as I slowly raise my hand and flip him off.

"You're such a brat," he says in frustration before stomping back into the house.

Whatever. At least now he'll lay off me about Hunter.

Dylan pulls back a little bit. "Did I get you in trouble?"

He runs his finger along my bottom lip, and I nip at it with my teeth. "He'll get over it."

"God, you have no idea how long I've wanted you," he

says. "Judah would fucking kill me if he knew I was here with you right now, but it would be totally worth it."

I raise an eyebrow. "Is that so?"

He nods, and it makes me smile. I can't see this ever turning into something serious, but maybe that's exactly what I need right now. A causal distraction who's easy on the eyes. Besides, this is what Judah wanted, right? He doesn't get to have all the fun.

It begins to get more heated as he positions me on his lap. By the lack of clothing separating us, I can be positive where he wants this to go. They say that the best way to get over someone is to get under someone else. Or at least Ollie says that. Maybe he's not the best person to be quoting right now.

So why am I really pulling back? Why am I hesitating? Why do I already know that tonight is going to end up like usual, with me lying awake at night and thinking about stupidly hot Hunter?

I kiss him once more softly. "Let's say we call it a night."

He grips my hips firmly and presses up against me. "Are you sure?"

I laugh once, removing myself from his lap. "Yeah, I'm sure."

He runs his hand roughly through his hair. "I'm not mad or anything. I'm sure we'll have plenty of time to get to know each other more." He winks at me before he slides himself out of the water.

I do the same and glance around, only now noticing that I didn't bring towels. I motion toward the pool house. "We can get dried off in there."

He nods and follows me over. I look back to the guest house and notice Hunter's light is on. Surely he wouldn't be spying on me.

I take extra time drying off and getting dressed with Dylan in the pool house. Just long enough to make a certain someone thinks more happened than it actually did.

After walking Dylan to his truck, I make my way back over to the pool to retrieve my bag. Hunter is standing just outside the guest house, glaring at me.

Me: 2 Hunter: 0

"What are you doing?" he asks roughly.

I reach down and grab my bag, barely glancing in his direction. "What?" My casual demeanor seems to piss him off more. *Good*. If he wants to act like I don't mean anything to him, then I can too.

"Is that what you really want? Another guy like Judah to make you feel special?"

I wrap my arms around myself as I stare back at his cold expression. "What's that supposed to mean?" His question makes me defensive. He obviously thinks I'm shallow and would only want to be with someone who would look good next to me.

He lets out a dark laugh. "Judah's gone for like five minutes and already you're back in the hot tub with some stupid jock?"

"Why do you care so much?"

He shakes his head in disappointment. "Because you're better than that. You know you're just using that guy to make Judah jealous."

I narrow my eyes at him and take a step closer. "It sounds like Judah isn't the one who's jealous right now." The look on his face confirms my accusation. Disdain mixed with equal parts guilt.

His eyes widen. "Are you saying that *I'm* jealous?"

"Seems that way to me."

Hunter laughs, but it doesn't hold any humor. "Elliot, do you have any idea how hard it is for me lying next to you every night knowing that I can never touch you?"

I laugh at the absurdity of what he said. "Hunter, you literally took a job as a teacher at my high school. Do you have any idea what kind of position that puts me in?"

He glances at the pool house. "Looks like you don't have any trouble getting into whatever position you want."

I struggle to pick my jaw off the floor. "Fuck you. I can do whatever I want and so can you. I don't care." I over enunciate the last part, even though I don't really mean it.

He steps closer to me and places his hand on my arm, his voice low. "If you don't care, then why are you shaking?"

"Because you're pissing me off right now," I say through clenched teeth.

He shakes his head. "No, that's not it. You feel something for me too, and it bothers you." His body moves closer so that only inches are separating us. "You don't really like that guy."

Did he just admit that he has feelings for me? It catches me off guard so much that I don't know how to respond. So I default to indifference.

"Well, you're wrong." I try to keep my voice strong, but it too comes out shaky.

He brushes a strand of hair from my face and studies my expression. It's like he's searching for an answer to a question he didn't even ask.

"You're not as complex as you think, Elliot," he says finally. "If you want to play games, I can play them, too."

I take a step back from him. "You already are."

He scoffs. "Oh, was it me dry humping someone in the hot tub a half hour ago?"

I laugh once. "No, what you did was worse."

This time, Hunter laughs bitterly. "I didn't do anything to you."

"You didn't even ask me how I felt about you taking that job."

He looks back at me with a confused expression. "I told you they offered the job to me on the spot, and I *need* that job."

"And you couldn't have asked for a day to think about it?"

I snap back at him. "You chose this. I have to see you not only at home, but now every day at school, and there's nothing I can do about it."

"What's so bad about that?" He sounds genuinely confused and frustrated, and that just pisses me off all the more.

And now, he's asking for me to tell him how I feel, what I want. If he'd asked that a week ago, I'd have let the dam burst. But now, it feels too much like begging.

"Forget it," I say.

His eyes cast downward for a moment before looking up at me again. "I need this job, Elle. I honestly didn't even think about how it would affect you. How it would affect—us."

I swallow all the hurt and anger stirring inside me and hold back the tears burning my eyes. I refuse to let him hurt me. "Well, you don't need to think about it. Because I'm not going to think about you." The words are out of my mouth before I can stop them. I know they're hurtful, but I don't care.

I hear him take in a sharp breath as I turn to walk away. I don't turn around to see his face, but even I know that was harsh. Although I may have won this round, it still feels like I lost.

8

SELFISH

Hunter

Standing outside my new classroom on Monday morning, I take in the typical high school chaos. To be honest, I don't miss it. One of the main reasons I became an English teacher was so that I could have something to fall back on in case my writing didn't pan out. So far, I made a good choice. I haven't written shit since college.

There's still almost ten minutes before class starts, but for some reason the teachers are supposed to monitor the halls for suspicious behavior. Couples being inappropriate, harassment, violence—that sort of thing. The first thing I actually notice is Elliot sauntering toward me, hand in hand with the tool-bag from the hot tub. She's been a ghost since our confrontation outside of the guest house last week and has apparently been spending quite a bit of time with Judah 2.0.

She struts beside him like she owns the place. Actually, she kind of does. It's amazing how heads turn to watch her, people go out of their way to say hi to her. Elliot Monroe stands on a pedestal whether she wants to admit it or not. Every move she makes is thoroughly scrutinized and I'm starting to wonder if she doesn't actually mind playing into it.

They stop at what I assume is his locker, and she leans seductively beside it. My eyes travel down her tight, pink sweater and skirt so short it should be illegal. Actually, I think it kind of is. I can't torture her as the guy she can't touch, but that doesn't mean there aren't other ways to get at her.

I take a step toward them, and she gives me a smug smile before pretending to pick at her nails.

"Miss Monroe, I don't think that skirt adheres to the dress code."

She looks up at me and then down to the small strip of denim covering her ass. "Oh, sorry." I watch as she proceeds to pull it downward, further exposing her perfectly toned midriff. The gleam of the ring in her naval catches my eye and sends a chill straight to my cock. *I'm in so much fucking trouble.*

"Is that better, Mr. Graham?" she asks, interrupting my impure thoughts.

I clear my throat. "Try to be a little more conservative next time."

"Yes, sir," she replies with a smirk.

I don't care if she was trying to be sarcastic or not, I like the way she said that. I walk back toward my classroom, just as the apparent new boyfriend takes off for class. He kisses her on the cheek before leaving, which I catch out of the corner of my eye. I also notice her eyes on me, not him.

I go back to pretending to prevent teen violence when the yappy little redhead appears at her side. Cameron Grey is the epitome of the obnoxious follower. She's always at Elliot's side complimenting her and telling her how amazing she is, all the while looking for a way to take over the throne. High school girls are bitches.

"So, I hear you and Dylan are like the new 'it' couple. I can only imagine how much Judah is going to flip his shit when he finds out," Cameron remarks.

I hear Elliot let out a sigh, but I don't turn to look at her. "Judah doesn't get to decide who I can and cannot date. Especially not now."

Date? She's already dating this guy? I know she's trying to prove a point, but really, how far is she going to take this?

"Don't you think that little display of everlasting devotion he left in your locker should make you believe otherwise?"

Elliot's looking at me again, and I pretend not to notice.

"I don't care." She slams the locker shut and continues speaking in a marginally louder tone. "The things Dylan can do with his tongue are worth the fight."

I've heard enough. If she wants to play dirty, class starts in five minutes.

I enter my new classroom and take a deep breath as the students start to pile in. Where does Elliot sit? Will she sit right in front of me so I have to try not to stare at her the whole time? Or does she sit toward the back as not to be noticed?

Elliot sneaks in right as the final bell rings and takes her seat near the back. I should've called that one.

I wait for the anxious chatter to die down before I speak. "As you all know, Mr. Young had to leave us." I pause as a scattering of snickers ensues. "So, I'll be taking over for the year. My name is Mr. Graham, and my first passion is writing. After reviewing the curriculum, I wanted to pick up with one of the classics, Wuthering Heights."

I turn to grab my copy from the desk behind me. "Has anyone read it?"

Several hands raise, including Elliot's. Of course she has.

"Okay, for those of you who have read it, if you could choose one word to describe it, what would it be?"

Silence fills the room, as expected. Nobody ever wants to volunteer their opinion. Elliot ducks her head slightly, and I smile.

"Elliot, what are your thoughts?"

She peers up at me defiantly as everyone's eyes shift to her. "Well, I would say that it's tragic."

"I would agree that is a fair statement. Care to elaborate on why you think so?"

She shifts slightly in her seat. I watch the way her chest rises and falls a little too quickly. I've caught her off guard.

"Although it's not how your typical love story would end up, I also find it to be sort of beautiful. That kind of soul shattering love isn't something everyone gets to experience."

I can help but laugh once. I'm starting to see a pattern here. "Interesting. So, you find beauty in Catherine's inability to express her true feelings to Heathcliff? The idea that this drives him to madness is beautiful to you?"

She shrugs. "It's a little dramatic, but yes."

I shake my head and take several steps forward through the rows of seats. "And you don't find her to be incredibly selfish? The way she pursues him regardless of the consequences?"

Elliot's eyes narrow slightly. "I guess that's left up to interpretation, Mr. Graham."

I can tell by her expression that I've rattled her. "Okay, then." I turn to walk back to the front, but I catch the heat from her eyes on me. For the remainder of the class, every time I glance in her direction, she's looking right back.

~

*J*t's beginning to get dark outside when I'm startled by an aggressive knock on my door. I know who it is before I even get up from my seat. Elliot's angry face meets me through the glass opening as I'm approaching. She's still in her track clothes, so I'm assuming she ran extra hard at practice just waiting to confront me.

I pull the door open, and she bursts in past me.

"I knew you were going to be an asshole," she grits out. She doesn't break stride until she reaches the kitchen.

I follow her, a slightly amused expression on my face. "I'm sorry. I'm not sure what you're referring to."

She turns back to glare at me. I lean against the counter while she rummages through my refrigerator. Her hands fly out in frustration. "Where's all the fucking beer?"

I laugh. "I didn't realize it was for a special occasion."

She rolls her eyes and reaches into the freezer and pulls out a bottle of vodka. Didn't think to look there. She twists off the cap, but I take the bottle from her before she can take a drink.

Her face scrunches up as she looks at me. "You know exactly what I'm talking about. First in the hallway, then that stunt you pulled in class—now this."

I stand up straighter and hold her gaze. "I wouldn't call it a stunt. I merely asked you a question. The fact that you're taking it so personally is something you should probably ask yourself."

She nods stiffly and then reaches out and steals the bottle back. "Okay, so you're insinuating that I'm some selfish, spoiled brat who has no regard for anyone else's feelings but my own."

I shrug. "I didn't say anything. You came up with that all by yourself."

She lets out an exasperated cry. "God, you really are a dick, aren't you?"

I laugh again and the memory of her hand wrapped around my cock flashes in my mind. It was only for a moment, but it's a memory I revisit often. "As you may recall, I'm a great, big one."

Elliot throws her head back and laughs. "Oh, you think you're so cute. And you call me immature." She pauses to take a large drink, sputtering a cough afterwards. "I'm not the one who started this."

She attempts to step around me, and I take the bottle from her hand again. If she expects to have a real conversation with me about this, I prefer she does it sober. "You really believe that, don't you?"

Her face falls a little and it almost breaks me. I don't want to fight with her or make her sad. That's what I'm trying to prevent.

"We've spent almost every night together for weeks and you've never once even tried to kiss me. You know that I'm having a hard time with the whole Judah thing and when I finally do go out with another guy you make me feel like shit about it."

I set the bottle down on the counter and step closer to her, invading her space. "Regardless of what you think, Elliot —I keep boundaries with you because I have to, not because I want to." I lower my voice further. "And you and I both know you're not dating that guy because you're trying to move on."

The hurt she feels is masked with hatred, and she narrows her eyes at me. "What makes you so sure?"

"You sure as hell didn't have a problem shoving the new version of Judah in my face." My tone gets louder. Her refusal to admit she's into me is starting to make me crazy.

She crosses her arms. "How can I shove anything in your face? You and I are nothing."

"We're not nothing, Elliot." I reach for her and she takes a step back. "Whatever we are or aren't, I'm still your friend. I still care about you. And I'm not going to stand here and watch you make the same mistakes over and over again."

"What I choose to do and who I choose to date is none of your concern. You have some serious issues to work out."

I run my hand roughly over my jaw. She's infuriating when she thinks she's right. Which is pretty much all the time. "I think the fact you were so quick to retaliate is the bigger issue here. I would have never done that to you."

She folds her arms across her chest tighter. "Really? And you think what you did doesn't count as retaliation?"

She's still standing so close to me I can almost taste her. It takes everything inside of me not to throw her down on the couch and fuck her until she forgets what we're fighting about.

I lower my voice before I speak again. "I think we both had our reasons for making irrational choices in the heat of the moment. The only thing we can do now is decide who ends this fucked up stand-off."

For a brief moment, I almost think I've gotten through to her, but then she shakes her head. "Well, it's not going to be me."

She takes off for the door again and I don't move to stop her. "That's your choice, Elliot."

She pauses but doesn't turn around. "You don't always get to be the one in control, Hunter."

I take a drink of my own just as she's slamming the door shut. That's where she's wrong, but I guess I'll just have to show her.

9

LOSING CONTROL

Elliot

"No way, Elle. The last time you and your asshole friends had a party you trashed the place. I had to pay overtime for the clean-up," Oliver protests. He's pointing his spoon at me from across the table like he has some kind of authority. It almost makes me laugh.

I roll my eyes. "You don't pay for shit." I throw a grape at him and he dodges it with a smirk. "Dad has them on his payroll any way."

He pauses for a minute, holding a spoonful of oatmeal mid-air. "You know, you really do sound like a brat. I thought I raised you better than that."

This time, I do laugh as I stand up from the table. "Ollie, if the roles were reversed we wouldn't even be having this conversation. You never gave a shit what destruction you caused in high school." I place my bowl in the dishwasher and turn back to face him. "I'm having a party this weekend and you're just going to have to deal with it."

"A party, huh?" Hunter says with a smile as he strolls into the kitchen. This living arrangement is starting to get on my nerves.

I cross my arms as he shoves in front of me to grab a glass from the cabinet. "Yes, and since you're both such mature grown-ups, you'll have to find something else to do Saturday night." I give Oliver a pointed look. "That means stay away."

Oliver and Hunter exchange a mocking glance, but I continue. "Listen, our parents never go away for a whole weekend. And last time they did I was at the beach with Cameron, so I didn't even get to enjoy it." I'm borderline whining at this point, but I don't care. Oliver always gets to do whatever he wants.

Hunter pops a bagel in the toaster, and I glare at him out the corner of my eye. "Don't you have a kitchen of your own that you can eat in?" I whisper harshly at him.

He leans into me slightly. "I would, but apparently all I have is vodka."

I shift my gaze to Oliver who appears to be distracted by his phone. It doesn't take much. I'm about to reply when Hunter's hand grazes mine as he reaches for the butter. Even that small amount of physical contact is almost enough to make me want to slam him against the wall and kiss him until I can't breathe.

His eyes meet mine, and I turn to walk out of the room, apparently causing Oliver to snap out of his trance. "Hey, this conversation isn't over, Elle," he calls to me.

"We'll see," I call over my shoulder.

∼

$\mathcal{B}$y noon, the news of my party has already spread across school. I catch Oliver glaring at me from down the hall, but it only makes me smile. Not only did I invite the essential people of the senior class, but also a large amount that graduated in the last couple of years. This would include most of his friends, making it extremely amusing to me that he and Hunter cannot attend.

I'm currently wearing Dylan's letterman's jacket over my dress. It's not a fashion statement I'd typically make, but the looks I've already gotten from Hunter are worth it.

He discretely grabs my arm to stop me when I try to walk past his classroom. His features remain even as he speaks, but his words are like ice. "I think you've made your point, Elle."

"I don't know what you're talking about," I reply.

He shakes his head and opens his mouth to speak again, but then thinks better of it. Before I can react, he pulls me into his classroom and shuts the door behind us. It's supposed to be lunch period so nobody should be looking for either of us at the moment.

His hand grips my waist firmly and he backs me up against the door. He presses his forehead against mine for the longest time without saying a word. The only sound echoing through the room is his ragged breathing.

"Did you sleep with him?" he asks.

"No." Our lips almost brush together as I whisper back to him.

The tension of his hands subsides, and he pulls back to study my face. "Are you trying to make me jealous?"

"Are you?"

He laughs once, but his face is like stone. "Yes."

His admission confuses me even more. Last night he was hell bent on proving how easy it was for him to forget about me. How he didn't think twice to do something that prevented us from being together entirely.

I bring my hands forward and place them flat on his chest. His muscles tense beneath my fingers. "If I'm only your friend, what do you have to be jealous about?"

His pale, blue eyes darken—turn lustful even. I know he wants me. It's obvious in the way he looks at me, the way he makes any excuse to touch to me even when we're not alone. What I don't understand is why he refuses to do anything about it.

Hunter's gaze sears me as it travels slowly down my body and back up to my face. He balls his hands at his sides, refusing to touch me anymore. "You know I want you." He cocks his head to me. "You fucking know that."

My heart skips a beat, but I don't. "Then why did you make a decision that means that you can't."

He sighs and then leans forward again, placing his hands on the door behind me. "Maybe I did it because I needed another reason to stay away from you."

There's more than one? How many reservations can a guy have?

I take another shaky breath and struggle to keep my composure with his mouth this close to mine. "What if I don't want you to?"

His eyes squeeze shut as if he's in pain. I move my hand from his chest and glide it along until it meets his waist. I want him to tell me what he's really thinking. Trying to figure him out is impossible.

He leans back a little and cups the sides of my face forcing me to look at him. "Does it turn you on to make me jealous?" He tilts his head, studying me closely. "Huh? Is that all this is to you—a game?"

I shake my head. "No."

His hands travel down my body as well, one of them slipping through my jacket and landing on my ass. He gives it a firm squeeze and pulls me against him.

"Are you upset that you got to touch me, and I never returned the favor?"

My pulse is in my throat while I flashback at my attempt to seduce him in my bathroom. I'm not sure what came over me, but I wanted him. I've never let myself give in to temptation like that before. But I don't regret it.

Hunter is still waiting for me to respond, and I don't know what to say. The air is too thick is this room. It's too quiet with only the sounds of our sporadic breathing.

"I don't want you to be jealous," I say finally. I look up into his eyes and he's watching me. Waiting for me to say what he wants to hear. Every guy is like that. They want to know that they have some kind of power over you, and I don't want to give it to him.

He moves one of his hands to my face again and holds my stare. "Then what do you want?"

The words get caught in my throat. I want to tell him what I'm really feeling so badly it hurts. On the other hand, the thought of his imminent rejection stops me from doing that.

"I don't know," I say instead.

He appears thoughtful for a moment, staring down at my lips. I hold my breath until he does something I don't expect —he kisses me. *Hard*. His lips crush against mine with a desperation that I thought only I felt. My hands grasp at his shirt, and I try to pull him even closer, but then he stops.

He pulls back from me and the expression on his face hardens, his eyes turn darker. "Go to class, Elliot."

Unexpected tears burn my eyes as I blindly fumble for the doorknob, but his features don't change. I manage to keep my composure while taking unsteady steps down the hallway to cafeteria.

Regardless of how I feel right now, I wanted him to kiss

me. He's not afraid to push the limits with me, and I like it. I need it. The effect Hunter has on me is staggering which only makes me want to fight harder.

I spot Dylan at our usual table in the back of the crowded room. I'm only ten minutes late, but it feels like everyone is watching me while I walk over to sit beside him. He smiles at me, and I release a breath I didn't realize I was holding. At least my face doesn't give away what my heart is feeling right now.

"Hey, where were you?" he asks.

I tuck a strand of hair behind my ear and force a smile back. "Ollie needed to talk to me about something." Seems plausible.

He nods. "You hungry? I can get you something." He motions with his head back to the near empty line.

My stomach clenches, and I let out an involuntary laugh. "No, not at all."

Because of who we are, whether we want to be or not—we're together. I didn't choose to start something with Dylan, he chose me. That's just the way it works around here. People expect this to be my most logical step after ending things with Judah. It's not what I want though. I want to be with the one who takes every bit of my air every time he kisses me. I want him to make my lungs burn until he does it again. The one who makes me feel beautiful and it has nothing do with how I look on the outside. He knows the real me and for the first time—I feel like that's okay.

~

I've been hiding in my bedroom since I got home from practice. Risking a run-in with Hunter is not something I can handle right now. He upped the stakes today, and I'm not sure what my next move is yet—or if I should even have one. He's not like Judah. The things we've done to each other wouldn't fly with a guy like Hunter. Maybe I should just swallow my pride this time and surrender? Tell him how I really feel instead of prolonging this torture.

After another thirty minutes of deep contemplation, I stand up from my bed and walk out to the balcony that overlooks the pool. I have a direct view to the guest house and can clearly see the light visible in the living room.

"Fuck it," I say out loud as I turn to go back inside. I take determined steps down the stairs with the full intention of ending this charade.

Just as I'm walking out of the side door, a car pulls up the driveway. I don't recognize it, so I stand with my arms folded across my chest and wait. My breath hitches in my throat when Regan exits the car.

She slings her bag over her shoulder and walks toward me with a bright smile plastered on her face. "Oh hey, Elliot. I was looking for Hunter. He said he's staying here."

"Yes, he is."

The words sound foreign coming from my mouth. I'm so caught off guard to see her standing here after he kissed me like that today. I know he was angry when I couldn't answer his question, but I never thought he would give up altogether.

She nods behind me. "Is he in there or—"

I swallow the lump in my throat and point across the patio. "He's in the guest house."

She offers another smile before walking past me. I take a step back closer to the garage door and watch as he opens his door. I can't hear what they're saying, but I don't have to. He pulls her into a hug, and she wraps her arms around his neck.

That sick feeling returns to the pit of my stomach, but I don't look away. I continue to watch as he motions her inside, and I swear I see him smile.

He may have won this round, but he just declared war.

BLAME IT ON ME

Hunter

I know exactly what it looked like to have Regan come over last night. Technically it wasn't even my idea. She called and asked if she could drop off a few of my things that I left there. We talked for a while, but that was about it. Nothing happened—although I'd bet anything Elliot thinks it did. Serves her right.

I sat up waiting for Elliot to turn the light off in her bedroom, but she never did. She either didn't sleep or she wasn't really in there. I can't be sure so I'm currently waiting to ambush her run this morning.

If I'm being honest, I might have gone too far yesterday. I guess it has a lot to do with Ollie's influence on her. She doesn't act like most girls, but I'm starting to think her tough exterior has its cracks. No matter what she does to try and hurt me I still want her. There's something between us that I can't really explain. It's real and honest and we don't need to play games in order to prove we should be together. I know we should—I just don't know how.

I'm beginning to wonder if she's even going to run today when I spot her slip out of the side door. Her long ponytail is hanging out of a baseball cap and she is actually fully dressed in a hoodie and track pants. It's still sexy even if she isn't trying to be.

She rolls her eyes when I jog over to meet her.

"Oliver coming with you today?"

"No."

"Can I come with you?"

She laughs once as she bends to stretch her leg. "Don't you have company to entertain?"

I shake my head. "She wasn't here for me—it's not like you think." I shove my hands in my pockets, suddenly feeling nervous. The anger coming off of her is radiating in waves so intense I'm half afraid she'll burn me.

Elliot continues to ignore me and stands up straight to put her earbuds in. "Like I said, I don't think about you at all. So, why would I care?"

She turns to walk away from me, and I pull the strings from her ears. "That's not true and you know it."

For a moment I think she's going to respond but then she takes off running down the driveway. I follow her of course.

We make it almost an entire mile and she still hasn't attempted to put her earbuds back in or say anything to me at all.

"Can we talk about this?" I ask as I keep stride with her.

She glances over at me quickly and then back to the road.

I sigh. "Okay, fine. I'll talk." I take a breath. "I'm sorry."

She lets out a huff but doesn't slow her pace, so I

continue. "This isn't fun for me, Elliot. We don't need to keep hurting each other."

It feels like she's running faster because my chest keeps getting tighter. "Say something," I demand forcefully.

"What you did last night—was bullshit," she spits out finally.

"What I did? What about what you've been doing with Dylan?"

She rolls her eyes again, and I want to scream. "Nothing even happened between me and Regan. I had to watch you make out with that guy for over an hour in the fucking hot tub."

She laughs once. "I didn't make you watch. You chose to do that all on your own."

"It was right outside my window, Elliot. Like I had a fucking choice."

"It's my house." She makes a quick turn up another hill and then continues. "I can do whatever I want."

She's such a brat. "So it's okay for you to hurt me, but when I do it right back then I'm the bad guy?"

I get no response this time, and I'm starting to get a cramp in my side. "Can you please just stop for a minute so we can talk about this? I can't keep running at this pace and have a conversation with you."

Elliot smirks. "Maybe you should work on your stamina."

I have a pretty good comeback ready when she begins to pull ahead of me. Breathing hard, I come to a stop and plant my hands on my hips and watch her disappear around the corner. I'm almost positive if I don't quit chasing her, she may never stop running.

e're almost through the entire class period and Elliot hasn't looked at me once. I know this because I've been looking at her almost the whole time. If I was going to be a dick, I could have called on her and made her talk to me, but I decide to leave her alone for a minute.

When the bell rings, I watch her shuffle her things together to make a quick escape. I'm not sure what comes over me, but I move to stand in front of her. "Elliot, could I see you for a moment?" I use my teacher voice, and I can tell she wants to roll her eyes.

"Alright," she says.

I wait until the few remaining students exit the room before I try to talk to her. She beats me to it. "Hunter, I don't have time for this right now. I have a test to get to."

She attempts to step around me, and I place my hand gently on her elbow. "Just give me a minute, okay?"

I see the tension in her stance as she nervously readjusts her bag over her shoulder and nods.

"Did I upset you yesterday?"

She raises an eyebrow. "Which part of yesterday are you referring to? The part where you manipulated me into thinking you actually wanted me or the part where you shoved your ex-girlfriend in my face?"

I swallow back the anger I feel from her insistence on never taking responsibility for her own actions. I lower my voice even further. "I'm talking about what happened in my classroom."

A bitter smile crosses her face. "That was the only part of yesterday I actually liked."

She tries to step around me, and I block her path. "I meant what I said this morning. We don't have to keep doing this."

74

She laughs. "If you really wanted this to end, you wouldn't have acted like a complete asshole yesterday."

I run my hand roughly through my hair. "What do you want me to do, Elliot? I'm trying to throw the flag here."

Her eyes cast downward for a moment before she answers. "It's too late for that." She pushes past me before I have a chance to stop her just as my next class begins to trickle in.

If I'm going to get her to stop, it looks like I'll have to take it up another notch.

~

I sit on the bleachers after school and watch Oliver yell at his team like an asshole. He loves attention even more than Elliot does, especially when he gets to act like a dick.

"That was pathetic," he calls through his hands. "Run it again!"

A series of grunts echoes over from several girls running laps on the track, and I fight a smile. Oliver walks over to me throwing his hands up. "Geez, these girls think they can just phone it in today or what?" He looks at the time on his stopwatch again and groans.

He takes a seat next to me and I laugh. "Don't you think you're being a little hard on them?"

He scoffs. "No, they love it. Girls respond best to aggression." He winks at me, and I laugh.

"If you say so."

It doesn't go unnoticed that Elliot isn't on the field. I'm about to ask him where she is when she comes jogging around the corner still pulling her hair into a ponytail.

Oliver stands. "Whoa, whoa!" he calls to her. "Do you just make your own rules now? Practice started twenty minutes ago."

Elliot shoots him a look as she begins to stretch. "I had a committee meeting. It was mandatory."

"I don't give a shit, Elle. You've been late all week. Now go run hurdles." He points to the track, and she narrows her eyes at him.

"You're joking?" she says with a huff.

"Nope. You want to be late, I'm going to treat you like everyone else." He blows his whistle at her, and I almost laugh again. "Get moving!"

She flips him off before reluctantly heading toward the track. I catch her glare in my direction for a moment, obviously not thrilled that I'm here.

Oliver shakes his head as he sits down again. "I don't know what's with her lately. She's always been difficult, but never like this."

I have a few guesses.

"I don't know, man."

My eyes drift back to the field where she takes her mark. Elliot takes off and makes it look fairly effortless until she trips on one of the hurdles. It goes three more before she stumbles again.

"What was that?" Oliver calls to her as he stalks back down the bleachers. "Get your head out of your ass."

She plants her hands on her hips as she breathes in and out harshly. "I'm sorry," she pants.

"Don't give me sorry, do it right. Run it again and if you trip over one more hurdle, I'll make you run sprints until you puke."

Now this kind of treatment would typically make most girls cry, but not Elliot. She gets a determined look on her face before heading back to the start. This time she doesn't miss a beat and breezes down the track.

Oliver claps his hands together. "That's what I'm talking about." He walks over and puts his hand on her shoulder. "See, now was that so hard?"

She shrugs him off. "Why are you being such a prick today?"

He lowers his voice, pulling her off to the side of the track. "Elle, what the fuck? You never fall."

I watch her eyes squeeze shut for a moment, and I can tell she's trying not to cry now. Oliver's face falls immediately. "Jesus, Elle. What's going on?"

She shakes her head. "Nothing."

"You're such a shitty liar. Now, tell me." He shifts right out of his dickhead coach persona into protective brother mode. "Is someone messing with you? You know I'll fucking kill them if they are."

Her eyes drift to me for a moment, and I swallow hard. The last thing I want is for Oliver to find out about this and murder me for it.

It goes another couple of beats before she finally answers. "No."

He lets out a frustrated sigh and pulls her into his side, hugging her against him. "Just go home today, alright? Relax or something and we can pick this up tomorrow."

Surprisingly she doesn't argue and walks slowly back to the locker room. The fact that her behavior has caught the attention of Oliver now has me worried. Even though I pushed her into this, I can't stand to sit back and watch her fall.

BREAKING RANKS

Elliot

I watch with disinterest as Cameron smears an excessive amount of make-up on her face. She really does try too hard. She eyes me through the mirror while I lounge casually on my bed, periodically scrolling through Instagram. I really should tell her, but I don't. We've always had a strangely competitive friendship.

"What's your problem today? You're about to have a party in like half an hour."

I shrug. "Nothing."

"Are you and Dylan not getting along?" She pouts her lips together after applying a questionable shade of lip gloss. I really should be a better friend and point these things out to her.

With a sigh I stand and walk over to my closet. "He's fine. I'm just not really that into him."

She looks at me like I'm crazy. "What more do you need, Elle? Practically everyone wants to date him and of course, he picked you."

I arch an eyebrow. "Was that sarcasm I detect?"

She rolls her eyes before going back to caking on another layer of mascara. "Seriously, you're never grateful for anything. You acted the same way with Judah."

I narrow my eyes at her. "Judah acted like a dick most of the time."

"Then why did you date him for years?"

I toss another dress to the floor after contemplating changing for the third time. "I don't know. It was easy I guess." I pause and chew on the tip of my fingernail for a moment. "We got along just fine and it never really went that deep."

Cameron laughs. "That deep, huh? I would say your sexual chemistry was pretty strong."

I roll my eyes. "Yeah, that's about all it was."

"So?"

"Don't you want more than that? A real connection with someone that actually means something."

She shrugs. "As long as he's hot I don't really care."

And I thought I was shallow.

∾

*A*n hour later, my backyard is filled to capacity. It's getting into late September, but the air is still warm enough for a few drunken idiots to swim around in my pool. I side step past a couple practically having sex on one of my lounge chairs and walk toward Dylan. He grins over at me, and I suddenly feel guilty. He's an innocent casualty in all this. I really should set him free before this goes too far.

He throws his arm around my shoulder and kisses the side of my head. "Hey, I was wondering where you got to."

I plaster a smile on my face because this is a party and I'm supposed to be having fun, right?

"I had to make my rounds. Say hi to everyone and make sure nobody drowned yet. You know, the usual."

"I hear that." He tilts his beer back while my eyes continue to scan around the party. Oliver is no doubt lurking around somewhere, although he's yet to be seen. He said that he and Hunter were going to the bar downtown, but he has a habit of popping up when you least expect him. It bothers him to no end that he can't go to parties anymore now that he's a teacher—and I love throwing it in his face. Both of them seriously need to grow up.

I'm starting to catch a nice buzz when a commotion over by the garages gets my attention. I walk away from Dylan to the crowd that has formed. As I get closer my heart drops when I see Judah's smiling face in the middle of it. This is the last thing I want to deal with right now.

He spots me almost immediately and pushes quickly through the group of guys surrounding him to get to me. "Babe!" He pulls me up into his arms and squeezes the air from my lungs. "God, I missed you."

I laugh nervously as I pull myself from his grasp. "Judah, what are you doing here?" I cross my arms to put some distance between us.

His eyebrows pull in. "I heard you were having a party."

"So, you just decided to drive seven hours to come to a party?"

He reaches out and touches my arm. "No, I wanted to see you."

"I thought the point of you leaving was that we wouldn't see each other."

Hurt flashes in his eyes, and I feel a pang of sympathy for him. Even though I don't completely believe his intentions are pure, this is the most he's tried in the entire time since we were together.

His jaw twitches slightly, and he leans in closer to me. "Elle, I heard you were fucking around with Andrews. I can't let you do that."

There it is. I reach my hand out and shove him back a little. "You'll never change, will you?" I release a bitter laugh. "I knew as soon as I started to see someone else, you'd be pissed."

I turn to walk away from him, and he spins me back around. "It's not about that." His voice is louder than I would like and the small crowd that formed around him is now an even larger one around us.

I throw my hands up. "Then what's it about, Judah? Ever since you left you've been acting like we were this epic love and that is so far from the truth."

"How can you say that?" he whispers.

"Because it's true."

I feel someone come up behind me, and I turn my head to see Dylan glaring over top of me. At this point I'm wishing for the ground to open up and swallow me whole.

"Leave her alone. She obviously doesn't want you here," Dylan grits out at him.

Judah clenches and unclenches his fist, and I take a breath. "Really, Andrews? You wanna go there?"

Dylan steps in front of me and gets inches from his face. "Yeah, I wanna go there." He pokes him in the chest. "You can't just show up and stake claim to her anytime you feel threatened. You left."

Judah lets out a dark laugh. "I'm not going to stand around and let her date a douchebag like you."

Seriously? *Let me.* I'm extremely tired of every guy in my life telling me what I should and shouldn't be doing. I step forward to intervene, but then take one back when Judah gives Dylan a forceful shove in the shoulder.

Dylan's face turns red and his eyes narrow. "She should be used to it." He leans in and gets closer to Judah's face. "She did date you after all."

Judah laughs again and some taunting cheers go through the crowd around us. They're both about the same height and have the same drunken testosterone running through their veins. Not a good combination.

Judah gets that cocky smirk on his face, and I know he's about to lose it. "That's your problem. You wish you could be me." He glances over Dylan's shoulder and locks eyes with me for a second before focusing his anger back on him. "— but you never will. Not even close."

I bring my hand up to cover my mouth, and my pulse begins to quicken. They're really going to do this, aren't they?

Dylan shoves Judah in the chest, and he stumbles backwards. Judah pops his jaw with his hand, his laugh more sinister. "You're going to regret that."

I'm about to try to stop them again when Oliver shows up out of nowhere and pulls Judah back by his collar. "Okay, pissing contest is over boys."

Judah shrugs him off, and Oliver laughs darkly as he leans into him. "You don't want to fucking start with me. I promise it won't end well for you."

Judah clenches his teeth but backs off. I almost breathe a sigh relief until Dylan unexpectedly takes a swing. *What the fuck?*

Dramatic cries ring out from the circle, and they start up all over again. Oliver gets back in the middle of them just as Hunter comes up behind me. He gives me a look of disapproval before stepping around and grabbing Dylan from Judah's grasp.

"Alright, that's enough!" Oliver yells over them. "Party's fucking over. Everybody go get alcohol poisoning somewhere else tonight."

Cries of disappointment echo through the crowd, and

Oliver waves them off. "That's right, I'm an asshole," he says with an amused expression while they stumble past him.

"I'm not leaving," Judah declares, crossing his arms.

I give a helpless look to Dylan and he shakes his head. "Alright, I get it." His lips press into a hard line, and I reach for his hand.

"I'm really sorry, Dylan."

He squeezes it once and then pulls back. "I'm sorry, too." As bad as I feel for him right now, I let him walk away. He's probably sorry he got involved in our drama in the first place. He doesn't deserve to be dragged into this anymore.

Oliver squeezes Judah on the shoulder with excessive force. "You gonna be cool now, dickhead?"

"Yeah, I'm cool."

Oliver gives a stiff nod. "Okay, then." He turns to me. "Are you okay?"

Hunter remains silent even though his eyes blaze over at me. I keep my focus on Oliver and give him a nod. "I'm fine."

"Clean this shit up," he says to me before patting Hunter on the back. "Let's go, man."

I see the hesitation on Hunter's face as Judah staggers closer to me. He holds my stare for what seems like forever before he reluctantly follows Oliver inside.

"Elle?" Judah says, pulling me out of my temporary trance. For the first time since he got here I take in how drunk he is. I reach out and place my hands on his waist while he struggles to stay upright.

"You can't keep doing this. You can't do whatever you want at school and then come home and freak out because I'm doing the same thing."

He takes a step back from me and straightens his stance. He runs his hands through his hair and lets out a long breath. "I know. I'm fucking sorry, I just can't help it." He shakes his head. "I don't want you to be with someone else. Especially one of my friends."

83

"This was your idea." I throw my arms out and then let them fall to my sides.

He steps closer, his voice low. "I think it was a mistake."

"You're right. We probably should have broken up completely."

His eyebrows furrow, and he shakes his head. "No, Elle." He steps closer to me. "That's not what I meant. I think this arrangement was a mistake."

The anguish in his eyes brings me pause. I know it's not just the alcohol talking, and I do feel bad for him, but something is holding me back. The ache that's been slowly building in my chest isn't because of Judah.

I take a deep breath. "I don't think it was."

Judah stays quiet for a moment, the muscle in his jaw slowly ticking. I hold my breath when he finally speaks.

"Do you want me to go?"

Considering that he's still somewhat swaying in front of me, I know that I can't ask him to do that.

"I can't let you drive like this."

His eyes are remorseful when they meet mine again. "You'll let me stay?"

I sigh. "I don't have much of a choice, do I?" I poke my finger into his chest. "You will sleep here and that's it. In the morning you're gone."

He nods quickly. "Just sleep."

I shake my head and then begin to drag him toward the house. I somehow manage to get him up the stairs with minimal complications. When we reach my bedroom he practically falls onto my bed.

"I'm sorry, Elle. I'll show you," he mutters and then curls himself against my pillow.

I clasp my hands on top of my head, and my frustration hits it's breaking point. "I'll get you some water. You're really going to feel like shit tomorrow."

His voice is muffled when he speaks again, facedown, and

no doubt slobbering, on my pillow. "You're so good to me, babe. I love you so much."

Huffing a bitter laugh, I step outside of the room and run directly into Hunter. He pokes his head over my shoulder and lets out a growl. "You can't be serious?"

The fact that he thinks I plan on sleeping with Judah is almost amusing, but I take advantage of it anyway. "That's none of your business."

He shakes his head. "You're better than this, Elle." The pleading look in his eyes almost takes my breath away, but I fight through it.

"Maybe I'm not."

His jaw hardens as he stares back at me, whispering harshly through his teeth. "Elliot, I am fucking begging you. Do not do this."

Even though it feels like my heart may physically break, I force a hard smile. "I'm calling it, Hunter. Game over."

It takes everything inside of me to step back from him and close the door in his face. That's the thing about war— the higher the stakes, the harder you fall.

LIFE LESSONS FROM OLIVER MONROE

Hunter

The basketball echoes loudly against the pavement, directly into my brain. It's the only thing I hear while I stare at Judah's truck still parked in the driveway. Oliver waves his hands in front of my face, catching my attention.

"Dude, you gonna shoot that ball or what?" he cries.

I grit my teeth and launch the ball toward the basket. It circles fast around the rim and bounces back at Oliver, and he laughs. "You fucking suck, man." He chuckles to himself while he jogs over to retrieve it. "You know, Hunter. For someone who used to play a lot of sports, you're pretty bad at them lately."

He dribbles past me and goes in for a perfect lay-up. "I

didn't play basketball. I played soccer, asshole."

He smirks, passing the ball back to me. "That's your problem. Soccer is for pussies."

I narrow my eyes, attempting to dribble around him, but he blocks me. "Come on, tough guy. Show me what you got." He moves quickly back and forth on his feet, taunting me. *Competitive motherfucker.*

I let out a growl, darting around him and shoot from the three-point line. I release a string of profanities when it bounces off the backboard and down the driveway. Oliver shakes his head before chasing after it.

My chest begins to burn again, and I can feel my cheeks getting redder as the heat rises up my neck.

"Calm down, man. It's just a game," Oliver remarks nonchalantly as he shoots another one, making it of course.

I run both hands through my hair, taking a calming breath. "I'm just off today."

"It's cool. Normal people have off days all the time." He winks at me before sinking another perfect three-point shot. "Not everyone can be awesome like me."

"Dude?"

"What?" he says with a laugh. He points his finger at me while he continues to dribble with the other hand. "That's your problem. You lack confidence."

"Fuck you, Ollie. I do not."

He nods his head mockingly. "Yeah, you do. You're too inside your head all the time. You need to relax and just let things happen." He proceeds to dribble the ball in and out of his legs in a figure eight. Now he's just showing off.

I glance down the driveway again and my nostrils flare. "What's he still fucking doing here, anyway?"

Oliver's eyebrows pull in, and he begins to dribble a little slower. "Who? Judah?"

My stomach drops when I realize my mistake. The wave

of emotions I've been feeling since last night are becoming increasingly harder to control.

He eyes me carefully. "Why do you care if he's still here?"

I attempt to shrug casually. "I don't. I just—he was such a dick last night I can't believe she let him stay here."

"Eh, he's always like that. Pretty sure she's used to it by now."

"Why do girls think that shit is acceptable? Like it's supposed to be normal or something."

Oliver smiles. "That's how girls are. It's like a twisted game that they get off on trying to tame you." He launches the ball to my chest, and I catch it. "Trust me, I should know."

I scoff. "Don't you ever want an actual relationship or are you just going to slut yourself through life?"

"Aw, Hunter. Are you jealous of all the mad game I have?" He steals the ball from me, and I let out a frustrated grunt. He dribbles it just out of my reach as he speaks. "I'm going to let you in on a little secret my friend. The way to set yourself up for a stress-free life."

His ego is about the explode. "Enlighten me."

"Glad you asked." He pulls his free hand into his chest. "Take my job for instance. I'm a physical education teacher. I'm talking dodgeball and shit." He leans into me. "It doesn't get any easier than that."

I nod. "Okay, so far I'll give you that."

He holds up a finger. "Second, I coach track. Running is like the easiest sport ever. A complete idiot couldn't fuck that up."

I actually laugh. He's beyond ridiculous right now. But once again, he has me laughing instead of breaking everything in the guest house, so I'm happy to have him.

He tosses the ball into the grass and grips my shoulder. "You need to get laid. I'm taking you out tonight."

I shake my head. "No, I'm not up for that."

He cocks his head. "Haven't you been listening to me at

all. I'm trying to help you." He throws his arm over my shoulder and begins to lead us back to the house. "And if I'm going to help you, you need to do what I tell you." He releases me with a shove, and I glare at him.

"Maybe it doesn't work that way for me."

His face falls a little, and I know exactly what he's thinking about. He grips the back of his neck. "Listen, man. I know you've got your shit to deal with still, and I want you to know that I'm here if you want to talk about it." He holds his hands up and gives a crooked smile. "I won't call you a pussy or anything, I promise."

My jaw tenses. "I don't want to talk about it."

"Okay, I get it. But I also know I'm the only one here that knows what you're going through." He pauses. "So, if you ever do want to talk about it. I'm here."

I nod slowly as my hand grasps the doorknob. I'm about to push it open when it's pulled forward for me.

Judah stumbles slightly and gives a lazy grin back at me. "Hey, sorry man. Rough night."

His bloodshot eyes still have a slight twinkle to them, and I struggle not to break his jaw. "It's cool," I say tersely.

He nods to Oliver. "Sorry about last night. You know how it is."

"Yeah, but I'm not sure how much longer Elle is going to put up with your shit. You're treading water my friend."

I close my eyes for a moment as the pounding inside my brain intensifies. It makes me incredibly angry that Oliver is so chill with him. If he only knew what I was thinking right now.

Judah shrugs. "We fight, we make up, typical Elliot. She'll be over it soon and on to the next fucking thing to bitch about."

God, I want to kill him right now. I bite the inside of my cheek until the metallic taste begins to fill my mouth.

"I'll see you next week, brother," Judah says patting Oliver on the back on his way past.

Oliver raises an eyebrow. "You coming back so soon? Gonna be racking the miles at this rate."

Judah laughs. "Yeah, but it's for Fall Festival. Gotta see my girl be crowned queen one last time."

I breathe forcefully through my nose and keep my jaw clamped shut. So, she is going to take him? Although, I worry it's not part of the game anymore. Maybe I pushed her too far, and she decided to give him a second chance? That thought alone makes my blood boil.

Judah finally pulls down the driveway, and I nudge Oliver. "Why do you let him talk about her like that?"

Oliver looks confused. Not a surprise, but it still pisses me off how oblivious he is sometimes. He shrugs. "He talks shit. Most of the time I think it's for other people's benefit to keep up some tough guy image or whatnot."

"It's still bullshit."

"Yeah," he says. "It is, but they're not serious. It's high school puppy love that's already starting to fade. A couple more months and I'll bet he won't even bother to come home anymore."

Oliver may seem confident about that, but I'm not so sure. He seems determined to prevent her from moving on with anyone, and I'll bet that he's a couple of months away from coming home for good. Maybe I'm just fighting the inevitable. For all I know Elliot could be thinking the exact same thing. Judah might be end game for her and everyone else is disposable.

"Second thought," I say suddenly. "You're right. Let's go out tonight, I need to let off some steam."

He smiles. "I'll knew you'd come around."

∿

The harsh morning light glares through my window and I roll over to shield my eyes. My face lands in something soft—and it's not a pillow. A seductive smile peers back at me from a blonde-haired stranger.

I roll onto my back and pinch the bridge of my nose as the events of last night come flooding back to me in a rush. The bar, doing shots with Oliver, making out with this blonde, more shots with Oliver, the Uber ride home— My stomach lurches when I spy the condom wrapper at the foot of the bed. *Fuck!*

"Sorry I stayed," she says and then she sits up and stretches her arms above her head. "Shit got pretty crazy last night, and I passed out." She turns and runs a finger down my chest. "You're something else, Hunter Graham. Surprising coming from you. You seem so gentle outside of the bedroom."

I laugh once. "I guess I'm full of surprises."

She leans down and kisses my cheek before pushing off the bed. "You sure are. Call me if you want to do it again sometime."

I watch her get dressed, resting my hands behind my head. I'm not going to call her; I can't even believe I let myself sleep with her in the first place. I promised myself that no matter what Elliot did, I wouldn't stoop to her level. And here I am, no better than she is. Maybe we deserve each other after all?

My new friend leaves a few minutes later, and I stumble my way through a shower. I'm thankful it's Sunday and I don't have to be subjected to seeing Elliot if I don't want to. I'll just avoid her at all costs until I have to face it tomorrow morning. My plan is out the window when I enter the living room in only a pair of sweatpants. Elliot is sitting on my couch, eyeing me with suspicion.

I swallow hard, taking in the anger in her eyes.

"What are you doing here?"

She keeps glaring at me with a hatred so harsh her hazel eyes look like they're on fire. "When I heard you were going out with Ollie, I assumed you'd be back quick. Ollie usually finds a distraction and bails on his wingman—but I never thought the one who needed the distraction would be you."

Instantly I feel like the biggest dick ever, but I'm pretty sure she's a fucking hypocrite right now.

I smile. "So, you can sleep with Judah and that's perfectly fine, but I'm to remain celibate for some reason."

She stands up to face me and crosses her arms. "First of all, I did not sleep with Judah. I slept next to him, there's a difference."

When I roll my eyes, she continues holding up a finger. "Second, you're the one always preaching about treating girls the way that they should be treated and yet you're perfectly okay with having a one-night stand with a girl you don't even know."

I shrug. "Your brother does it all the time."

Elliot laughs. "Oh, he's your hero, eh? You wanna be like Ollie?" She takes a step closer. "How many actual relationships has he been in?"

I pause, trying to think of just one. When it goes too long, she laughs again.

"There isn't any. He can't commit to anyone, and that's okay, but it's certainly not how I want to live my life anymore."

I reach for her, but she pulls back. "Elle, I'm sorry."

She shakes her head, tears pooling in the corners of her eyes that I know she won't let fall.

"It doesn't matter. This whole thing was a mistake." She grabs her bag and heads for the door quickly. I move to stand in front of her.

I place my hands gently on her waist. "Elle, what was a mistake?"

"Being friends with you. I can't anymore."

It feels like I just got punched in the balls. "You can't be serious. We were always friends."

She takes a step back, out of my arms. "Not anymore. From now on when you see me, you look the other way. Talk to me in class if you have to, but that's it."

I lower my voice. "You don't mean that."

Her breath hitches in her throat and she hurries toward the door again. Hurting Elliot is something I never wanted to do. Playing games and acting irrational is dangerous. Especially when you might be in love with the person you're trying to beat. .

13

THE POWER OF SILENCE

Elliot

*O*liver enters the kitchen with a smirk. "Good morning." He holds his arms out dramatically before making his way to the fridge.

I shoot him a look. "What are you in such a good mood for?"

He shrugs before taking a large bite of an apple and speaking with his mouth full. "Can't a person be genuinely happy?" I narrow my eyes at him, and he laughs. "Apparently not." He makes his way to the table with a handful of questionable breakfast choices. "Did you get your car back from the shop yet?"

"No, it won't be done until tomorrow. Why?"

"I have to leave early today so if you need a ride, you'll

94

have to get one with Hunter," he says causally while browsing the paper.

Goosebumps prickle down my spine when he says his name. "I'd rather fucking walk," I mutter under my breath.

He lets out a whistle, looking up at me. "Whoa. What'd he do to you?"

My cheeks flush. I can't believe I said that out loud. "Nothing," I say quickly. "I'm just feeling off today, I guess."

Oliver laughs. "That's funny because he said the same thing. Maybe you two can go be miserable together."

I pour myself a much needed cup of coffee and ignore his comment. He looks over at me and grins again.

"What?" I ask, slightly irritated.

"Well, we went out Saturday night so he might be feeling a little better now if you know what I mean." He waggles his eyebrows at me, and I think I may be sick. I know exactly what happened during their guy's night out. The only problem is—I have no right to be upset about it.

"Oliver, I don't fucking care. I'll get a ride with Cameron."

He shakes his head. "Geez, Elle. You're so moody lately. I can tell you're back together with Judah."

My mouth drops open. "I'm not back with Judah. Who told you that?"

"Um, Judah basically did. He said he was coming home next weekend to take you to that dance when me and Hunter were playing basketball."

That explains why Hunter went out with Ollie. I guess that means he tagged himself back into the game.

~

*C*ameron stands beside my locker shifting around on her feet. Knowing her, it's because she has something to say that she doesn't think I will like. It's nothing new, but I don't have time for her drama right now. I have more important things to worry about.

"What's up?" I ask as I dig around for my notebook.

She shakes her head, staring down at the strands of hair she has pulled between her fingers. "Nothing."

"It's not nothing. Just tell me."

I hear her sigh. "Well, since you're not going to Fall Festival with Dylan anymore I was thinking—"

Her voice trails off and I laugh, standing up and closing my locker. "You can go with him, Cam. I don't care."

Her eyes widen when they meet mine. "Seriously?"

"Yeah, why would I?"

"Because you two just broke up."

I laugh again, although none of this is amusing to me. "It's not a big deal. I don't even want to really go with Judah, but his impromptu appearance at my party left me with few options."

Cameron lowers her eyes again, and I'm seriously starting to get a migraine. "Did you tell Judah I was having a party?"

She doesn't look up at me.

I throw my hands up. "Cam! Why would you do that? You know how he is."

"I'm sorry, okay." Her pale green eyes are pleading when she finally looks at me. "He was on the group text I sent. It was too late by the time I realized."

Honestly, I don't really believe her. It makes sense that she would want to sabotage me and Dylan after that comment she made before the party. What she doesn't realize, is that it caused this war between me and Hunter to escalate further. I'm not even sure what we're fighting about at this point, but I refuse to let him win.

I take a breath. "Alright. I don't care how it happened, it's done, and there's nothing we can do about it now." I throw my bag over my shoulder and turn to walk to class.

She doesn't follow me, and I'm glad because I'm on my

way to sit through forty-five minutes worth of glares from Hunter. Not how I wanted to start my Monday. That's a lie. I already miss his face so much I can barely stand it.

By the time I walk into the room most of the people are already there. Hunter is standing at the front talking to one of my classmates with a smile on his face. He doesn't turn to look at me, and it strikes me as odd. He always does.

I don't realize how long I'm standing here, and not moving, until his voice snaps me back to reality. "Elliot, is there something you need?" The bored tone of his voice makes my stomach flip—and not in a good way.

I look up at his expectant expression and everyone else's as well. My eyes meet his briefly before I shake my head and walk back to my seat. He remains casual as he walks around his desk to grab a paper, like he didn't even notice me.

"Okay, I was very pleased by everyone's essays from last week," he begins. I watch him walk back to the front of his desk and lean against it. "It seems you've all got a good understanding of the important plot points. That will serve you well for the midterm in a couple weeks."

A series of groans goes around the room, and he laughs. I hate the way his stupid, perfect hair falls into his eyes when he laughs.

He continues speaking but I can't hear him anymore. It would appear I'm paying attention to every word of his lecture, but I'm just watching him. I watch the way his eyes light up when he gets excited about a certain topic. The way I can still see the outline of his perfectly sculpted biceps when he bends his arm to write something on the board. Most importantly, I watch the way he never looks at me, not even once.

~

Typically, I'm not the type of girl who sits around and cries, but tonight I can't help it. I've been curled up on the couch since practice let out watching sappy chick flicks while spontaneously bursting into tears. My parents are working late as usual, so I don't need to worry about controlling my sadness from anyone—except for Ollie, but I haven't seen him either.

I'm in the middle of a particularly emotional outburst when Oliver strolls in out of nowhere. He's casually dressed in an old T-shirt and jeans, which makes me think he wasn't out doing anything too important. His face shifts from the typical mildly amused expression he walks through life with, to distressed as soon as he sees me. "Elle? Are you okay?"

He quickens his pace over and takes in the balled-up tissues thrown around. "Jesus, are you having some sort of breakdown?"

I shake my head but don't answer when another sob threatens to escape.

His expression remains skeptical. He stares down at me until recognition crosses his face. "Oh! Do you like need some chocolate or something? Would that make you feel better?"

I roll my eyes and throw a tissue at him. His face scrunches up in a disgust and he dodges it. "No, that's not why I'm crying."

He runs his hand along his jaw for a second and then shifts to anger. "Did Judah do something? Do I need to drive down to Ithaca and break his legs?"

"No, it's not Judah," I choke out.

He throws his arms up and then plants then on hips. "I'm running out of ideas, Elle. You're going to have to help me out here."

I shift on the couch, drawing my legs in closer to me. "It's nothing, Ollie. I'm fine."

"You're not fine. I've never seen you like this, and it's freaking me the fuck out." He bends down closer. "You have to tell me so I can fix it."

"You can't fix it," I say in a whisper.

Oliver scoffs at me. "Elle, did you forget who you're talking to? I can fix anything."

I almost smile a little as I shake my head. "Not this."

He lets out a sigh before grabbing a throw pillow and flopping down on the chair beside me.

I raise an eyebrow and sniff once. "What are you doing?"

"Well, I'm going to sit here and watch this stupid movie with you until you either feel better or decide to talk to me." He turns to me with a serious expression. "—and you know how much I hate *The Notebook* so I'm hoping that happens sometime soon."

I start to laugh, and he smiles. "I'm just kidding, Elle. Take your time. Rachel McAdams is fucking hot."

As much as I still feel like crying, Ollie always has a weird way of making me feel better. There's no way I could ever tell him about Hunter. He would probably kill him if he knew that's why I was so upset. Even though that would be an easy way to end the game, that's not what I really want.

Being ignored today by Hunter hurt worse than anything up until this point. A part of me thinks he knows that. The only thing worse than not being wanted, is not being thought of at all.

14

ATTENTION

Hunter

I couldn't sleep last night. All I could think about was how difficult it was to keep my eyes away from Elliot for an entire class period. If it had lasted even one second longer I would have broken. Even though I never glanced in her direction, I could sense her presence everywhere. It's always like that when she's in the room. I felt physically ill when the bell finally rang.

Today is worse. She never came at all. I know for an absolute fact that Elliot is serious about attendance, so it's a rare occasion when she doesn't show. Although it may seem like a bad idea, I can't help but go to Oliver's office after class. I need to know that she's okay even if it draws attention to me.

As I'm about to step inside his doorway, a small orange basketball flies at my face. I barely have time to catch it before it lands straight into my nose.

Oliver laughs loudly and then stands up from his chair. "Nice catch, man. Where were those reflexes the other day?" He grabs the ball from my hands and motions to the basketball hoop nailed above his door. "I've been working on the logistics, but I haven't got it down yet."

He bends and moves the small garbage can underneath it over a few inches. He holds up a finger before quickly moving back to his chair and shooting again. This time he sinks the shot and it lands perfectly in the can below. His arms fly up in victory. "Finally! That took me all morning to get right."

I laugh, retrieving the ball and passing it back to him. "I'm glad your morning was productive."

He bounces the ball on his desk and smirks. "It's a hard job, but somebody's got to do it."

I grip the back of my neck nervously and then take the seat in front of him. "Is Elliot okay?" I ask the question quickly before I get a chance to change my mind.

His smile fades almost immediately and the sick feeling in my stomach intensifies. "I don't know, man. She was so upset last night she wouldn't even talk about it." He pauses for a moment, appearing to be deep in thought. "I mean, she usually tells me everything. I hate the fact that I can't help her."

I struggle to swallow the lump that forms in my throat. I have to keep the conversation going even though I'm positive it's because of me. "What do you think it is?"

After another moment of contemplation, I see his neck twitch and his expression turns darker. "I don't know, but I can promise you one thing. If I find out some fucking guy is messing with her..." His voice trails off, and he clenches his fist. "I'll beat him within an inch of his life—and then I'll make him fucking apologize for it."

I nod slowly. "Yeah, man. I'm with you there." It's more than a struggle to keep my voice even but somehow, I manage.

~

*B*y the next day, Elliot's name is all I hear in the hallway. Rumors about her health have caught like wildfire and everyone speculates about where she's been. Some of them even started up a collection in her name. After all, how can a kingdom run without its queen?

My personal favorite is that she ran off with Judah and is currently spending the week at Cornell. If I didn't live twenty feet away from her, I would have drove down there to see for myself.

By noon I've talked myself out of faking sick for the rest of the day to go home and see if she's okay. The sight of her strolling down the hall after lunch period quite literally takes my breath away. By typical Elliot standards, she looks flawless, but her eyes seem somewhat hollow to me. Her smile isn't as bright as it usually is, and it kills me.

I watch groups of people flock to her and inquire about her absence. She effortlessly brushes it off with a laugh as if all is well. I can't keep my eyes off of her even though I know I need to walk away. She never glances in my direction even though I'm only about ten feet away from her. I guess I kind of deserve that.

When the warning bell rings, I can't stop myself from walking over to her when everyone begins to hurry to class. She drapes her bag over her shoulder and turns to face me. "I'm sorry I missed class. I'll make up whatever assignments I have, okay?"

Her eyes are desolate when she looks up at me. I shove

my hands in my pockets to keep from reaching from her. I want to comfort her and take away every ounce of sadness I caused—but I can't.

"I don't care about that Elle and you know it."

"Then what do you care about?"

I glance around the hall quickly and then back to her. "*You*," I whisper fiercely.

She rolls her eyes. "Really? Because I think you made it perfectly clear you don't."

"I'm only doing what you asked."

She laughs bitterly. "You act like this is so easy for you."

"It's not fucking easy for me," I growl almost too loudly. Despite the apprehension I feel about having this conversation here I lean in a little closer, lowering my voice again. "Elliot, you have no idea what I've been going through these past few days. I'm not sure how much longer I can do this."

Her eyes scan my face for a moment before she responds. "You know, that might actually mean something to me if I believed you."

If my classroom wasn't full right now, I'd drag her in and show her how much I really mean it. I can't get the words out fast enough before she slips past me. "Better get to class, Mr. Graham."

I take in a breath and count to ten before I slowly make my way to my next class.

～

*O*liver decides he's in the mood for pizza tonight and convinces me to come to the main house to join him. I know the real reason is because he wants to get the enormous one that is cut into square pieces. He says they taste better that way. I don't have the heart to tell him otherwise.

"So, my father asked me about finding some seasonal help

for the lodge this winter. It seems he lost a lot of the college students from last year," Oliver says after taking an exceptionally large bite.

"I could ask around," I suggest and then reach for another slice.

He nods while he continues to chew. "I think Elliot is going to work up there. She said she needs a distraction." He shakes his head. "Her life is pretty perfect to me, so I don't know what she'd need to escape from."

I pause to take a drink from my water so I don't choke. I know exactly what she wants to escape from. "Maybe I could help out, too. I don't really have much to do on the weekends, and I should probably do something to show my gratitude for having a roof over my head."

"Dude, he doesn't care. I'm basically the only one who ever stayed over there, and it wasn't for sleeping." He winks at me, and I cringe. No matter how many times I change the sheets, that thought will always cross my mind.

He shrugs. "Fuck it. I could go up there, too. We could run the lifts and check out the ski bunnies that are only in town for the weekend."

"Sounds like an activity you might enjoy."

He shoots me a look. "You used to enjoy shit like that too. I'm seriously getting concerned for your manhood. You're acting really out of character lately."

The only way out of this is to feign innocence. "You're right, man. I'm so done with relationships. Bring on the lonely housewives on vacation."

He raises his hand. "That's what I'm talking about. Finally!"

I don't leave him hanging and return his high five just as Elliot walks into the kitchen. She doesn't show her face for days and chooses this particular moment to emerge. *Perfect.*

The look of abhorrence on her face confirms she heard

the latter part of our conversation. She pours herself a drink while pretending to ignore us.

Oliver nods to her. "Elle, we got some pizza if you're hungry. The good kind." He holds his slice up dramatically to demonstrate. "See, square."

A smile cracks on her face, and she nods. "It tastes better that way."

He shoves me in the shoulder. "Told ya, dickhead. I'm not the only one."

I just shake my head and then take another bite. Elliot surprisingly sits across from me, and I involuntarily hold my breath. I have to remind myself to exhale before I pass out.

"So," Oliver says tossing a slice on her plate. "You ready for the dance on Friday? All the little bitches in my third period class were speculating if you'd be overthrown today. It seems Cameron's been campaigning pretty hard."

Elliot wrinkles her nose. "Whatever. I honestly don't care if she does. Who wants to sit on a float all summer anyway?"

Oliver's eyes widen. "Are you serious, Elle? You fucking hate to lose."

She shrugs nonchalantly before locking her eyes on me. "Some things just aren't worth fighting for anymore."

My jaw clenches and I fight the urge to break her stare. She knows damn well I can't say anything right now. A smug smile crosses my face when I suddenly get an idea. "That's a shame, Elle," I say, cocking my head slightly. "I somehow got talked into chaperoning that dance, and I would hate see a bitch like Cameron win."

"Truth, man," Oliver chimes in, between bites. He shoves the rest of his slice into his mouth. "She really is a dick."

I can almost see the color begin to drain from Elliot's face as she forces another bite. If she thinks she can hide from me, I'll just have to be everywhere she is.

"Well, I'm sure Judah would be upset if I didn't win. He's been really supportive lately."

My blood pressure begins to rise just from the sound of his name escaping her lips. I have to hand it to her, she recovers quickly when backed into a corner. I'll just have to make sure the next time I do it, she has nowhere to

15

BE CAREFUL WHAT YOU WISH FOR

Elliot

*H*unter's conversation with Ollie yesterday really pissed me off. Either he was putting on a show for my brother's benefit, or he's not the guy I thought he was. Judah is another story. The dance is only a couple of days away, and I kind of feel like we're at a crossroads. We can't continue to go on like this without making a decision. Do I take him back completely or end things once and for all? After sitting on my patio for several hours, I'm no closer to a resolution.

The light in the guest house is off, and I haven't seen Hunter since I got home from practice. I'm not sure why it bothers me that I don't know where he is, but it does. Having him here is comforting and frustrating at the same time. I like him always being available to me, but ever since we started this war, things haven't been the same. I miss my friend. I miss the person I could talk to about anything and never have to worry about being judged by him.

The truth is, I don't really feel close to anyone. Cameron is technically my best friend, but her motives aren't always clear. Sometimes I swear she hopes for me to fail so she can be better than me at something. Ollie has always been my go-to person for basically anything. The only problem is, I can't talk to him about Hunter and it kills me. Sure, he would most likely get over it after freaking out for a minute, but then he would say 'I told you so' because it turned out exactly the way he said it would. A disaster.

I'm about to give up and go inside when I hear footsteps behind me. I turn my head to see Hunter walking over from the guest house. He must have been home after all. I turn back to the pool, dangling my feet in the water.

He sighs and then sits down beside me. He doesn't say anything for a minute, and my heart starts to beat faster until he does. Out of the corner of my eye, I watch him roll his pant legs up and slip his feet in the water next to mine.

"Are you okay?"

His voice is soft, and when I look over at him, his eyes are filled with sincerity. I can't remember the last time I looked in them and saw something other than anger or disappointment.

I shake my head. "No, I'm not." He bites his lip, but doesn't respond, so I keep going. "Are you?"

After a moment, he looks at me again and shakes his head.

I take a shaky breath. "I miss you."

When a tear starts to fall from my eye, he catches it with his thumb. He leans in and kisses me on the cheek, cradling my face with his hand. "I miss you, too."

"Then why are we fighting?" I whisper.

He shakes his head again. "I don't even know anymore, but I hate it." He brings his hand down and rests it on my leg. My stomach clenches at his touch. It never used to be that way. We used to hug and touch each other all the time and it was playful—it didn't mean anything. Now it feels like it does.

Even though I'm afraid to, I reach my hand over and lace my fingers through his. When I look up at him, he's staring down at our hands, and I'm terrified he's going to pull away. But he doesn't. He gently runs his thumb across the back of my hand instead.

"Hunter, I'm not sure what's going on between us, but I can't live with us being nothing." He looks up at me at my words, but I don't stop. "And maybe I understand your reasoning for not wanting to be together." I pause and take a deep breath. "That's why I might give Judah another chance."

The muscle is his jaw ticks, but he doesn't say anything. Slowly, he pulls his hand back and runs it through his hair. "Judah, huh? You think things will be different this time?"

I shrug. "I don't know, but I feel like he deserves a second chance."

He stares off across the pool, avoiding my eyes. "If you think he's changed, then maybe you should."

My eyebrows pull in. "Really? You're not going to tell me what a huge mistake I'm making and how much my life is going to suck if I do?"

Hunter laughs and it eases the heaviness building in my chest. "Elle, I was never trying to make you feel like you can't make your own decisions." He reaches over and tucks my hair behind my ear, speaking close to my face. "All I want is for you to be with someone who treats you the way you deserve."

I find myself staring at his lips. If he leans forward anymore, they would be touching mine. Before I can contemplate that for too long, he pulls back and stands up from the pool deck.

He tugs on the sleeve of my T-shirt. "Come on," he says, nodding back to the guest house. "I need to find out what happened to Chuck and Blair. I don't like it when she's with Nate."

With a laugh of my own, I stand as well. "You know, for someone who claims to hate my favorite show, you sure know a lot of details."

Hunter shrugs, his eyes lighting up with amusement. "I can't help it. They're growing on me I guess."

I bite my lip so I don't say, 'I told you so'—but it doesn't stop me from thinking it.

~

*T*he decision to watch TV on his bed was mine. Even though we made this friend pact pretty clear, I still enjoy testing his willpower. I'm lying on my stomach with my feet crossed behind me. The shorts I have on are smaller than most underwear I own. He can't see my T-shirt at the moment—but there isn't much to it.

I catch a heady glance in my direction from time to time that he tries to play off and fails. When another episode ends, he sighs dramatically.

He sits up from his position on the bed and rakes his hands through his messy blond hair. It's sticking up on one side from laying on the pillow, and I find it absolutely adorable.

"I don't think I can take much more of the back and forth between these two. It's exhausting."

I roll over to my side, exposing my bare midriff. His eyes follow right where I want them to. "There are still two seasons left. Plenty more time for drama."

He laughs. "For someone who claims to avoid drama, you

sure like watching it." He motions toward the paused screen. "Why can't they just be together? They obviously want you to believe they have this tragic, can't-live-without-each-other, type of love, and yet every time they get close, something happens, and they just—don't." He lifts his hands up and drops them to the bed with another sigh.

"That's the thrill isn't? Will they, won't they? It keeps everyone entertained." I wiggle my fingers at him, expecting a laugh, but he doesn't give me one.

Instead, his expression turns darker when he looks down at me. I almost cringe. "I won't live my life that way. If I want something, I'm going to make sure they know it."

I trace the pattern on the comforter we're laying on with my finger, not meeting his eyes. "Is that so?" I look up and lock eyes with him. "For some reason, I don't believe you."

Without so much as a warning, he shoves me onto my back and pins my arms above my head. My heart starts to beat so fast I can barely catch my breath.

His voice is rough when he speaks. "Is this what you want? You want me to fuck you right here in this bed—because I want to."

"What's stopping you?" My voice barely makes it out in a whisper and his chest rises and falls sporadically against me.

He keeps my hands locked behind my head, but removes one to trail a finger down my cheek to my lips.

"This mouth," he breathes. "I think about how perfect your lips are. How soft they would be against mine." He leans forward and nips my bottom lip with his teeth and almost growls his next response. "How much I want them wrapped around my cock."

My insides instantly turn liquid, and I involuntarily thrust my hips up against his erection. He obviously finds me attractive. Maybe he just wants me for his own sexual pleasure? Pushing things further, I pull one of my hands free and slip it down the front of his sweatpants.

He hisses when I touch his skin and I slowly run my hand up and down the length of him.

"Don't do that," he says harshly.

I tilt my head to him. "Why not?"

He leans down and speaks close to my lips. "If you need a release, I'll give you one—but I can't have sex with you."

I stop my movements and pull my hand back. "That doesn't make any sense."

He smiles. "It makes perfect sense. I can please you and walk away, but if I get inside of you, that's it. I won't allow another man to touch you and we both know what's at stake here."

My eyes cast away from him. Every time we get close to intimacy that would actually mean something, he pulls back. Fooling around is one thing, but Hunter is making it very clear that I'm not the type of girl he wants around for the long haul.

I feel him watching me and his finger hooks my chin. Slowly, I look up at him through my lashes. "Talk to me, Elle. Tell me what you want."

That's a loaded question, and I'm not entirely sure what he's really asking. Does he want to know what my heart is feeling or my body?

My body decides quicker, and I grab his hand, pushing it down to the part of me that has the deepest need right now. He leans in and kisses my neck while sliding his hand into the waistband of my shorts. His fingers graze across my panties and I'm already clawing at his back, almost begging him to continue. He kisses a path back to my lips and his mouth hovers above mine.

"I want to taste you." He kisses me once and then swipes his tongue inside my mouth. He pulls back after another slow, lingering kiss. "Is that okay?"

The smile I give is forced. I know that what he's about to do will feel amazing physically, but emotionally—I'm not so sure. I want Hunter to want me for me, not because he thinks I'd be banging in bed. Despite all of that, I nod anyway.

I keep my reservations to myself as he lowers my shorts and positions himself between my legs. My uncertainty starts to melt away when his tongue makes small circles in my most sensitive areas. I try to imagine that he actually loves me. When I run my hands through his hair, I picture him telling me that between kisses as he licks his way up my center.

He looks up at me suddenly, and I meet his gaze. "A little taste is enough for me to know what I can't have, Elle." He licks me once more. "And you're so fucking sweet."

I push my conflicting thoughts away as the pressure between my legs builds faster. My hands grip the comforter, and he moves on top of me so I scream my release into his mouth. It's been building for so long and happens so fast that I barely have a chance to really enjoy it. It's an empty victory for me. Being this way with him puts us no closer to what I really want, and I know that. He basically admitted to me that he thinks I'm manipulative and never really serious when it comes to relationships.

He works his fingers inside of me for a moment longer until I come down, kissing me softly.

"You feel better, Elle?" he asks pressing his forehead against the side of my head, his breathing labored.

I've never had anyone make me feel like a whore, but right now, I do. I mean nothing to him. I'm just his friend who occasionally spends the night. At the end of the day, all of the flirting, the causal kisses—mean nothing. One day he'll find someone his own age that will pique his interest and he'll be gone.

All I do is nod. That's all I can do. If I tried to speak, I might cry and then he'd be really confused. The simple fact is —I think I'm falling in love with him.

16

SURRENDER

Elliot

The dance started twenty minutes ago, and we're still standing in the parking lot. Judah is passing around a flask while reminiscing the old times with our usual crew. Typically, I don't mind being late and making an entrance, but for some reason I'm annoyed by it. My mind keeps drifting to Hunter and the fact he's inside right now probably looking amazing in a suit and tie. My mind takes that image to a dirty place, and I find myself distracted.

Judah grabs me by the waist and pulls me over to him. "Babe, I'm so glad you decided to let me come with you. This is going to be a great night."

I force a smile, and he leans in to kiss me. I keep it brief because I've been trying to be cautious about getting his hopes up. Even though Judah is a dick, there's been something different about him lately. A part of me wishes he would have been like this when we were dating. Who knows where we would have ended up if he had put in this much effort before.

After some convincing on my part, we finally make our way inside. Fall Festival is basically the kick-off to our month-long celebration during October. The queen's job is to show up at events, smile of course, and help sell apple cider and pumpkin themed crafts. It was one of the highlights of my year last fall, and now I could care less what happens. Priorities change I guess and being the center of attention doesn't exactly hit the top of my list anymore.

We make our way toward the middle of the room, and I spot Cameron and Dylan in amongst a small section of our group. Apparently, some people felt the need to take sides. I wave to her, and she gives me a skeptical smile back. It almost makes me laugh what a big deal this is to her. Dylan eyes me and then shifts his gaze to Judah, glaring at him. Judah gives him a cocky smirk and moves his hand lower and rests it on my ass. Well, at least some things never change.

I discretely remove his hand from me and give him a quick peck on the cheek. "I'll be right back."

He nearly growls back at me as he presses me firmly against his side. "Don't be too long, babe."

As I'm making my way to ladies' room, I spot Hunter out of the corner of my eye. The first thing I notice is the fact that his dark green tie matches my dangerously short dress perfectly. When his eyes connect with mine it's obvious he likes it. His stare burns into me while he pretends to be engrossed in a conversation with Mr. Daniels, the art teacher. I brush a strand of hair behind my ear before disappearing around the corner.

Surprisingly, there's no line and I make it in and out fairly quickly. When I step back into the hallway, Hunter grabs me by the arm and pulls me down a dark corridor. I'm so taken off guard I don't open my mouth to protest when he scans the hall before opening the door behind us. Satisfied no one saw, he pushes me inside.

I take a step further into the room and notice it's a large storage closet for extra band instruments. He still doesn't say anything while he locks the door and flips the light switch off. The small window in the corner of the room only provides a dim glow across his face.

Hunter closes the distance between us with a few determined steps and grips my waist firmly, pushing me back until my ass hits the edge of a table. "I can't watch you with him," he says finally, his voice a low growl. "I don't like it."

His words make me angry. Last night he said he couldn't be with me and now he's saying that he doesn't want to see me with anyone else.

I shove my hand against his chest, putting distance between us. "You don't know what you want."

His eyes are hooded as he stares down at my hand. "I know what I want is wrong." When he looks up at me, I brace myself for his rejection again—but instead, he threads his hands through my hair and pulls my face to his. "But I don't fucking care anymore."

Without another word his lips crash over mine, and he kisses me so hard he steals all the air from my flailing lungs. He lifts me up onto the small table and pushes my dress back to expose my panties.

He steps between my legs, his breathing already labored. "Do you want me, Elle?"

My response is automatic. "Yes."

He smiles, slipping the fabric to the side and inserting a finger slowly. I moan when he slips his finger all the way inside, dragging it slowly in and out as he watches my face.

My breathing is reduced to short pants when he adds a second.

He leans in closer to my face, his fingers still working inside of me. "Tell me."

The words I've been so desperate to say are out of my mouth before I can think twice about it. "I want you." My voice breaks despite my best attempts to keep it steady. He's driving me crazy, and he's barely even touched me.

He pulls his fingers away and I hear the distinct sound of a foil packet. His hand grips my hip, and he positions himself directly in front of me. "Tell me again."

"I want you, Hunter."

There's something feral in his eyes when I say his name. For as many times as I thought about being with him in this way, I never envisioned it being like this. He kisses me like he's starving and I'm the only thing in the world that could possibly satiate him. I'm clawing at his shirt, grabbing at his arms—anything to bring him closer to me faster.

He tilts his head to the side so he has a full view as he presses inside of me. I hold my breath and then release it in a quick burst. He keeps one hand on my hip and the other tangles in my hair as he rocks into me.

"*Fuck*," he grits out.

My nails dig into his sides, earning me another strangled grunt. He kisses me again, his mouth rough over mine.

"You feel so fucking incredible," he whispers over my lips.

I can't say anything back because I'm trying so hard not to be loud. If I opened my mouth right now, I'd surely get us caught.

The rhythm he maintains is slow and measured. Thrusting gently inside of me and pulling slowly back out. He's trying to draw out the pleasure, but I find myself getting lost in him. The soft grunts he's making, the heat from his body being connected to mine—it's all too much.

I allow myself to surrender to this feeling and almost lose it altogether. I'm so close to the edge already, I bite down on his shoulder to keep from screaming. He groans and it vibrates directly into my chest. He starts to move faster and the tightening in my core intensifies. Unable to hold back any longer, I come hard and his hand cups over my mouth to muffle my cries.

I'm blinded by the waves crashing over me and he shudders his way through his own release. When I catch his gaze again, he's watching me. The intensity in his eyes makes my entire body shiver.

He kisses me softly once before pulling away. I lean back on my elbows and continue to breathe like I just ran a marathon. I watch him fasten his pants and tuck his shirt back in before sitting up on the edge of the table. For some reason I'm afraid to speak.

Slowly I slide myself to the floor and pull my dress back into place. He opens his mouth to speak, but I lift my hand to stop him. "Please, don't give me some speech about how we can't be together." With a fluff of my hair, I grab my clutch from the table. "I really can't handle that right now."

He nods once before turning for the door. My heart beats out of my chest when I realize he won't say anything at all. He pauses with his hand on the doorknob. "I know that's what I should say, but I'm not sure if I can." His eyes meet mine before he continues. "You better get back out there before anyone notices you're gone."

I don't get a chance to respond before the sound of the door slamming behind him startles me. He seems angry and that makes me think he already regrets it. After barely finding the strength to collect myself, I exit the room in just enough time to be crowned.

~

$\mathcal{M}$y heels click loudly on the pavement as I walk up the driveway after Judah dropped me off. I convinced him I wasn't feeling well and that he should go to the after party without me. He reluctantly agreed when I promised to call him later. That was a lie. How could I possibly think about being with Judah again when literally all I think about is Hunter?

I almost walk directly to the guest house, but something stops me. It's not a game to me anymore, and to be honest, I'm not sure it ever was. What's been happening between me and Hunter always felt so much more than that. The worst part is—I don't know how to handle those feelings. I've never had them before.

After changing out of my dress, I've been staring out of my window down to his. The lights are still on, and I've been home for almost two hours now. It's like I can't move even though I want to. When my phone buzzes with an incoming text, I jump. My heart pounds in my chest as I swipe the screen to unlock it.

Hunter: You don't even cuddle afterwards? Savage.

A laugh escapes me so forceful I cover my mouth with my hand. The tears that follow aren't from sadness. He knows this is hard for me, and despite how frustrating I know I'm being, he's still trying to make me feel better.

I don't sit and wallow in my doubt any longer. I barely glance in the mirror on my way to the stairs. I make it through the house as quietly as I can and practically jog across the patio to the guest house. The lights that were on before are now off except for the small lamp in the hallway.

The pounding in my chest resumes when I enter his bedroom and see him lying on his back in the darkness. He removes one of his hands from resting on his chest and pulls the covers down by his side.

When I hesitate again, he smirks at me. "Don't make me beg, Elle."

My legs suddenly feel weak, but I will them to move forward and crawl under the covers next to him. He turns and pulls me to his chest and then kisses the side of my head. I relax against him, instantly feeling calmer.

We don't say anything for the longest time. He runs his hand through the back of my hair, and I cling to him, desperately searching for the words I want to tell him. They're on the tip of my tongue when he speaks first.

"I hated leaving you like that, but that's not what I planned on happening when I pushed you into that room."

My heart constricts in my chest. He regrets it. The last thing I want is his pity, so I decide to let him off the hook.

"It's fine. I know it didn't mean anything."

His hand freezes in my hair and he cranes his neck back. "Elliot, look at me."

I press my face into his chest for a moment before picking my head up and catching the shock on his. "What?" I whisper.

His brows furrow and then he leans down and cups the side of my face with his hand. "How could you think being with you like that didn't mean anything?"

I shake my head and try to pull away from him, but he holds me so I can't. "Don't do that," he says softly. "Stay with me in this moment. Tell me what you're thinking—*please*."

My eyes squeeze closed, unable to face him. "I don't want to be a casual fling to you. I want more than that."

I'm still too afraid to open my eyes, and I feel his lips on my cheek. They move to my lips, and I release a strangled sigh into his mouth. He kisses me once more and then runs his thumb across my bottom lip.

"Look at me, baby."

The softness of his words makes my eyes flutter open. He smiles and continues to caress the pad of his thumb along the side of my face. "Elliot, you literally mean *everything* to me. How could you not know that?"

I take a shaky breath. "You never told me."

"I know my actions may seem confusing to you, but this is a first for me." He stares directly into my eyes as he speaks, and it paralyzes me. "I've tried to stay away from you, but I don't think I can anymore."

Panic creeps its way inside of me again, and my hands grip his waist to keep him close to me. "I don't want you to. I don't want anyone else but you."

He smiles, but there's still sadness behind it. He brushes the hair from my forehead and continues to study my face. I don't know what he's looking for, but I've never been more honest in my life.

He swallows roughly. "I don't want you to be with anyone else." His hand slides down my side and hooks my leg, drawing it over his. He leans down and presses his forehead to mine. "I want you here with me. Just me."

"That's all I'm asking for," I whisper over his lips.

With our bodies tangled together like this it's easy to forget about all of the things we still need to talk about. I still have no idea what he thinks he's saving me from by not being with me. The talk I had with Ollie on the bleachers flashes in my mind, and as quickly as it comes, I push it away. I don't want to think about all of the reasons we shouldn't do this. All I want is to feel as good as I feel right now. It's a risk I'm willing to take.

17

LANDING IN THE BUNKER

Hunter

*E*lliot's hand is creeping slowly down my stomach. My eyes remain closed, and I pretend not to notice. When she reaches the waistband of my boxers, she laughs. "I know you're awake, Hunter."

"I was waiting to see where you were going with that," I say with a smirk and then roll her brusquely to her back. She lets out a squeal in response, and my heart skips a beat. These are the kind of games I'd rather play with her.

Her lips find mine, and I start to get lost in her all over again. One thing I can be sure of is the harder we fight, the harder we make up. When her hands begin to travel south once more, I have to stop her.

"As much as I would like to hold you hostage here all day,

I have plans with Oliver to play golf at the resort this morning."

She squeezes her hand around me in response. "Oh really? You'd rather shoot balls with my brother today?"

I let out a deep groan, and thankfully, she loosens her grasp. "You know that's not true."

Elliot gives me a knowing smile before planting a chaste kiss to my lips. "Let's hope so."

She gets up from the bed and starts to pull on her jeans. "Speaking of Ollie, we should probably think about finding a way to tell him."

"You're right." I let out a sigh and run my hand down my face. "I hate keeping things from him. He's bound to get suspicious with the amount of time we've been spending together."

Elliot laughs from inside the hoodie she's still pulling over her head. "I don't know if you noticed or not but Ollie's not the most observant person." She fluffs her hair and glances in the mirror behind my door. "I love him and all, but he's pretty self-involved. If it doesn't somehow directly affect him, it won't enter his radar."

"Elle, this most definitely directly affects him. You're his sister, and I'm supposed to be his best friend." I stand up and grab a T-shirt off the chair. "He's going to lose his shit."

Her eyes drift to the floor then back to me. "It may not be for the reason you think." The unease in her voice confuses me a little.

I finish pulling on a pair of jeans and go to her. "What do you mean by that?"

She shakes her head and gets a look of sadness on her face, borderline shameful even. "Ollie's not as much concerned about you destroying this than he is me doing it."

I smooth the line that forms across her forehead with my fingers and kiss her gently. "Why would you think that?"

Her eyes cast down again. "Because it's true."

"Hey, look at me." I wait until her eyes meet mine again before I continue. "Whatever happened before doesn't matter. You and me are something different."

"I feel like all of my relationships up until this point were shallow. I've never really wanted something to work out as much as I want it to with you. What if I mess this up, or I hurt you?"

Something in the tone of her voice makes me wonder if Oliver told her more about my past than I would like. It's not really a conversation I want to get into right now, so I decide to brush it off. "You won't, I promise."

~

*E*lliot sneaks back over to the house twenty minutes later, and I wait another five before walking over to meet Oliver. He's standing in the driveway dressed like the posterchild for sports endorsements. His dark, brown hair is gelled to perfection and there are crisp lines in his shirt and pants. He goes all in no matter what he does, I'll give him that.

"Hey, man," I say as I approach.

A grin spreads across his face and then he shoves his golf bag in the back of his truck. "You ready to learn a thing or two about the art of golf?"

I scoff. "I play golf pretty well thank you very much."

He pops the collar on his polo shirt. "Okay, but I've been told by more than one person that I remind them of a young Tiger Woods."

I give him a questioning look. "It might not be for the reason you think."

He laughs and gives a shrug. "Hey, either way, I'll take it."

I'm about to reply with an excellent comeback when a familiar truck pulls in the driveway. Judah hops out with a smile on his face carrying a brown paper bag. Even though my eye begins to twitch, I try not to jump to conclusions.

"What's up?" he asks, swaggering over like he owns the place.

"Oh, me and Hunter are about to tear up the golf course at the lodge. What are you doing here? I half expected Elle to just be stumbling in after she clenched the crown two years in a row."

Judah laughs, and I shove my hands in my pockets so I don't punch him. "Nah, she's not feeling well." He reaches into the bag and pulls out a container. "I got her this disgusting soup she likes from the Chinese restaurant and her favorite candy from that store downtown."

Oliver raises an eyebrow. "Geez, you're really laying it on thick."

Judah shrugs. "I have to. I really messed up when I left. I didn't realize how much I love her, and now I can't stop thinking about it." He pauses for a moment and grips the back of his neck. "I'm thinking about transferring next semester. I can't be that far away from her anymore."

"Dude, that's something you should probably discuss with her first," Oliver remarks patting him on the back. "That kind of thing will most likely scare the shit out of her."

He nods slowly. "Yeah, I know. I have to hope that what we had still means something to her. I'm willing to do whatever it takes to convince her I've changed, that I want to be better for her."

I'm scared to see what my face looks like right now. The blinding rage surging through me is almost impossible to control at this point. I close my eyes for a moment to regain my composure until Elliot's voice makes them snap back open.

"Judah, what are you doing here?" She crosses her arms when she comes to a stop right beside me. I fight with everything I have not to grab her and show Judah who she belongs to now.

He smiles a little, clearly nervous. It's really strange actually. I almost believe him at this point. I've never seen him be this sincere about anything. "I brought you some things to make you feel better. I was worried—you never called me back last night."

I release a breath at the fact that she didn't call him to come over. It's shitty for me to automatically go to a place of doubt with her, but considering how their relationship was up until this point, it's kind of hard not to.

"I fell asleep."

"That's okay, babe," Judah says as he places a hand on her arm. "I'm here to take care of you."

Oliver tugs on my sleeve, but I can barely tear my eyes away to look at him. "Let's hit the road. These balls aren't going to drive themselves." He smirks again and nods toward the truck.

I steal a glance back at Elliot, and she shoots me an apologetic look. I can't be sure how I will my feet to move away from them, but the sight of her and Judah walking back to the house is something I carry with me.

❧

*O*liver is currently knelt beside me as I line up my putt. To say that the first nine holes were a disaster would be an understatement. I tighten my grip on the club and try to clear my mind for a moment.

"Okay, Hunter. This is a distance putt, but you can make it. Open your stance a little and stand up straight."

I grit my teeth but do as he says.

He stands up from beside me. "Now, just give it solid consistent contact—but not too hard," he adds.

My eyes focus on the ball, and I line up my shot.

"Remember, you *are* the ball," Oliver whispers before taking a step back. It's a good thing too, because now I kind of want to hit him instead.

I take in a breath and attempt to tap the ball, but instead I send it soaring straight off the green. "Fuck!" I can feel my face becoming redder, and I give the putter a forceful toss toward the hole.

Oliver's hand clasps my shoulder. "That wasn't too bad. You lacked control, but aside from that, good form."

I shrug him off. "Alright, Ollie. I fucking get it."

He laughs. "I'm sorry, man. You're so serious all the time." I watch him walk over to his marker and set his ball, inches from the hole. "You know what your problem is?" he asks over his shoulder.

I cross my arms over my chest. "No, but I bet you're going to tell me."

He flashes me a crooked smile before effortlessly sinking his putt. "You always let your emotions control your mood. There's obviously something bothering you." He turns back to me and gives a shrug. "You could tell me what it is, and maybe I can help."

Oliver walks to the hole, retrieves his ball, and then starts walking back to me. His concern for me is nice and all, but I'm still not at the point where I can be honest with him. I hate the fact that I'm keeping something this huge from him. I have no idea what to expect when he does finally know the truth. He's kind of unpredictable sometimes.

He stands beside me and clasps my shoulder again. "Come on, tell me. I'm sure it's an easy fix."

"Not everything in life is an easy fix, Oliver."

He raises an eyebrow and lets out a whistle before stepping back from me. "See. That's what I'm talking about. You need to go with the flow, let things comes as they may and just roll with it."

"God, Ollie. I seriously can't take your bullshit philosophies on life today." I pinch the bridge of my nose and take a few breaths.

When I open my eyes again he's looking over at me with a shocked expression. "You think I'm full of shit?"

I shake my head. "No, man. I'm sorry. It's just not a good day for me."

He nods. "It's cool."

I put my hand on his shoulder. "No, it's not. I shouldn't take it out on you."

Oliver flashes a smile and pats me back. "Seriously, it's fine." He walks over to the golf cart and loads his club before turning back to me. "You know I may seem like it's all glitter and fucking rainbows all the time, but I get down sometimes too. What's important to remember is that there are some things we can't control. When that happens, you have to trust it will work itself out, and if it doesn't, then we were never meant to have it anyway."

"That's the most sense I've ever heard you make."

A smug smile crosses his face, and he shrugs. "I'm a fucking genius. The sooner everyone realizes that the better off we'll all be."

I can't help but laugh. "So true, man."

The next nine holes aren't any better, but somehow, I manage to keep my rising temper in check. I never thought I would say this, but Oliver is right. If fate meant for Elliot and I to be together then no matter what obstacle we face we should be able to overcome it. Even though it seems that literally every force is trying to pry us apart, I have to believe we were brought together for a reason.

18

DODGING BULLETS

Elliot

The look on Hunter's face this morning when Judah showed up is still burned into my mind. After all the progress we made last night I'm worried he will take it the wrong way. I know I need to have a conversation with Judah about Hunter, but it's not like I can actually tell him that we're dating. No matter what we do, it still has to be a secret. If I tell Judah I'm dating someone else, I know how he is. He'll dig until he finds out who it is, and I can't let that happen. I wish I could talk to Ollie about this. What's worse is that all of this could have been avoided if I could just tell him. He's a reasonable guy, maybe he won't even get mad?

I've been alternating between pacing back and forth across the kitchen and peeking out into the driveway through the window for about two hours now. How long does it take to play a round of golf?

My phone buzzes on the counter, and I almost leap to grab it. Hunter hasn't responded to any of my texts all day. My heart drops again when I see it's from Judah. He's relentless. I click the message off without fully reading it and take a seat at the kitchen table. I've been pacing for so long, I'm driving myself crazy.

I'm about to go upstairs and call it a night when headlights flash through the room. I remain seated and wait for one of them to enter. Even though I can barely stand it, I can't exactly run out there and jump into Hunter's arms.

Two minutes and thirty-eight seconds later, Oliver strolls into the kitchen. "Elle, what are you doing sitting here in the dark?" He shoots me a look before walking over and flipping on the light switch.

So much for not seeming suspicious. I was so wrapped up in waiting for him I didn't even realize it got dark outside. I fold my hands on the table. "I was just sitting here thinking and lost track of time." *Also sounds suspicious.*

He nods before grabbing a bottle of water from the fridge and leans back against the counter. "Did Judah tell you about his plans for next semester?"

I sigh. "Yes. What's his problem lately?"

Oliver takes a drink before responding. "He loves you."

I raise an eyebrow. "How can you say that? You know Judah as well as I do."

"Exactly.

"Oliver, he does not love me. He's upset about the fact he can't have me whenever he wants anymore."

Oliver shrugs as he replaces the cap on his bottle. "I don't know. I've never seen him act this way before. I think he's serious." He pats me on the shoulder on his way to the living room. "Let him down gently, killer."

After sitting in stunned silence for about five minutes, I

make my way over to the guest house. I take a deep breath and knock on the door.

Hunter opens it immediately. "Hey, I was wondering how long it was going to take you." His smile and warm reaction throw me for a loop.

"Aren't you mad?" I ask.

He looks behind me and then pulls me inside. "No, of course not." His arms wrap around me, and I inhale his comforting scent. He smells like soap combined with something woodsy and it calms me.

"I texted you and you never answered."

He pulls back and kisses me on the forehead. "I'm sorry, baby. I was in such a hurry this morning I left my phone."

Okay, solves that I guess. The bigger question is why is he taking this so well? Any other guy would have freaked out by now and demanded to know why Judah was really here.

I pull back to study his face. "I didn't mean for that to happen this morning."

"I know. It's okay, seriously."

My face scrunches up and I take a step toward the kitchen. "You're acting weird."

I hear him laugh from behind me as I browse the refrigerator for alcohol. With all the drama over this past weekend, it feels necessary.

He leans forward over the breakfast bar on his elbows. "Listen, I talked to Ollie today and he made me feel better. What he said made a lot of sense actually."

I turn around to face him, snapping the top off of a bottle of beer. I'm almost positive my mouth is hanging open. "Ollie made sense? There really must be something wrong with you if you are starting to agree with his logic."

Hunter laughs again, and I take a long drink. "Elle, the point is, if I let every little thing bother me then we are never going to make it. Even though I want to physically hurt the guy, I can't help it if Judah keeps coming around. Not until we don't have to keep this a secret anymore."

I set my beer down and walk around the counter. He pulls me into him and places a kiss in my hair. "How long do you think it will have to be this way?" I ask.

"At least until you graduate. I'm not sure how accepting people will be of me dating my student."

All I can do is hold onto him tighter. With so many odds stacked against us already it would be easy to want to run away and not have to deal with the inevitable heartbreak. What bothers me the most is what I don't know about Hunter, and there's only one person I can ask.

~

The next couple of weeks go on without any major conflicts. I somehow managed to talk Judah out of transferring schools next semester. He didn't take it very well at first, but his calls have been dwindling, so I'm hoping he gets the idea it's really over.

I'm just about to head to practice when I notice Hunter still inside his classroom. I walk quickly down the hallway to his open door, knocking twice. When he turns to look at me a smile crosses his face. "Don't be late for practice, Elle. Oliver will make you run hurdles again."

"Well, I just wanted to talk to you, Mr. Graham." I walk over to him and run my hand down his tie.

He visibly swallows. "I like the way you say that."

"Hmm, do you?" I step a little closer and he glances over my shoulder. "Maybe you should give me detention? That way I can skip practice and you can bend me over your desk."

Hunter's eyes turn darker with my words. I think the thrill of getting caught excites him. If I'm being honest, it excites me too—but he already knows that.

As if he can read my thoughts, he grabs my hand and

casually runs it down the front of his pants. "You see what you're doing to me? You're being very bad, Elliot."

I trace my hand along the hardened outline through his pants. "Maybe you should punish me?"

He lets out a deep groan and tilts his head to me, speaking close to my ear. "You should go to practice, baby. If you don't, the things I want to do to you right now will get me fired."

I release my hand from him and smile. "Later."

I'm still smiling to myself when I step out into the hall and directly into Dylan. He grins when I look up at him. "Sorry, I didn't see you there."

I step around him and stop at my locker to get my bag for practice. For some reason he's still right behind me. "Elle," he says hesitantly. "I've been meaning to talk to you."

Not what I want to deal with right now. "Well, I'm late for practice. Can it wait?" I don't wait for his reply. I sling my bag over my shoulder and start walking toward the gym. He keeps in step beside me.

"It's just we never talked about what happened," he says quickly.

I laugh once. "What's there to talk about?"

He shoots me a look. "We used to be friends, and now you don't even talk to me anymore. I can tell you're mad at me over what went down at your party."

I raise an eyebrow. "Shouldn't you be the one who's mad?"

Our footsteps echo through the empty gymnasium and I continue toward doors that lead to the field. He grabs my arm to stop me. "I know Judah can be an asshole, and yes I was mad that you took his side, but I didn't realize how bad it was."

I let out a sigh and shift my bag to the other arm. "Okay, what are you talking about? Everything's fine. Judah is gone, and he's going to stay that way."

He lets out a laugh and runs a hand through his hair. "Oh, Elliot. You have no idea do you?"

My irritation is growing by the minute, and I'm running out of them. I glance at my watch and see that I have five left before Ollie goes into full blown dick mode. "Dylan, just tell me what's going on."

"Judah has been asking around, trying to figure out who you're with. He's threatened basically everyone, and all the guys have been watching for him. He's becoming completely unhinged over this."

I sigh and pat him on the shoulder. "I can handle Judah. Don't worry about it."

He grabs my arm again before I make it another step. "Elliot, I'm not afraid of him."

"Okay..."

"I'm just saying that you don't have to be alone because Judah's acting like a psycho," he adds.

"That's nice of you and I'm glad you still want to be friends, but I want to be alone right now."

He nods and releases my arm. "I understand." The smile perks up on his face again. "But if you ever change your mind, I'll be here."

I give a tight smile. "That's nice of you, Dylan. Thank you."

By the time I finally make it onto the field it's already after four. Looks like I'll be running hurdles after all.

19

HAUNTED

Hunter

$\mathcal{M}$y dad called yesterday. I haven't spoken to him in at least a year, and I've only seen him once since my mother and I moved here from Texas right after I turned sixteen. It's funny how no matter how hard you try to run, your past always finds a way to catch up with you. Even though I sent his call to voicemail it's all I've been able to think about. Elliot has been working hard to put me in a better mood. She always has an innate way of sensing when something is bothering me even if I try to hide it. She can't help me with this, and I don't want her to.

The next night I wake up in a cold sweat with Elliot gently shaking my arm, alarm written all over her face. There are some things that I don't want her to see, and this would be one of them.

I'm slightly disoriented, staring blankly back at her for a moment. It's been a long time since I had a dream like that. I can almost taste the blood clogging my throat when I try to take a full breath.

"Hunter, are you okay?" she asks softly. The distress radiating off of her is still palpable as I nod. "Are you sure? You were—"

"I'm fine," I interrupt a little too loudly. I take another quick breath and collect myself, turning toward her. "I mean —I'm okay, baby. I'm sorry."

Her hand is clutching her stomach as she remains up on her knees at my side. "You scared me. I couldn't wake you up." She slowly sinks back into the covers and curls against my side again.

I wrap my arm around her while I continue to try to catch my breath. "It was just a dream, everything is fine."

Elliot pops her head up, searching my face. "Hunter, you're still shaking. Does this happen often—do you want to talk about it?"

I shake my head. "No, I'm fine. Really."

She doesn't look convinced, but she also doesn't press further. Instead of lying down beside me again, she gets up from the bed.

"Where are you going?"

"I'm going to get you some water," she says, pulling on a pair of sweatpants.

I sit up quickly and throw the comforter aside. "Elliot, get back into bed. I said I'm fucking fine, will you just let it go?"

Her face contorts in disbelief. "Hunter, you were literally screaming. If you don't want to talk about it, that's fine, but I'm trying to help you."

I throw my hands up and stand up from the bed, walking past her. "I don't need your help right now." I know my words come out harsher than I intend them to because her face falls.

She wraps her arms around her tiny frame and nods. Causing her to feel that way almost breaks me, and I curse under my breath as I walk back to her. "Baby, I'm sorry." I kiss her forehead and then her temple before pulling her into my arms. "Okay? It just caught me off guard is all. I'm sorry."

Her face presses harder against my chest, her voice barely a whisper. "I love you. You can talk to me about anything."

My arms stiffen around her. *Elliot loves me?* I pull her back a little so I can see her face. I heard her plain as day, but I want to hear it again.

"What did you say?"

She wipes a tear from her eye and smiles. "I said—I love you, Hunter."

Leaning down, I kiss her once softly. "I love you, too." I wrap my arms around her and hold her against my chest again. "So much."

As much as I try to stop it, a tear begins to fall down my cheek. What will she think of me when she finds out who I really am?

~

*W*alking up onto the warped floorboards of the front porch I frown at the screen door still hanging off its hinges. I told that lazy piece of shit I'd fix it the last time I was here, but he insisted he would get to It. Looks like I was right again.

I take a breath before knocking twice. It goes so long I almost knock again before my mother answers the door. "Hunter," she says with a small smile. "I wasn't expecting you." She waves for me to come inside, and I take in her tired eyes. She looks ten years older than she's supposed to, and I know the reason.

"Sorry, I was going to call but—"

"No, I'm really glad you're here," she says cutting me off. "Can I make you something to eat or a drink maybe? I just made a fresh batch of tea."

I nod as I walk into the small kitchen and take a seat at the table. "Tea sounds great."

My acceptance makes her smile a little brighter, and she grabs a glass from the cabinet. "Russ isn't here right now. He got a new job and it keeps him on the road for most of the week. I'm sure he'll be sad he missed you."

That's highly doubtful. In the almost five years since they've been together, I can't remember a single conversation between me and her boyfriend that I would consider to be amicable. "Tell him I said hi when you talk to him." Sometimes it's better to keep the peace rather than admit the truth.

She nods as she continues to pour my drink. "How's Regan doing? You haven't brought her around lately."

I scratch my head as I take the glass from her hand. "Oh, we kind of broke up. I'm actually living at Ollie's right now."

She smiles again, taking the seat across from me. "Such a nice boy he is. I always enjoy when he comes by." I almost laugh. Oliver really puts on a show for her when I bring him with me. You would think he actually had manners.

"Yeah, he's something alright."

"Well, what happened with this one?"

I shrug. "She wasn't the one for me I guess."

The look on her face tells me she knows there's more to my visit than some girl. A mother always can, they are programmed that way. "So, that's it then? Nothing else new going on?"

I take another drink because my mouth suddenly feels dry. "Dad called a couple days ago." I pause and gauge her reaction. She folds her hands together but keeps her features even. Ever since they divorced, she always tried to keep things as casual as possible for me considering the circumstances surrounding it. "When's the last time you talked to him?"

"Um, I talk to him a good bit about you. He's always asking how you're doing."

I laugh, but not out of humor. "But he doesn't ask me though. I haven't spoken to him since last summer."

"You know it's hard for him to communicate with you. That doesn't mean that he doesn't care."

My mother has been making excuses for him since I was old enough to listen. Her choice in men hasn't changed as I would assume it seldom does for most women. My jaw clenches. "Well, what does he want?"

Her eyes drift to her intertwined hands and then back to me. "He wants you to go visit him. I think it's a good idea. It's time you two hash things out finally. You only get one father, and everyone deserves a second chance."

The weight of her words lands heavily on my chest. I'm not sure I have even an ounce of forgiveness in me for that man. I stand up from the table and lean in to kiss her on the cheek. "I'll think about it, okay?"

≈

When I make it back to the house, Elliot is sitting on a lounge chair with her legs pulled up under her chin. I know my behavior over the past couple of days has been unsettling, but I'm not ready to talk about it.

"Hey," I say as I make my way over to her.

A genuine smile crosses her face, and it hits me hard for some reason. I sit down below her and pull her legs across my lap. "I missed you today."

She grabs my face gently, pulling me closer. Her kiss is soft and measured as opposed to the urgent nature in which we usually greet each other. It's like she's assuring me that everything is going to be okay without needing the words the say it.

"I always miss you, no matter how long you're gone." She pulls back and searches my eyes, so I force a smile.

"Is Oliver home?" I ask, changing the subject.

"No, he said he had some extracurricular activities he needed to attend to, and I didn't ask him to elaborate further." She laughs. "I don't want to know."

I pat her leg with a laugh. "It's probably better that way."

Elliot leans into me and wraps her arms around my neck. Even though I know she wants to, she doesn't say anything. She's treading lightly around me now, and I don't blame her. I always expect her to be so open with me and yet I can't offer the same in return. Eventually I will have to tell her, but for now I'll just try to keep my darkness inside where it belongs. Locked deep down where it can't hurt anyone ever again.

20

AMBUSH

Elliot

liver crunches pretzels in his mouth loudly beside me while I stare down into the driveway below. "Do you have to do that right now?" I ask in frustration.

He shrugs. "What? This is entertaining."

Judah is standing in my driveway, tears streaming down his face, begging me to come outside. I'm almost positive he's wasted. Oliver and I have been watching from the upstairs window for the past five minutes. This unfortunate event was brought on by a series of unanswered calls and texts. Evidently, letting him down gently isn't going to happen.

"Elliot?" My dad asks from behind me.

I turn to see him cross his arms with a slightly amused expression on his face. "Care to explain to me why the quarterback who won us State last year is currently crying outside my window right now?"

My eyes drift back to the driveway where Judah is now on his knees with one hand on the pavement. I cringe slightly. "I think he's upset."

My dad rolls his eyes. "You think? What did you do to the poor boy?"

"Dad, seriously?"

Oliver raises his hand like an idiot. "I know."

I glare at him out of the corner of my eye, but it doesn't stop him from chiming in. "Elliot broke his heart, and now I'd say he's losing his shit."

My dad laughs once. "Well, would you mind going down there and putting him out of his misery." He places his hand on my shoulder. "I just talked to Jeff this afternoon while we were working out the plans for the new building. He said Judah's not adjusting very well to being away."

Judah's father, Jeff and my dad have been friends since they were kids. Not only do they work together on a number of projects at the resort, but we also spend quite a bit of time with them socially as well. It makes it extremely awkward now that things are ending so badly between us.

I swallow back my frustration. "Fine."

He pats me on the back. "Thank you. You know how I feel about public displays of emotion, especially from such a big guy."

Oliver laughs. "Yeah, Judah really does look like a pussy right now." He throws a pretzel at me. "You destroyed him. Savage, Elle."

"Seriously, Ollie. You're not helping." I pinch the bridge of my nose and take a few breaths. I never imagined things would escalate this far. My mind drifts to Hunter not twenty feet away from all this. I can only imagine what he's thinking.

I hear Oliver laugh again. "The only thing that would make this even more poetic is if it started to rain right now."

As if the heavens heard him, thunder strikes across the sky and rain begins to pour. Oliver's hand flies up to his mouth. "Oh my God," he whispers through his fingers. "He can fucking hear me."

This causes me to laugh. "If that were true, I'm pretty sure you would have been struck down by now."

He nods. "You're probably right." He shoves another pretzel in his mouth and smirks again. "You do need to go down there. I'm even starting to feel bad, and that's pretty hard to do."

I let out a sigh. "Alright, I'm going." I give Oliver a shove away from the window. "Don't watch either."

I can still hear his snickers from the same spot as I walk down the stairs. Before I push the door open, I throw my hoodie over my head. Judah looks up immediately and rushes over to me. The scent of whiskey permeating off of him nearly knocks me to the ground.

"Elle, listen—babe, I'm sorry. You have to listen—"

He grips my arms tightly, and I almost wince. "Judah," I sigh, looking up at him. "Why are you doing this?"

"You haven't been answering my calls."

"We broke up. That's how this works."

He shakes his head. "No, that's not how this was supposed to happen." His eyes squeeze shut. "This is not how this was supposed to end."

My heart clenches at his words. It was never my intention to hurt Judah. I never want to hurt anyone, especially someone that I love—and I do love him, but I know he's not the one.

I gently place my hands on either side of his face. He opens his eyes and all of his sadness pours out to me. "I'm sorry, okay? I know this is hard, but I think it's for the best."

His eyebrows pull in. "I *can't* accept that. You're all I think about. I'm going fucking crazy, Elle."

That much is obvious. The only question I have is why?

143

He never seemed to care the entire time we were together, and I have *never* seen him cry. I tug his arm and drag him forward under the side porch awning out of the rain. He stumbles with me, and I sigh.

"I don't want you to be upset, but I'm not going to change my mind."

He throws his hands up and then grips them in his hair. "No, you don't mean that. Not after everything we've been through." He takes a shaky breath and then moves closer to me. "You love me—I know you do."

My stomach keeps clenching tighter at his torment. Regardless of my feelings toward him, it's breaking my heart to see him like this. I place my hand on his face again to keep him steady. "Judah, listen to me. I love you, okay? We just can't be together anymore."

His face relaxes for a moment and then shifts right back to agony. "Elliot, I tried so hard to get over you—but every girl I've tried to be with has made me realize that I can't."

I roll my eyes. He's still in there. He shakes his head quickly and pushes me back against the wall, caging me in with his hands on either side my head. "No, I'm not done yet. I know I fucked up—I *know* that." He takes a shaky breath. "But we can fix it. I know we can."

My heart pounds, and I place my hands on his chest, but he's too strong for me to move him away. "Judah, I know you're upset—but I can't do this anymore."

He shakes his head and leans in closer. "Not until you hear me."

I close my eyes for a moment to regain my composure. "I hear you."

He presses his face against my neck before pulling back to look at me. "Remember that night at Christian's bonfire—remember how we promised to always be together? You said you didn't want to be with anyone else."

"Judah, that was over a year ago, and at the time—"

He shakes his head, cutting me off again. "No, you fucking promised, Elle. How can you just walk away from us like that?"

His question makes me want to scream, but I can't argue with him when he's this drunk. I'm not the one who left. I'm not the one who wanted to explore our options this year. He decided that, and now he has to live with those consequences.

I take a breath when he leans further into me. "You're not thinking clearly. You need to go back to school and start moving on with your life—"

He grabs me by the waist and pins me back against the wall again. "I don't want to go back. I want to stay here with you."

"You can't give up everything you've worked so hard for. I would never let you do that."

Judah shakes his head again, refusing to hear what I'm asking. "No, I'm not leaving."

I close my eyes for a moment and try to think through this until the weight is suddenly lifted. Hunter still has a grip on the back of Judah's hoodie when my eyes pop back open. "She said leave her the fuck alone." He releases him with a shove and then looks to me with concern etching his features. "Are you okay?"

I nod, but Judah starts to stumble back toward us. "Who the fuck do you think you are? Why are you here all the time?"

Before Hunter can answer, Oliver steps out from inside the house. "Hey, come on now Judah." He throws his arm around his shoulders. "Let's go for a little drive, brother. Sober up a bit."

Judah looks to me and then back to him. "I can't leave. Not until she talks to me."

Oliver gives his shoulder a squeeze. "She'll talk to you. Just later, okay?"

Judah doesn't look convinced and shakes his head before staggering back toward me. Hunter immediately moves between us, and Oliver raises an eyebrow.

"Elle," Judah slurs. "Promise we'll talk about this. Say that you'll call."

I nod quickly. "I'll call you later."

Judah's nostrils flare, and I can see the tension in Hunter's shoulders as he clenches his fist. "No, say you fucking promise."

My voice is nearly broken when I reply, "I promise."

Oliver pulls him back again. "Come on, man. We need to get you together. You're falling apart." He laughs to himself while tugging Judah toward his truck.

I watch as he helps him into the passenger seat before walking back over to us. "I'm going to take him for a little ride. You seriously need to get a better handle on this."

My eyes drift back to the truck where Judah is already slumped down in the seat with his hand covering his face. "I don't know what to do."

Hunter steps closer to me and glares at Oliver. "*You* should put an end to this. He can't fucking treat her like that."

Oliver pats him on the shoulder. "I got it, don't worry."

Hunter laughs coldly and shrugs him off. "Do you? Every time he does something crazy you act like he's your best fucking friend." He leans in closer to Oliver. "He could seriously hurt her and then I'll fucking kill him."

Oliver nods, his features shifting more serious. "Okay, I'll take care of it. Just relax."

Hunter takes a step back, and Oliver exchanges a look with me over his shoulder. I wait until he makes it back to the truck and begins to pull down the driveway before I speak. "You shouldn't have done that."

He spins around to me with an incredulous look on his face. "Are you kidding me right now?" He points over his shoulder. "Judah is crazy. I can't stand by and watch him hurt you, Elle."

I take a step toward him and wrap my arms around his waist. "You also can't act like that in front of Oliver. Is that how you want him to find out about us?"

"No, but if it comes to your safety I would." He places his hands on the sides of my face. "If anything ever happened to you I...I wouldn't be able to live with myself."

I lean forward and kiss him once. "It won't, I promise."

He shakes his head. "You can't promise that, Elliot. No one can, but I'm going to try."

The look on Hunter's face is overwhelming. I never once thought of Judah as a threat, but I can see how someone on the outside might view it that way. It's clear I need to get a better handle on the situation before it spirals completely out of control and destroys us all.

EXTRACTION POINT

Hunter

*A*fter the scene that played out earlier today, Elliot decided it was best to stay in her own bed tonight. I'll admit that my behavior may raise a few flags to Oliver, but I couldn't help it. I've seen first-hand what blind rage mixed with alcohol can do to a man, and I'm not about to let it happen to her.

It's just after midnight when Oliver's truck finally pulls into the driveway. A group of guys showed up hours ago to collect Judah's vehicle so I figured he would have been home a long time ago. I watch him look to the house and then turn quickly in my direction. I meet him at the door.

"Ollie, what took you so long?" I ask, pulling the door open.

He gives me a stern look and steps past me. "You were out of line today."

I let out a stunned huff of air before closing the door. "Are you joking? I'm the one who was out of line?"

Oliver turns to me and crosses his arms. "For you to insinuate that I wouldn't protect my sister is beyond ridiculous."

I shake my head and take a step toward him. "Listen, man…"

"No, *you* listen," he says harshly, cutting me off. "I always have Elliot's best interests in mind. There is nothing I wouldn't do for her. I know Judah. He's young and clearly upset right now, but I have no reason to believe that he would physically hurt her."

My eyes widen. "Was I the only one who was here today? He had her backed against the wall out there and you did nothing to stop it."

"I was right there watching the whole thing. I stepped in when I thought he was getting a little too pushy."

I scoff. "Yeah, after I already pulled him off of her."

Oliver throws his hands up. "Why are we fighting over this? Everything is going to be okay now. We had a long talk, and once he stopped crying and sobered up, he started making some sense again."

I laugh. "Judah made sense. Really?"

He nods. "Yeah, the back and forth between them has really been getting to him. Elliot is extremely manipulative whether she intends to be or not. Some guys can't handle that."

I cover my mouth with my hand for a moment. I'm about to say something I'll regret. Oliver takes a seat on the couch and clasps his hands in his lap. "She's my sister, and I love her, but she's quite selfish. I can't say anything really because I act exactly the same way. We're cut from the same cloth." He shrugs, and I clench my fist involuntarily.

He laughs once. "This is not the first time something like this happened. Last year her and Judah broke up, and she started dating some guy from the swim team to make him jealous. After that whole ordeal the guy stalked her for weeks. It's like she doesn't realize the way her actions affect people or even cares."

My mind is completely blown right now. I can't believe that Oliver is almost defending Judah. "So, you're saying this happened because Elliot brought it on herself."

He shakes his head. "No. Listen, right or wrong, I would defend her above anyone else. I not so subtly explained to Judah that a repeat performance will not be tolerated. I'm just saying it didn't surprise me it came to this."

Honestly, it shouldn't surprise me either. After the games we played I saw firsthand how vindictive she can be. But the part that Oliver is missing is the side of her that you can't see. It's a front so she can protect herself from how she really feels. Not to mention her most substantial role model is a glorified playboy. That would cause anyone to have a skewed sense of what a relationship is supposed to be like.

Oliver stands and walks over to me, extending his hand. "I'm glad you were there today. She's lucky to have two guys that care that much for her."

I shake his hand in return. "Anytime."

He smiles. "Good." He pats me on the back on the way out. "I'll see you tomorrow."

The way that Oliver views Elliot should be unnerving to me, but for some reason it isn't. This is what she wants you to see, and the fact that even her own brother does, proves just how far she takes it. I don't for one second think we've seen the last of Judah, I just hope I will be there next time he comes around.

*E*ven though we've tried to be extra careful this week, it wasn't enough to keep her completely away. She's currently curled up beside me on the couch as I sit through another episode of this stupid reality TV show she loves. It's a pain I'm willing to endure. I would stare at a blank wall if she asked me to.

"Hunter," she says suddenly. I look down at her as she pulls herself into a sitting position. "I feel like we should talk about the other day."

I lace my fingers with hers and pull her hand to my lips. "Are you still upset?"

She shakes her head. "It's not that…I mean yes, that was upsetting, but I'm more concerned about you."

My eyebrows pull in. "Me? Why?"

Her eyes drift to our hands. "I made a lot of mistakes with Judah. I misinterpreted his feelings for me, and even though he has his share of flaws, I really hurt him."

I tilt her chin up with my finger. "Elliot, you're defending the guy that wanted an open relationship with you so he could fool around at college. I don't feel bad for him."

She laughs a little. "Okay, that may be true, but isn't it weird that it didn't bother me at all?"

I shrug. "How deep can a relationship be if it's just based on sex?"

Elliot bites her lip, and I instantly feel like a dick.

"I don't think our relationship is that way if that's what you're thinking."

"Hunter, you can't even talk about a dream that you had. There's so much we don't know about each other."

I take a breath and square my shoulders. "Okay, ask me what you want to know. I'll tell you anything." I say a silent prayer that she doesn't start where I know she wants to.

"Alright, what's your favorite color?" She smiles, and I let out a nervous laugh. I love this girl.

"Green, what's yours?"

"I'm a girl. It's pink."

I hold up a finger. "Not all girls like pink, Elle. Just saying."

"Okay." She pauses before her next question, chewing on her bottom lip again. "Why don't you want to talk to your dad?"

My jaw twitches, but I push it down. If she needs to know something about me then that's what I have to do. "My father and I are very similar—and it scares the shit out of me."

Her eyes hold mine, almost pleading with me to continue. "He has a very short temper and likes to control everything. We used to fight constantly, and it was difficult for my mother. It then caused them to fight and uh—things got ugly. More than once."

She places her other hand on top of mine. "Is that why you came here? To get away from him?"

As much as I want to tell her, I'm not sure I can handle the look on her face when I do. For now, I take the easy way out. "Pretty much."

"Is that why you think Judah will hurt me?"

All I can do is nod as I struggle to swallow the lump in my throat.

She hesitates again, and I can tell she doesn't want to ask her next question. "Do you trust me?"

"I want to say yes, but I won't lie. It's my initial reaction not to. That's something I can't control. For the longest time I refused to let anyone get close to me." I take a breath and pull her closer. "But with you, I can't seem to get close enough. I can't really explain it. It's just something I feel."

She leans forward and kisses me once. "I feel that too. I'm afraid I'm going to screw this up somehow, and I don't want to do that—not to you."

I smooth back the hair that falls in her face. "If you and I are going to work we need to trust each other. I don't want to play games with you, and I don't want to have any secrets." The lie slips so easily off my tongue even I'm surprised.

"No more secrets?" She repeats the question for conformation.

I fight to keep the emotions from my face. "No."

She shifts herself onto my lap, and I immediately twist my fingers through her hair, drawing her into me. Her kiss is urgent again, and I match her intensity. It always seems that way no matter how good things are going between us. Almost like we're on the verge of disaster.

I stand up from the couch with her still in my arms, and she wraps her legs around my waist. Her lips never leave mine until we fall onto the bed. I don't want to be forceful with her tonight. I want to take this slow.

Although I can tell she likes aggressive sex, I don't want to control her right now. I just want to love her. When everything feels so uncertain, I want to be the one who makes her feel safe.

22

BREACH

Elliot

My eyes scan the bleachers while I jog in place. Hunter is seated right behind where Oliver is standing, and he smiles at me. Without thinking, I wave, and Oliver points his whistle at me with his stern coach expression. I roll my eyes and start to stretch.

It's already mid-season, and we're still in first place. For as competitive as Oliver and I are, we would like to keep it that way. I'm about to take my place on the line when I spot our typical crowd plus one person who shouldn't be here. Judah has a ball cap pulled low on his head with a hood over top of it. He must really think I'm an idiot not to recognize him.

Oliver jogs over to me. "Okay, Elle. You got this."

I nod toward the bleachers. "Judah's here."

He turns to look behind him and then back to me. A scowl forms of his face as he places his hands on my shoulders. "Don't let him distract you, okay? I'll be right here the entire time. I will walk you out when we leave. He won't get near you if you don't want him to."

I shake my head. "I'm not afraid of him. I just don't know what to say anymore."

"You said what you needed to say, right? It's up to him to accept it now."

"He's so broken because of me. I feel terrible."

Oliver scoffs. "He'll be fine. He's just having a hard time with all of the changes this year. I'll talk to him again tonight. Make sure he's okay."

I nod as I release a shaky breath. "Okay."

He gives me a smirk and pats my shoulder. "Hunter's here, too. We got this."

Even though I smile back, guilt swirls in my stomach. I would never forgive myself if Oliver lost his relationship with Hunter over this.

He releases me, and I go to the starting line. I exchange one last glance with Hunter before I take my mark. There's something about that moment before the starting gun goes off. Everything seems to fade out around me, and my vision becomes singular. The only thing I can see is the finish line, and the only thing I can think about is how fast I need to cross it.

The shot rings loudly, and I take off down the track. I never hesitate; it's such a natural reaction for me to surge forward when something is chasing me. My lungs are barely warmed up as I easily take first place several seconds before everyone else.

Ollie cheers louder than all the others. He also shouts some language that would typically get someone in his position fired, but for some reason no one ever questions him. I guess it wouldn't seem right if he didn't.

He raises his hand to me as I jog back to his side. "Elle, you fucking smoked them! Good job."

I laugh and return his over enthusiastic high five. He turns to verbally assault the rest of the team as I grab my water bottle.

Hunter winks at me from the bleachers, and I can't hide my smile. It's cut short as I watch Judah stroll down the stairs toward me. He's flanked by most of the current football team, which surprisingly includes Dylan.

Judah doesn't take his eyes off of me as he casually swaggers to the parking lot. It's like he's almost taunting me now. They are still his friends, but there's no reason for him to be home so much. That worries me. As disturbing as he's acting lately, I don't want anything to affect his performance at college.

My eyes drift over to Hunter who is visibly on edge. I think back to the conversation I had with Ollie the day I decided to go after him in the first place. The warning he gave me is still so prominent in my mind even though I have no idea what it means. I need to know what Ollie's not telling me if I have any chance at protecting him.

~

*M*y palms are sweaty as I close my hand to knock on his door. I wouldn't just enter Oliver's room unannounced. You never know what you'll find.

He answers with a stupid grin. "What's up?" His smile fades. "Elle, why are you crying?"

I shake my head and another sob rips through my chest. He opens his door wider and pulls me inside. He guides me to the chair next to his bed. "Sit down. Talk to me."

The tears keep falling even though I try so hard to compose myself. "I'm sorry," I choke out.

He kneels in front of me, his face scrunching up in confusion. "Elle, what are you sorry for?"

I pull at the torn fabric on my jeans, unable to meet his eyes. "You have to tell me—I need to know."

My sentences are coming out short and clipped, but I can't help it. I start to cry harder.

"Elliot, you are seriously scaring the shit out of me." He shakes my knee back and forth. "Just tell me. I won't be mad whatever it is."

I shake my head again. "You—you don't mean that."

He clenches his teeth. "Yes, I do. I can't promise I won't hurt the person who did this to you, but I won't be angry with you."

My eyes lock on his. "You can't hurt him either."

I watch Oliver's throat bob as he swallows. "Hurt who?" The ominous tone of his voice almost makes me flinch.

I close my eyes. "Hunter."

I can practically hear all of the air escape from his lungs as he stands in one quick motion. "You've got to be fucking kidding me?"

"Ollie, you promised—"

He slams his fist into his chest. "I didn't think you were going to tell me that!" He runs his hand through his hair. "Jesus, Elliot. What were you thinking?"

His words make my tears fall faster, and he sighs loudly and then walks back over to me. "Elle, I'm sorry."

"No, I deserve this."

He shakes his head in determination. "No, you don't. I overreacted. A lot of thoughts are going through my head right now. I can't process them all."

I sniffle loudly and wipe my face on my sleeve. He sighs again and stands to get me a box of tissues. "Here, now calm down and explain this to me."

Oliver sits on the edge of the bed facing me while I try once again to collect myself. He folds his hands in his lap, plastering a falsely serious expression on his face. "Okay, what exactly is the nature of your relationship?"

I give him an irritated look. "Seriously, do you even have to ask—"

He stands abruptly from the bed again, cutting me off. "Nope. I'm gonna kill him."

My reflexes kick in, and I leap from my chair to grab his arm. He's much stronger than I am so he drags me with him a couple steps. "Ollie, you can't!"

He looks down at me with a murderous expression. "Elliot, let me go. He should have known—"

"Oliver, I *love* him!"

Instantly, Oliver stops pulling away from me and his eyes widen. "What did you say?"

I take in a deep breath, releasing my grip from his arm. "I said, I love him. I love him so much that it physically hurts." I rub the throbbing spot on my chest, and it starts to beat faster. "And I can't go one more day not knowing. You have to tell me what he's hiding from me. I can't be the one who breaks him—I just can't." I lower my face into my hands when the sobs start all over again.

Oliver's arms come around me, pulling me into his chest. "Elliot, I'm the only one who knows," he says softly.

My hands grip his T-shirt as I look up at him. "That's why I'm asking. *Please*, Ollie."

His expression is conflicted. He stares down at me for the longest time, contemplating what to say. He takes another deep breath. "What do you want to know?"

I take a step back to prepare myself. "What happened to him? Something happened that he won't talk to me about. I know it has to be really bad, but I need to know."

Oliver starts pacing. If there is one quality that I know for sure my brother possesses, it's loyalty. Selfishly, I also know that if it comes down to a choice between us, Ollie would choose me.

He pauses for a moment and runs his hand down his face. "Did you ask him about it already?"

I nod.

"And he didn't want to tell you?"

I shake my head.

He lets out a frustrated grunt, taking a seat on the edge of the bed. He motions with his head to the chair. "Sit down. This is going to take a minute."

On unsteady legs, I walk over and sit across from my brother. His eyes meet mine with a sadness I've never seen before from him. I inhale one more uneven breath and prepare myself for the worst.

23

OUTSIDE THE WIRE

Hunter

After the track meet, I spot Judah still in the corner of the parking lot. Elliot is getting a ride home with Oliver so at least I know she's safe. It still doesn't change the fact my patience has run out. I clench and unclench my fist while I watch him finally get into his truck and pull out of the parking lot. Five seconds later, I crank the ignition and follow him.

Fortunately for me, Judah pulls into an alley beside the liquor store. I park one block over and let my truck idle. I know this is a bad idea, but if Oliver's going to pretend like it's no big deal then somebody needs to show this asshole that it is.

He has a cocky smirk on his face when he exits the store

with a brown paper bag tucked under his arm. His face is concentrating on his phone while he attempts to text and walk at the same time.

I shake my head. Of course he's drinking again. I don't think the kid's been sober since Elliot broke up with him. It's a dangerous combination—alcohol and heartache. It makes you do crazy, irrational things. Sometimes unspeakable things you can never take back. I won't let anything happen to Elliot because of this behavior.

When Judah gets back into his truck, I pull out and follow him exactly where I knew I would. He maintains the speed limit and stays inside the lines the entire way to Elliot's driveway. Hopefully, he hasn't started yet. It will be easier to get him to leave without resorting to violence. I don't want to hit him, but my patience is running thin.

I park against his bumper and jump out of my truck. He slides out of his vehicle casually and turns back to me and laughs.

"How did I know it was you again?" Judah says sarcastically and then reaches across his seat for the small brown bag. He twists the cap off the bottle and takes a long drink. "What's your fucking problem with me?"

I cock my head to him. "Elliot already made it clear to you she doesn't want to see you. You need to stop this."

He laughs again. *Right in my fucking face.* "You don't know what you're talking about, man."

"I think I fucking do."

Judah runs a hand along his jaw, studying me for a moment. "Why are you so concerned with what's going on between us?"

It must be something he sees in my face because his grin widens as he tilts the bottle back once more. I watch him twist on the cap and place it on his front seat. "You're fucking her, aren't you?"

The anger burns behind my eyes as I glare back at him.

"When a girl tells you no, it means no. If you can't understand that then I'm going to be forced to explain it to you." I lean into him and he keeps his stance in challenge. His nostrils flare. "Trust me, motherfucker. You don't want that."

Judah shoves me back, and I laugh under my breath. "You think I don't know what's going on here? This is what she does."

My pulse starts to beat into my neck, and I clench my fist at my side. "I'd shut the fuck up if I were you. Last warning."

His eyes turn darker. "Don't you get it? It all ends with me anyway. Everyone else is just a casualty. Dylan, obviously, now you—you're just collateral damage." His eyes lock on mine. "She always comes back to me."

"Not this time," I grit out. My fist clenches so violently I'm surprised my knuckles don't crack.

Judah looks thoughtful for a moment and then a smirk spreads across his face. "I was the first person to have her. Did you know that?" He takes a step toward me, and I take a breath. "And I'm going to be the last."

That's when I lose it. My fist flies at Judah's face so forcefully his head snaps back against the open door. Blood immediately begins to pour from his nose after I land hit after hit. He manages to get one to the side of my face, but I don't even feel it.

The white noise continues to ring in my ears until he collapses to the ground. I wipe the blood from my face before landing a kick straight to his ribs. I find the will to stop for a moment and catch my breath. The weight on my back and the screaming from beside me brings me all the way out it. My eyes scan around, and I find a distressed Elliot clutching her chest with one hand.

"Stop!" Ollie growls in my ear.

I realize he's the one pulling me away, and I don't even remember him walking out here.

My chest heaves in and out, and I shrug him off. Judah

groans from the pavement and Oliver gives me a forceful shove on the shoulder. "What the fuck, man?"

I stumble sideways, but my eyes cut to Elliot knelt beside Judah, horror on her face. He still didn't really move too much yet. I must have really hurt him.

With tears in her eyes, she's looking back to me while resting a hand on his chest. "Why did you do this?"

"I'm sorry," I say, still struggling to take full breath. "He was saying horrible things about you."

Her face contorts in disgust. "So you beat the shit out of him?"

The look in her eyes destroys me. I've seen it before, and I never wanted to see it from her. Oliver clasps my shoulder, but I don't turn to face him.

"Go to take a walk, man. Chill the fuck out for a minute."

The tone of his voice doesn't make it seem like something I can argue. My entire body is shaking, and I can't tear my eyes away from Elliot. She's still on her knees at his side and he's starting to come around and mumbling incoherently. If she could just look at me and let me know she's okay I could walk away a little easier right now—but she doesn't. She cradles his face in her hands and speaks to him in a soothing tone.

I can't watch anymore, so I stalk off down the driveway. When I make it back to the guest house, I walk straight to the bathroom. I pull my blood-spattered shirt over my head and glance in the mirror. My hands grip the edges of the sink, and I study the cut across my lip. It's going to be hard to hide that one. He must have gotten one good elbow in that I was too enraged to notice.

Reaching into the drawer beside me, I grab a towel and wet it in the sink. As I'm wiping the blood from my face, I take in the eyes staring back at me. They're as hard and cold as the ones who created them.

With a fresh T-shirt on, I make my way back to the living

163

room as a hard knock lands on my door. My shoulders tense before I see Oliver looking through the glass. I pull it open slowly. "You gonna hit me?"

His expression is unreadable as he holds my gaze. "Can I come in?"

I wave him inside with an impassive look on my face. Might as well get it over with. This night can't possibly get any worse.

Oliver steps past me and continues to look me over with extreme scrutiny. He nods once. "When were you going to tell me?"

My heart instantly sinks. I'm not sure how to react. Did he figure this out on his own or did Elliot tell him? My mouth runs dry when I attempt to swallow. "About what?"

He runs his hand over his head and laughs. "That's how we're going to play it, huh?" He takes a step toward me. "You should have been the one to tell me—not her."

I take in a breath. I really wish she was here right now. My mind races as I try to figure out why she felt the need to confess to Oliver without me. "I'm sorry."

"Sorry?" He laughs again. "All those times I was trying to help you out and it was all over my sister. If I would have known, I would have told you what a bad idea this was."

I scoff. "Why? What's the big deal if we're together?"

Oliver looks at me like I'm an idiot. "For starters, she's your fucking student."

I laugh once. "She's so much more than that and you know it."

He rolls his eyes. "If I fucking knew we wouldn't be in this situation in the first place. You're my best friend—you're supposed to tell me everything." His eyes narrow as they meet mine. "She was in there talking soul shattering love. You better not be fucking her around."

I pull my hands into my chest. "I'm not, Ollie. I swear. I love her, too."

"Wow." He throws his hands up and then rubs his temple. "I don't even know what to do with this."

"Listen, this is real. We're in this together, completely. It's what we want."

He shakes his head. "Completely, huh? So, that means you told her everything. She knows everything about you."

I bite the inside of my cheek and he nods. "That's what I thought." He walks over to me and looks me directly in the eyes. "You know how I know that?" I shake my head, and he continues. "Because she asked *me* to tell her."

My lungs feel like they collapse for a moment as I struggle to take another breath. "Did you?"

He throws his arms up again and drops them heavily at his sides. "I didn't want to, and I almost did, but then you two showed up and decided to have a brawl in my driveway. What were you thinking?"

"I wasn't thinking. I just reacted." I step closer to him, my hands still shaking. "He's going to hurt her. He's crazy."

"He's not crazy. He's a dumb kid who can't handle losing the love of his life."

I laugh sarcastically. "The love of his life? He's treated her like garbage since they started dating. He doesn't deserve a girl like Elle—he never did."

His eyes soften a little. "I know you care about her." He pulls his hand into his chest. "I care about her, too."

I clench my fist, the anger coursing through me in waves. "I fucking love her." I get right in his face. "Do you understand me? I *love* her. I will do anything that I have to do to protect her."

Oliver holds his hands up. "Whoa. Calm down, killer. Judah is not the enemy."

My mind is completely blown right now. I can't wait to hear his rationale on this one. Oliver takes a deep breath and leans on the edge of the couch. "Hunter, they've been back and forth for years—you know that. This is probably the worst time for her to get involved with someone else. She's young, she doesn't know what she wants."

When I open my mouth to protest, he stops me. "And that's okay. She needs to make mistakes and figure things out on her own." He pokes me in the chest. "And if you love her as much as you say you do, then you need to be patient with her. She's not as strong as she appears to be."

I breathe a little calmer and nod once. "I can do that."

Oliver laughs. "Can you? You really put the beat down on the poor kid."

I grip my hands in my hair and pace around the small living area. "I know. I fucked up."

"You sure did."

I look down to him in shock. "You're supposed to make me feel better."

"Only when you're right." He stands up and shrugs and then places his hand on my shoulder. "Right now you're totally in the wrong, dude. Apologize to Judah and pray he doesn't spread this around to their friends. You could be in a world of shit."

To be honest, that's the least of my worries. Elliot could barely look at me. What if what I did was so horrifying that she never speaks to me again? That thought alone makes me physically ill.

So, I wait. I wait for her to come to me and pray that she gives me a chance to explain.

POISON AND WINE

Elliot

udah winces when I press the damp washcloth to his lip. "Sorry," I whisper. I attempt to move as gently as I can around the cut. He peeks up at me, and I keep my gaze averted. If I look at him right now, I won't be able to hold it together anymore.

"Elle?"

I swallow the lump in my throat. "What?"

There's a long pause and I finally lower my eyes to his. "Are you with him?" he asks.

When I don't answer fast enough, he pulls the rag from my hand, catching my full attention. He tosses it to the table. "You are, aren't you?"

Ignoring him, I reach for the bag of ice lying next to the

bloody washcloth and place it to his cheek. "You're already swelling up. It will look even worse if you don't take care of it now."

He grabs my wrist gently. "Elliot, please. Tell me that I'm wrong." I look down at him and see the panic in his eyes. "Tell me that you're not in love with him." His throat bobs when he swallows. "At least tell me that."

I'm not sure why it's so hard to admit it to him, but it is. He sees it in my face though. I can't hide that. My feelings for Hunter are too strong now to be denied anymore.

I take a step back from him and lean against the counter, gripping the edge to hold my balance. "I'm sorry," I say again and then take a shaky breath. "I don't know what else to say."

He looks at me like all the air has been knocked out of him. "How could you do this?"

"How could *I* do this?" I ask. I stand up straighter and draw my hand into my chest. "You're the one who wanted this."

Judah stands up from the chair abruptly and instantly regrets it, clutching his side. He lets out an angry breath through his nose. "I never asked for this. You weren't supposed to fall in love."

"What was I supposed to do, huh?" I cross my arms over my chest. "Sit around and wait for you until you banged every girl that made your dick twitch out of your system."

He shakes his head roughly. "No." His eyes lock on my mine, and the intensity in them brings me pause. "You were supposed to miss me."

My eyebrows pull in. "Miss you? How was any of this supposed to make me miss you?"

His eyes lower to the tile floor for a moment. "I wanted you to come with me." He looks up and gives me a guilty look. "I thought it would make you want to come to Cornell next year."

"Why would this make me want to do that?"

He narrows his eyes slightly. "I sure as hell didn't think it would make you bang your English teacher."

"Fuck you, Judah," I say , stepping forward. I point my finger at him. "It's not like that and you know it. He's our friend."

Judah laughs bitterly. "Not my fucking friend. Hunter and I were never bros." He cocks his head to me when I lower my hand. "I was cool with him because of you. That dude never looked at me right." He laughs again and then locks his eyes on me. "I never liked the way he looked at you either."

"Things were completely innocent between us until recently."

Judah throws his arms out in frustration. "Yeah, so what changed? Don't you think I had a right to know?"

"Are you serious right now?" I point between us. "You and I were over. I didn't have to explain anything to you."

Judah's jaw clenches. "Dating someone and being in love with them are two completely different things."

I cross my arms around myself and look away from him. "I didn't mean for it to happen. I was just so—so tired of pretending I wasn't sad." I look back to him, and the anger I saw a moment ago is replaced with regret. "He took that away for me. It didn't hurt so much."

"If you were hurting so badly—" His voice trails off, and he takes a shaky breath. "If you were hurting at all because of me, you should have told me." He takes my face gently in his hands. "I shouldn't have to tell you how much you mean to me, but I will. I'll tell you every day how much I love you and how much I need you in my life. If you have to stay here next year, then I'll wait.

My eyes well up, and I choke on my own air. "Why are you telling me this now?" The words come out in a strangled whisper, and I watch his eyes squeeze shut like I wounded him.

"It's not too late," he says, mostly to himself. His eyes flick open again as my first tear falls. "Tell me it's not."

If I opened my mouth to speak, I know my words would break into a million pieces. I never wanted to hurt Judah—mentally or otherwise, but it *is* too late. I've already given my heart to someone else, and I have no intention of taking it back.

Judah sees my struggle, and a tear falls down his cheek. "Okay," he says, his voice thick. He grabs the rag from the table and wipes the rest of the blood from his lip before reaching for his hat. He slips it on backwards and starts toward the door, pausing with his hand on the doorknob.

"If he's what you want, I won't stand in the way of your happiness." He turns over his shoulder. "I won't say anything either. I may not give a shit about his future, but I sure as hell care about yours."

Without another word, he slams the door behind him, and I slowly lower myself to the barstool. The tears are falling steadily now, and I'm not sure if they'll ever stop. Judah is being the guy I always wanted him to be, and Hunter is acting like a jealous, psychopath. I know that's not how he really is. I *know* him. I've spent countless nights staying up with him, getting to know every corner of his heart and have never found a single part of it to be impure.

Something must have really set him off, and I need to find out why.

～

I don't go to the guest house after Judah leaves. I need time to think. I'm sure Hunter is upset, too—but I don't know what to say to him. Judah has gotten into fights with guys over me before, but this was different. It's not causal like it was before, if you can even call a fight casual. The emotions behind those blows were intense. They both feel like they are losing me, and the simple fact is, one of them already did.

I will always love Judah, that's something I can't take back. He's a part of me forever whether Hunter likes it or not. When this all began, I never expected to fall so hard and so deep for someone else, but I did. The love I have for Hunter consumes me and terrifies me at the same time. In the past few months, the dynamic of our relationship has changed so much that I'll never be able to go back to being his friend. You can't love someone the way that I love him and do that.

I'm lying on my side, staring at the blank screen of my phone. He didn't even text me. Maybe what Judah said really hit a nerve and now I'm too much trouble for him? Despite the fear of rejection, I type out a text and send it quickly. I shove my phone face down, and my heart pounds while I wait for his reply.

Me: Can we talk

It goes so long that my chest almost seizes up completely —but when I pick it back up, I see those three dots flashing.

Hunter: Door is open

I practically jump from my bed and pull on a pair of sweatpants. After twisting my hair on top of my head, I quietly slip down the stairs and out of the back door.

All of the lights are off in the guest house, and I slowly push the door open. I scan around the room and don't see him anywhere. I walk further down the hall and peek in the bedroom. He's lying on his side facing the wall.

I slide in behind him, wrapping my arms around his waist. I place a kiss on his cheek, and he sighs. "I love you, Hunter," I whisper.

His hands lace with my mine, and he brings them tight to his chest. He's shaking, and I can't tell if it's from his recent rage or something else.

"I'm sorry," he says softly.

I pull one of my hands away and run it through his thick, blond hair. "You know that I only want you, right?" He doesn't answer, and it causes my stomach to drop further. I take a shallow breath. "Hunter?"

He turns around to face me, resting his hand on my hip. His eyes are so sad it breaks my heart instantly. "This is really hard for me."

"All relationships are hard sometimes," I say softly.

He shakes his head. "No, not for me. I've never loved anyone before—I never let myself love someone the way I love you."

"Why?"

His eyes shift away from mine and down to the space between us. "What did Ollie tell you about me?"

"Nothing," I say quickly. I grab his face, so he has to look at me. "He told me nothing, and I'm glad he didn't. I want to hear it from you."

Hunter laughs bitterly. "You don't know what you're asking for."

"You're right," I say, letting go of him and inching back a little. He mirrors my position and rests on his elbow. "I don't know what I'm asking for because you never really let me in."

He sighs and then reaches for my hand. His fingers thread back and forth through mine slowly, but he doesn't meet my eyes. "I didn't grow up like you did. I didn't have a family to teach me things like love." His gaze lands on mine. "My father is a horrible man. That's not just me being cynical, there isn't a decent bone in his body."

"Is that why you don't see him?"

He laughs once. "I can see him any time I want. That's

why we're here—my mother and I. She followed him when he got sent to prison."

Prison? A million scenarios run through my mind of what he could've done and why Hunter obviously feels responsible for it. I'm not even sure what to say. He's watching me, waiting for a response, so I work to keep my features neutral.

"Why?"

He blows out a long breath and leans in to kiss my forehead. He pulls back a little and looks in my eyes. "You sure you want to hear this?"

I grab his face and kiss him hard. I try to put every ounce of love I have for him into it, so he knows how invested in this relationship I really am. He kisses me back for a moment and then laughs against my lips. "Is that a yes—or?"

I nod. "It's a yes. I want to know every part of you. Even the ones you're afraid of."

"I wanted to protect you from that," he whispers. His voice is nearly broken, and I find myself on the verge of tears again.

Instead of breaking down and losing it, I give him a small smile and gently cup the side of his face. "Well, I want to protect *your* heart." I lean over and kiss him slowly. "Please, let me."

25

IN THE BLOOD

Hunter

The vulnerability in her eyes paralyzes me. She's scared, too. It's not just me that's terrified I won't be enough. We're both scared neither one of us is capable of providing the other with what they need. Maybe we're not —or maybe we're two perfectly flawed people with so many rough and torn edges they'll fray and fit together beautifully.

I gently smooth the hair back from her face and lean down to press my lips to her skin. "It's yours, Elle." I grab her hand and place it on my chest, and my heart pounds against it. "That's not a question, that's the problem." I take an unsteady breath. "I'm so fucking in love with you that it brings out the worst part of me."

She shakes her head. "There isn't a worst part of you. You're a good guy—"

"I'm not," I say, cutting her off with a bitter laugh. Her eyes are incredulous when they meet mine, but I don't falter. "I'm not, Elle. I had a shit life for most of it, and I struggle with the aftermath that it caused."

Elliot's face tenses. She's trying not to react to what I'm saying. I know she wants to protect me from judgment, but it will come anyway. A story like mine always does.

I roll over on my back and lace my hands across my chest. My eyes fix on the ceiling, so I don't have to see hers while I speak. "Where do I begin?" I sigh heavily and the bed shifts beside me, and I feel her move closer. Her fingertips inch toward mine, and I slide my hand over to meet them. "I used to get in trouble a lot as a kid. Getting into fights at school or at a friend's house—didn't matter where really, I was usually hitting someone."

Another bitter laugh escapes me. "My father taught me how to fight. It mostly came from him beating on me, but I learned a thing or two."

I smirk at her in an attempt to lighten the mood, but she's not amused.

I sigh. "I was like this all through school until I hit ninth grade. I was gone more with soccer and stuff so that left more time for him to focus his rage on someone else." I clench my fist and grit my teeth when I think of my mother. "I wasn't going to let him hit her. You never raise your hands to a woman—especially not someone you love."

I risk a glance over at her, and there are tears in her eyes. Unable to stand it any longer, I turn on my side and tuck her into my chest. "I would never hurt you, Elliot. *Ever*."

"I know," she whispers.

I lean back so I can see her face, gently cupping her check. "You have to know that. Everything I do is to protect you. The way he acts—I don't like it. It fucking scares me."

She leans back from me a little, and I move my hand down to rest on her hip. "Judah's not scary, he's sad."

I shake my head. Sadness leads to anger and anger leads to violence. It's only a matter of time before he loses his shit, and I'm not going to stand around and wait for it to happen. Especially since she's with me now. It's my most important job to keep her safe.

"Sad or not, it's not right the way he was acting." I press my finger to her lips when she starts to protest. "What I did wasn't right either." I lower my hand. "I know that."

Her face softens, and she lowers her eyes to the space between us. "I'm glad because I never want to see that again." She looks up at me with a more serious expression. "I mean it. Judah and I are going to be in each other's lives. Our families are long-time friends, and he's my friend, too."

I don't understand how she thinks they can remain friends after this. He's clearly still in love with her, and I would bet anything he's not okay with her and I being together. That's assuming she told him everything.

I'm about to ask her about it when she speaks first. The concern is back on her face again. "What happened? Why is he in prison?"

I laugh once. "I guess you're not going to let this go, huh?"

She shakes her head, and I take a deep breath. "Okay, well —my father is serving time for felony assault on a minor." Her eyes widen, but I keep going. "It would have been attempted murder, but my testimony prevented that from happening."

Elliot brings her hand up to cover her mouth. It's shocking when you say it out loud—*murder*. Do I think he wanted to kill me? Absolutely, but I couldn't bring myself to admit it. Who wants to admit their father hates them so much they nearly beat them to death?

"I spent two months in the hospital after we got into it

one night after practice. He was drunk as usual and pushing my mom around the living room. I stepped in and tried to be a hero, and he showed me I wasn't."

I shrug like it's no big deal, but Elliot's crying. She feels bad for me, and I never wanted that. I never wanted her to know this of me, to know what I'm capable of. I'm sure that was already shot to shit after she saw what I did to Judah.

She wipes under her eyes and reaches for my hand again. She brings it up to her lips and kisses it gently. "I'm sorry that happened to you. I'm sorry you had to go through something like that."

I lean down and catch her lips briefly. "It's okay, baby. I'm okay."

That's probably a lie, but she doesn't call me out on it. I've never really talked about my past to anyone—besides Ollie, and that's not exactly a good thing. They suggested a therapist after the incident, but I never saw one. Call it pride or just being a stubborn kid, but I wasn't about to sit in a room with someone I never met before and pour my heart out. Fuck that.

Her eyes drift away from me for a moment. "Judah isn't going to say anything about us."

"How do you know?"

She looks back to me. "Because he promised."

"And you believe him?"

"Yes."

I lower my head into the palm of my hand, feeling like an idiot for losing it on him. The last thing we need is to draw attention to ourselves when we still have five months until graduation. If it gets out that we're seeing each other, it will be detrimental for both us.

She runs her hand along my back in an attempt to comfort me. Comfort *me* after what I did to us.

I look up at her. "I'll apologize to Judah. I'll set shit straight with him, and hopefully it will be enough."

Elliot's fingers trail along the side of my face. "It makes me very happy that you're willing to do that. I promise he's not a bad guy."

My stomach twists at her words. She's right. Judah is not a bad guy. Sure, he has his faults just like the rest of us—but at the end of the day it's becoming more and more clear that maybe he is better for her. Despite the stupid teenage bullshit they go through, they have a strong history, and they care about each other. She may love me now, but what about next time? How will she feel if I can't control myself some other time and really hurt someone? I don't want to end up like my father, but it doesn't seem like that far of a stretch.

~

The next morning Elliot is still cuddled beside me when I open my eyes. It's almost light outside, and I curse under my breath for agreeing to run with Oliver. The only time you can count on him to be punctual is when a sport is involved. Work, meetings, any kind of date—you're pushing your luck.

I sigh when I glance at the bedside clock. *Ten minutes.* I rub my eyes with the balls of my hands and then nudge Elliot gently. She stirs, but doesn't move much and mumbles something I don't quite make out.

I lean down and kiss her cheek. "Wake up, baby. Ollie will be here soon."

"So," she says, her face half in the pillow. "He already knows."

I laugh. "Yeah, well I don't want to rub it in his face too much, too soon. I have a feeling I'm on his shit list."

Elliot rolls over to her back and gives a small smile. "That's a guarantee." When I frown she lightly slaps my side.

"Don't worry, I'm sure I am, too. We're both heartless liars in his book."

"He didn't need to know. It was our business if we wanted to be together." I stand up from the bed and reach for my pants. I lock eyes with her while pulling them on. "Besides, I needed to be sure it's what you really wanted before I risked pissing off my best friend."

Elliot scoffs and sits up against her pillow. "Of course it's what I really wanted. You're the one who kept me away."

My eyes soften toward her. I don't want to fight about this. I'm still not even sure we should continue this after what happened last night. There's too much attention being drawn to us, and I'm not willing to risk her future over it. But then my heart steps in and prevents me from doing the right thing. I know what we're doing is wrong, but I can't stop myself. Not since I allowed her to get so inside my head. She feels like a part of me even more now, and I don't think I can give that up.

Elliot rolls her eyes and hops off the bed. I watch her shimmy into her yoga pants and consider texting Ollie that I'm sick. He'll never buy it, but a different organ is now doing the thinking for me.

She's still angry though, glaring over at me and crossing her arms. I walk over and place my hands on her elbows, leaning in to kiss her forehead. "I should've never done that. I love you. I've been in love with you for so long I don't even remember how it started." I tip her chin up with my finger. "I'm going to make this right. All of it."

She nods.

"I mean it, Elle. I'm going to be the guy you need. The one who makes you feel safe, the one you always have to rely on no matter what."

She smiles. "You really have no idea how much you already give me." She loops her arms around my neck, and her lips linger over mine. "You're everything I want."

I'm not sure how much I believe her, but I kiss her like I do. I kiss her like everything is right with the world, and I have the only thing that matters right here in my arms. Only one part of that thought is true. I'm still working on the other one.

26

DOUBLE STANDARD

Elliot

The buzz around school on Monday morning is that Judah got jumped. From what I've heard so far, he's been pretty tight lipped about it. I knew he wouldn't say anything, but it makes me nervous how much people are talking about it.

We're only five minutes into lunch period and the theories are already flying. Cameron is still sitting across from me even though we barely speak anymore. I know she somehow thinks I'm angry over Dylan, but I actually find it ridiculous. You can't even consider the minimal time we spent together dating, and I basically gave her my blessing.

When I look up from my barely touched salad, her green eyes bore into me with accusation. "You're awfully quiet."

She takes a sip of her iced latte. "Or don't you care what happened to Judah?"

I glare over at her. "Of course I care what happened to him." I glance around at the curious eyes surrounding me at the table. Attention usually doesn't make me uncomfortable, but right now I feel like I'm on trial.

Poppy Lincoln leans in from beside me. "So what did happen?" She twirls her spoon around in her yogurt before taking a small bite. Of all the girls in our group, Poppy loves gossip the most—especially the juicy kind that involves her friends. Like I said—sharks.

"I have no idea. Judah and I aren't really talking at the moment."

Cameron scoffs, and I raise an eyebrow. She catches my look of disdain and squares her shoulders. "Your little arrangement not working out anymore?"

My stomach clenches. I'd rather not get into it with her in front of everyone. "We broke up."

"Kind of convenient don't ya think?" Holden chimes in from down the table. Holden Parker is one of Judah's best friends, and if anyone is going to choose sides, it's going to be him.

I instantly get defensive. "What's that supposed to mean?"

He shrugs. "I don't know, maybe Judah got into it with whatever guy you're dating. You haven't exactly been around lately."

"So that means I must have some secret boyfriend nobody knows about?"

"Seems reasonable."

"Whatever." I direct my attention back to my salad, aggressively poking my fork into the lettuce, but he doesn't let it go.

He leans forward across the table at me. "Did you know he's in danger of being on academic warning next semester?"

My stomach knots further, but I don't look up at him. I

was worried something like this would happen. Judah never mentioned his grades were in jeopardy. It's not what I would expect from him. He's always been smart and barely had to study. He must have taken our separation way harder than I realized—or he's been drinking too much. My guess is that it's a combination of both.

When I don't acknowledge Holden, he laughs once. "And he got suspended from the team for missing too many practices."

This causes my anger to spike. I pick my head up and narrow my eyes at him. "And how is any of that my fault?"

He motions toward me dramatically. "You're the fucking reason. If he hadn't been coming home so much because of you this never would have happened."

Dylan nudges him from beside Cameron. "Hey, man. That's not cool." He nods to me. "It's not Elle's fault Judah's acting irrational. Every time I've seen the dude in the past couple of months he's been wasted. I'll bet he picked a fight with the wrong guy and got his ass handed to him."

Holden sputters a laugh. "You would defend her."

Cameron stiffens in her seat, clearly pissed that Dylan would speak up for me. Poppy's spoon is poised mid-air, and everyone else is just staring at us waiting for the next outburst to erupt. So much for staying out of the drama.

I catch Ollie walking up out of the corner of my eye, but Holden doesn't see him. He points his finger at me with a sneer. "You've been fucking him around since the beginning of the semester. I bet he caught you fucking someone and finally snapped." He gives Dylan a shove sideways. "Wouldn't be the first time."

A few things happen at once. Dylan clenches his fists and prepares to punch Holden for shoving him. Cameron gets a scowl on her face because now she thinks Dylan and I slept together, and I didn't tell her. Holden's smirk disappears from his face when Ollie grabs him by the back of the neck. I just sit there, unable to process all the bullshit that got spouted at this table in the past five minutes.

Oliver gives a dark smile and leans down to Holden's ear. I can't hear what he's saying, but I watch the color drain from Holden's face. He nods quickly and then glances in my direction. "I'm sorry, Elle. That was out of line." His voice trembles a little and Ollie loosens his grip.

"Alright. Come with me." He motions upward, and Holden lets out a nervous laugh.

"Where are we going?"

Ollie's jaw ticks, but his face remains stoic. "Let's go."

I'm starting to panic. "Ollie."

He doesn't look at me. He keeps his gaze on Holden. "Mr. Parker wants to cause a scene during my lunch period, we can take this out in the hallway. Let's fucking go."

Holden's eyes meet mine once more before he pushes up from the table and stalks toward the doors. Ollie gives a menacing look around at everyone and then turns and walks away without another word.

"Shit," Dylan breathes. He shakes his head with a laugh. "Good thing Ollie's a teacher. Teacher's don't hit people."

My stomach drops again, and I discreetly scan for Hunter. It's not his period to monitor lunches so he has no reason to be here. Even so, that never really stopped him from sneaking in to wink at me or do something cute to make me smile.

I breathe a little easier when I don't see him. Abandoning my tray, I get up from the table and sling my bag over my shoulder. I think I hear Poppy call my name, but I don't stop. I keep going until I make it to Ollie's office on the other side of the building.

When I push open the door, I expect to see him and Holden in a heated discussion or a headlock—but the room is empty. The knot inside of me twists tighter at the thought of Ollie being stupid enough to assault someone over me too.

I set my bag down on the floor next to his desk and sit back in his comfy office chair. I pull my legs up under my chin and try to formulate some kind of way out of this. It's only a matter of time before they find out about Hunter and me. He could go to prison, lose his teaching license—so many bad things that he doesn't deserve. I'm sure bad things would happen to me too, but nothing that would ruin me. I'm not trying to get into a particularly good school, and I could always work for my parents even if I don't go to college.

That's the difference between us. He has so much more to lose, and that's not fair. Why should either one of us have to sacrifice something all because we love each other?

My thoughts are interrupted by the door flying open and Ollie storming in. He doesn't notice me at first because the light is still off, and I watch him struggle with the knot in his tie, swearing under his breath.

"You okay?" I ask in a small voice.

He jumps and then looks down at me with a laugh. He reaches over for the light switch and flicks it on. "Jesus, Elle. I'm on edge right now if you haven't noticed."

"I gathered."

He sticks his finger in the knot to loosen it further. "I hate game days at school. On top of everything else I have walk around like a douche wearing a tie all day."

I smile. "I think you look very professional."

He gives a sarcastic sneer. "Yeah, well, I feel like an asshole." He plants his hands on his hips and gives me a hard look. "You okay?"

I sink back into the chair a little and lower my legs. "I'm fine, I guess."

Ollie shakes his head and moves around the desk to sit on the edge next to me. "He won't fuck with you again."

My eyes widen. "You didn't—"

Ollie laughs. "I'm not an idiot. I didn't hit him. I just gave

185

him a strong warning and some very interesting detention activities that will take quite a while."

"You can't tell Hunter."

Ollie taps his head. "Again, I'm not an idiot. We're barely through the last assault and battery. No need to add a second."

It must be something he sees in my face, because his face falls, too. "I'm sorry, Elle. Guys are terrible. They can sleep with whomever they want and be some kind of God, but if a girl does it—well, Holden is an asshole."

"I didn't sleep with Dylan."

He holds his hands up. "I never said you did."

"You insinuated you believed him."

Ollie shakes his head. "No, I didn't believe him. I know you're not like me, but I also know that's how guys think. Judah probably thought the same thing, and that's why he had such a problem with Hunter."

I twist a long strand of hair around my finger in front of my face, avoiding his eyes. "He has a problem with Hunter because he knows that I love him."

Ollie's voice is soft. "You told him that?"

I nod.

He blows out a long breath. "And he was okay with that?"

I laugh and look up with him. "Of course not, but what's he going to do? He made his bed, now he has to lie in it."

He chuckles and stands up from the desk. "Good one."

He pulls his tie off and throws it around a hook by his door before turning back to me. He gets his serious brother expression on, and I prepare myself for more bullshit or some actual brotherly advice.

"Elle, I need you to really think about what this could do to Hunter if it all goes to shit."

"I know that!" I say, almost too loudly.

He holds up a finger. "Let me finish." I clamp my mouth shut and he grins. "I'm your brother and more than willing to help you. Lie, steal, light assault—I'm down for basically anything, but you need to remember one thing."

"What's that?"

"If you do get caught, and Hunter goes away, you won't have him then either."

My heart nearly dies at the thought of Hunter going away for any period of time, let alone forever. I clutch my chest and try to soothe the ache already burning.

Ollie's sees my pain and sighs. "Be careful from now on. That's all I'm asking."

27

IF YOU SAY SO

Hunter

*E*lliot has been acting weird since she got home from practice today. Typically she comes over after showering and does her homework on my bed while I grade papers. Today, however, she's doodling circles on the top of her page and sighing every few minutes. Kind of adorable, but it's driving me crazy wondering what's wrong.

I set my pen down and stand up from the chair at the small desk by the window. I sit down on the bed beside her and gently run my hand down her back. "Are you okay?"

She nods, blackening the edges of her latest creation. I give a sigh of my own and pat her on the ass. "Come on, tell me. I'm a big boy. I can handle it."

Elliot shoots me a skeptical look, but then rolls over onto her side. "Promise you won't get mad."

I hate when people say that. It almost always means that whatever you are about to hear will piss you off. That being said, I already promised to be there for her when she needs me and part of that is not acting like a dick when she tells me something I may not like.

I take a deep breath. "Okay, let me have it."

She sits up the whole way and crosses her legs in front of her. Her eyes remain wary. "I'm serious, Hunter. You can't freak out, and I don't like keeping things from you, so I want to tell you."

My pulse begins to quicken. Since our current situation is still precarious, I'm afraid of what she's going to say.

"I promise."

She laughs once. "Okay, well remember that in a few minutes." She flicks her long, dark hair over her shoulder and meets my eyes. "Holden started a rumor at lunch that Judah got into a fight with my new boyfriend."

My stomach drops a little further. "Do they know who?"

"No," she says.

This time, I breathe a sigh of relief. I reach over and squeeze her shoulder. "Okay, we can handle that. Judah said he isn't going to say anything, and you trust him, right?"

"Right."

She answers automatically, but her tone lacks enthusiasm. Something's *not* right.

"What else happened?"

She turns her eyes away from me toward the window. "You're going to get mad."

I'm already mad imagining all of the horrible things she could possibly tell me. The fact that she's upset at all right now is reason enough for me to find the person who made her this way and teach him a lesson—but I'm not going to do that. I'm going to take a deep breath and think everything through as it comes.

I grab her hand. "Elle, look at me baby." Her eyes shift back to me, and I bring her hand up to my lips. "Let me fix it, okay? Whatever it is, you should never be afraid to tell me something."

The look in her eyes is desolate and it destroys me. What could have possibly happened today to make her feel this way?

She takes a shaky breath. "I don't want to ruin your life."

My eyebrows pull in, confused by her admission. I tug her closer to me and wrap my arms around her. "What could make you think that?" I kiss the side of her head. "Huh?"

She sniffs like she's been silently crying. "The guys are determined to get to the bottom of what happened to Judah. If they find out..." her voice trails off with a strangled sob. She grips the front of my T-shirt, looking up at me with tears in her eyes. "You could get in serious trouble. Like trouble you can't come back from."

I know the risks of being with her. I've weighed them in my own head too many times to count, but they don't matter anymore. I want her, need her even, and I'm too selfish to let her go now.

She squeezes me tighter and lays her cheek against my chest. "I just got you. It's not fair if I lose you already."

"You won't lose me, Elle." I lean back and tip her chin, kissing her once. "You won't. No matter what happens, I'm not going anywhere."

She kisses me back harder, gripping the back of my neck. I work my lips over hers to calm her, but it calms me too. Being near her is enough to take away any doubt that we belong together. I know we do. All that's left is to figure out how.

~

*A*s promised, Oliver and I are running the lifts and helping with the tubing park at the resort this weekend. Elliot is inside bartending which I'm not exactly thrilled about. All that keeps running through my mind is drunk vacationers making lewd comments and eyeing her like she's on the menu.

"Whatcha thinking about over there, Mayweather?" Oliver smirks at me as he loads inner tubes onto the conveyor.

"Nothing." I attempt to keep my tone casual, but he sees right through me.

He lifts his beanie and looks me in the eye. "You know what pisses me off the most?"

I raise an eyebrow, and he shakes his head. "Every time you were in one of these pissy little moods it was about my fucking sister."

"I'm sorry. I should have been honest with you."

He nods. "Yeah, you should have." He stops throwing the tubes on the belt for a minute and readjusts his gloves. When he's done, he looks up at me with a serious expression. "First and foremost, Elliot is my main concern. If I think you've stepped out of line with her in any way, I won't hesitate to retaliate. You've put me in an awkward position here, man."

I run my hand roughly down my face. "I know, I really do. And I wouldn't expect anything less." I pause for a moment and attempt to swallow the growing lump in my throat. Just the thought of someone causing her harm—myself or otherwise—wrecks me more than I ever imagined. "I promise you that I would never hurt her. I mean that, Ollie."

Oliver nods again, and his expression softens. "Let's hope not. Because if you do, the way Judah looks right now will seem mild compared to what I do to you."

I don't blame Ollie one bit for feeling that way. My own need to protect Elliot forced me into doing terrible things. I just hope that was the last of it, because I would hate to see what I would do to him if it happens again.

He's quiet for a moment and then turns to me, the somber expression back on his face. He starts messing with his hat again. I brace myself for what he's about to say. "Listen, man. I know you have strong feelings for Elle—"

I start shaking my head, and he laughs a little. "Ollie, I already told you. I love her."

He nods. "Yeah, you said that—but I'm worried."

I'm starting to think there's something I don't know. Elliot was acting weird all week and now Oliver can't spit out whatever the fuck he wants to tell me. That's not like him. He's never afraid to say what he's thinking.

I sigh heavily and toss another discarded tube onto the conveyor. I square my shoulders when I turn back to him. "Just fucking tell me."

He takes a breath. "There was an incident during lunch period yesterday."

"Yeah, I know. She told me."

Oliver blows out a long breath, clearly relieved. "Okay, good. I didn't want you finding out that little shit called her a whore while you're at school and beating him to death in the hallway."

My blood instantly boils, and my jaw starts to twitch. "What did you say?"

The low tone of my voice makes Ollie visibly flinch. "Um, I thought you said she told you."

He takes a step back when I take one toward him. "Who said it?"

Ollie braces his hands on my shoulders and looks me dead in the eye. "I'm going to tell you and then you're going to count to ten and forget about it, okay? I got it covered."

My posture remains rigid. "Who?" I ask again, but this time I try to speak more calmly. His expression is skeptical, but he releases me and sighs.

"It was Holden, but—"

I pull away from him abruptly and stalk toward the parking lot. Ollie jumps on my back like a spider monkey before I make it three steps. I drag him with me for a few more until the weight of him face plants us both into the snow.

He's still clinging to me, and I struggle to push him off. We catch sideways glances from several skiers on their way past, but he just laughs.

"Get off of me," I growl and then give him a forceful shove.

He falls onto his side, still smirking. I push myself up on my knees and grab a handful of snow before throwing it at his face. He dodges it with another chuckle, clearly amused with himself.

I brush my pants off when I stand and turn to glare at him while he does that same. "What the fuck is wrong with you?"

He grins at me. "It was the quickest way I could think to stop you."

"Stop me from doing what?"

He rolls his eyes. "Building your criminal record, obviously." He walks over and gives my shoulder a squeeze. I fight the urge to punch him. "You need to chill. I know you want to murder that kid, but you can't."

My nostrils flare. "You said you took care of it. What did you do?"

He releases me and then shrugs. "I threatened him—and then I told Judah."

Now I'm really going to hit him. "Why the fuck did you tell him?"

He looks at me like I'm some kind of idiot. "Because, genius. Judah can take a swing at him and not serve time for it."

I cross my arms, extremely uncomfortable with Judah being involved further. "I don't know, man. I don't trust him."

Ollie scoffs. "I know him. He's just as pissed as you are right now. He'll set him straight."

"And what if he wants to tell the truth?"

Ollie shakes his head. "He won't hurt Elliot. Exposing you, exposes her too. He would never do that to her."

It's total bullshit that I'm supposed to put all of my faith in someone who, I not only assaulted, but is definitely in love with my girlfriend. It doesn't exactly put one's mind at ease. Ollie senses my tension and sighs.

"Listen, I know you don't like him, but you have nothing to worry about. Underneath all that chauvinist exterior, he's a good dude, and he cares about her." His eyes drift away from me for a second and then he clears his throat. "And, uh —she cares about him, too. So you need to make shit right with him."

He readjusts his hat once more and turns back toward the conveyor. I don't say anything back because I know he's right. If I don't make nice with Judah then there's always going to be the worry he'll change his mind and destroy everything I have. I know I'm the one who put it all at risk, and I have to be the one to fix it.

GLASS HOUSES

Elliot

inter break couldn't have come at a better time. The constant tension among my friends now is stifling to say the least. Who would've thought that my break-up with Judah would have so much effect on everyone when he isn't even here? It just goes to show how petty high school really is and how much I can't wait to be done with it.

I'm powering through the last hour of the day when Cameron breezes past my locker. I glance up from exchanging textbooks and see her come to a stop and turn around. I cast my eyes away from her, but she walks up to the locker beside mine and leans back against it.

I ignore her, continuing to rummage through my things

and hoping she'll go away. I don't want to deal with whatever she has to say right now. My prayers go unanswered when she speaks.

"Didn't see you at Holden's last night. I take it you two are still fighting."

My hand pauses on my notebook, and I laugh under my breath. "Well, it was a Thursday, and I've been really busy with practice."

"Never stopped you before," she snaps back at me.

I close my locker hard and sling my bag over my shoulder. When I turn to face her, she flinches back, but I force a smile.

"Why do you care?"

She shrugs, clutching her Bio book to her chest. "I don't know. I've never seen you guys be so hostile toward each other."

"Well, he's being a dick so—"

I attempt to step around her, but she blocks my path. "Judah was there. He's home for break—but you probably didn't know that since you aren't talking to him either."

I grit my teeth. "What's your point, Cam?"

She stands up straighter. "He said he got into a fight with a couple of guys outside of the liquor store. Seems odd, but whatever right? Why would he lie?"

This conversation is beyond frustrating. If she's digging for dirt, she's not going to get it. "I have no idea."

"There's a lot of things you don't seem to know lately."

I cross my arms, losing every bit of patience I have left. "What's that supposed to mean?"

She leans in closer to me. "It seems Hunter has a mysterious cut on his lip the same week Judah gets the shit beat out of him."

My pulse skyrockets, bounding through my veins. I struggle to keep my face impassive. The last thing I want is for her to connect the two and get outed by my supposed best friend.

"Doesn't seem strange to me. Hunter and Ollie go out drinking all the time, and you know how they get."

She huffs under her breath. "He does live in your guest house now. It's awfully convenient that he moves in practically the moment Judah leaves for school."

"Alright," I say, putting my hand up to stop her from talking anymore. "I'm done with the third degree. Judah and I are over, I'm not seeing anyone else, and I don't have time for this petty bullshit right now."

Cameron shifts around on her feet, and the tension subsides from her face. She looks almost sad for a moment.

"Well, I wouldn't have to make such leaps if you actually talked to me anymore."

I laugh once. "You're the one who's walking around pissed off for no reason." I throw my arm out to my side. "I don't even want Dylan, so if that's what this is about—"

"It's not," she says quickly, cutting me off. She tucks a long, red strand of hair behind her ear. "Not really. I just have no idea what's going on with you, and we used to be so close. It hurts, Elle."

The heaviness I already felt in my chest multiplies, and I sigh. It's true I've been distant from everyone—*except for Hunter*—but this is so new for me, and it's not like I can talk to anyone about it. I've never let myself get so wrapped up in someone before, and I don't know how to make it stop—or if I even want it to.

"I'm sorry, Cam," I say, my voice softer.

She looks down and picks at the polish on her nails. "It's okay."

I shake my head and gently put my hand on her shoulder. "No, it's not." When she looks up at me, I offer a small smile. "I'll try to be more social during break. I'll come to Holden's this weekend, and we can hang out like old times."

This gets her to smile and for some reason it makes me nervous. I haven't trusted her intentions lately. Well, I kind of never did but it wasn't something I wanted to admit. I hate when people say someone is jealous of them. It makes them seem full of themselves, and I'm really not. It could seem like I have everything from the outside, but from the inside it's very different. I have all the same insecurities everyone else has—I was just taught not to let them show.

"I'd like that," Cameron says after a moment. She glances down at the phone clutched in her hand and then types off a quick text while smiling. She looks up at me again and flips her hair over her shoulder. "Okay, I'll see you Saturday then."

"Yep, Saturday."

I watch her walk away for a minute, strutting around like she knows something that I don't. I don't like it. Not at all.

❧

*D*eciding that we should probably get our stories straight, I drive past Judah's house on my way home. His truck is in the driveway, so I pull in behind it. I'm not even out of my car yet when I see him walking down the cobblestone sidewalk.

Judah's house looks a lot like The Lodge. Large glass windows, sharp peaks and edges, and covered in natural stone. It makes sense because his father designed both of them. That's another thing that brings us together. We both know what it feels like to have people think we have everything handed to us. Being born into a moderately wealthy family comes with more backlash than people would assume. We have to work twice as hard to get any kind of respect for our accomplishments.

That's why I'm so disappointed with how he's been acting. I know the last thing he ever wants to do is disappoint his father, and I'd hate to be the reason why he does.

He's wearing a Cornell hooded sweatshirt, and his ballcap is pulled down low on his head. My heart drops when he gives me that familiar crooked smile as I'm walking up to him.

"I didn't expect to see you."

I stop in front of him and cross my arms around myself. "I'm worried about you."

He laughs under his breath and stares over my head. When his eyes flick down to mine all traces of happiness to see me are gone. "Well, I'm fine." He nods to my car. "So, you can go back to the guest house with Hunter and quit worrying about it."

I take a breath. "I get that you're still mad—"

"Mad?" he says, cutting me off. He takes a step closer. "I'm not mad, Elliot. I'm..." his voice trails off, and he shakes his head before taking a deep breath and blowing it out forcefully. "I don't know what I am, but mad doesn't really describe it."

I reach forward and place my hand on his arm. He tenses under my touch but doesn't pull away. "Then what are you feeling, because Holden told me about what's been going on at school." I draw my hand back and laugh once bitterly. "Quite dramatically I might add."

Judah's jaw ticks. "Yeah, don't worry about that." He locks his eyes on mine. "I set him straight. He won't disrespect you like that again."

Swallowing back the residual hurt I feel, I nod. It still pisses me off that Holden accused me of sleeping around and hurting Judah while I'm sure it's perfectly okay if he was doing it.

"Elle, I'm serious." He speaks more firmly when I don't answer. "He's my best friend, but I'd knock him the fuck out if he says anything like that to you ever again."

"It's fine," I say. My voice sounds slightly exasperated because I'm already so tired of defending myself and pretending like I'm fine. I'm not fine. The guy I'm so desperately in love with is risking everything to be with me and all I'm doing is causing more problems for him.

Judah laughs. "I know you're not fine, babe." I look up at him and he grins. "You think I don't know you?" He steps into me and nudges my arm gently. "Come on. Tell me."

He always says this to me, and he believes it. Only, it's not the truth. I've held more things inside than I've ever let out before. It's not that I lie about it exactly. The only person I'm really protecting is myself. If I don't appear to ever be hurt, then it isn't real, is it?

So, I try to be as honest with him as I can. But, how can I possibly talk to him honestly about how I'm feeling right now? I still see the hurt in his eyes when he looks at me. He can smile all he wants, but it's not real. Despite my best attempts, I know I blindsided him with this.

"It's okay," I say. He gives me a skeptical look, and I flash a quick smile. "Seriously, I don't even give a shit what Holden or anyone else thinks." I take a breath. "—but I do care what you think. I haven't really talked to you since—uh, since that night in my kitchen. You were upset."

He takes a step back and messes with the bill of his ballcap. His hands fall with a shrug. "Yeah, of course I was upset. That doesn't mean I'll go back on my word and tell people about it." He laughs under his breath and keeps going. "It's not exactly something I would brag about."

I arch an eyebrow. "What do you mean by that?"

"You expect me to tell a bunch of dudes that I find out my girl is dating someone else and then that guy beats *me* up?" He chuckles again. "I'd look like a punk."

I'll ignore he just referred to me as *his* for a moment. He's clearly still reeling from what happened and needs a chance to fully process it. But suggesting our break-up was a hit to his ego pisses me off.

"That's what you're upset about?" I huff. "That you lost the fight?"

"No, Elliot," he says roughly. "You also ripped my fucking heart out—so there's that, too."

If I were being honest right now, I'd tell him it physically hurts my heart to hear him say that. I never wanted that for him. So, instead I lower my eyes from his and whisper, "I didn't come here to fight with you."

After a moment, he sighs, but I don't look at him. "I don't want to fight with you either. It's going to be hard enough at dinner next week."

The reminder of the upcoming holiday makes my stomach dip. We always have the Holloway's over for Christmas eve dinner. Even before Judah and I started dating, our fathers have been close friends.

I catch his gaze again. "They don't know about Hunter."

He looks at me like I'm an idiot. "I figured that."

"Well, I wanted you to know that he's going to be there. I didn't want it to be a surprise."

He laughs bitterly. "What? Sitting next to you at dinner while you play footsies with your boyfriend under the table?" He shrugs mockingly. "No, won't be uncomfortable at all."

I slap his arm with the back of my hand. "I would never do that."

"You would never do what?"

"Rub it in your face like that."

"Okay, Elliot," he says sarcastically. He gives me a hard look and then turns to walk away. "Because that would be so much worse," he mutters under his breath.

I stand there for a moment and watch him stalk up the sidewalk. It feels like he's taking this harder than I expected. I'm sure people will think I should have seen this coming—but I didn't. The Judah I knew six months ago would have never acted this way. He finally decides to show me he really cares and it's too late. That's what hurts the most.

29

PRESSURE

Hunter

$\mathscr{I}$'ve never been one for holidays. I'm sure it has something to do with the way mine usually went. My father would get drunk, pick a fight with my mother, smack me around a bit, knock over the Christmas tree in a whiskey fueled rage—normal stuff like that.

That's why I was so nervous when Elliot said her parents invited me to Christmas dinner. I've spent holidays with them before, but never under these circumstances. It's hard enough to pretend around everyone else, but now I have to be face-to-face with her family and basically lie to them. It makes me feel like shit considering all they've done for me over the years. There were many nights where I would have needed to sleep in my truck if it wasn't for their generosity.

Oliver seems to think it'll be fine. It's not reassuring considering he feels that way about pretty much everything. His outlook on things is skewed by the privilege he's known his whole life. He doesn't understand how important it is to make a good impression on his family. The last thing I want is for them to perceive me as some charity case who can't get his shit together. When we do finally tell them, I don't want them to worry I won't be able to take care of Elliot the way they would want.

I stand in front of the mirror, scrutinizing the outfit Elliot picked out for me earlier. It's no surprise this dinner is somewhat formal, and she wanted to make sure I felt comfortable. To be honest, I'm not sure I'll ever be comfortable in her world—but I'm willing to try.

Heels click on the floors outside my bedroom, and I smile. "I'm almost ready," I call over my shoulder. I rush through securing the dark grey tie over my black button-down when she appears in my doorway. I lose my breath for a moment. When Elliot is actually trying to be sexy, instead of just naturally being that way—she burns you.

She hikes up one stocking covered leg and leans along the door frame. "You like my dress?"

I bite my lip while I admire the short hem of her long-sleeved, lace dress and matching red satin heels. The stockings come just above her knees with a tiny little bow on the side. She looks like a present. My mind races through a dozen scenarios that all involve blowing off dinner.

Then Elliot laughs, and my eyes lock on hers. "Do I look like Christmas?" she whispers.

I take a few steps toward her, and she stands in front of me with that seductive look in her eye. Her hand grips my tie, and I reach for her ass. "You certainly look like something I want to unwrap." I glide my hand up the back of her dress, running my fingers along her bare skin. I lean in and kiss her once. "But I doubt we have time for that."

She smiles and tugs on my tie a little harder, bringing our lips inches apart. "It's going to be awfully hard to keep my hands off of you for an entire dinner." She nips at my bottom lip with her teeth and releases her hold. Her expression changes into something less seductive and more modest. Her hands smooth out the collar of my shirt as she speaks. "I know these aren't the most ideal circumstances, but I'm really happy you're spending the holiday with my family. It feels complete with you here."

I get that swelling in my chest again. It's like she knows how I'm feeling without me needing to say it. That's how connected we are now. For every doubt that creeps into my mind, there's a million little reasons why I shouldn't listen to them. Seeing her smile right now is the biggest one. I'd sacrifice pretty much anything at this point to make her happy.

Turning back to the mirror, I give myself one last look. She's fixing her hair when I turn back to her, and when her eyes meet mine, she smiles again. "What?"

I take a step forward and brush an errant curl from her face. "You know, you do look like Christmas." I gently kiss her cheek and then press my lips below her ear. "My favorite one."

$\sim$

*T*he main house is decorated like a Hallmark movie on steroids. I wouldn't even know what that meant, but Elliot's been making me watch them for almost a month now. I think she secretly likes happy endings.

I walk past the third fully dressed Christmas tree, and I haven't even made it to the dining room yet. They host a party after dinner that Oliver and Elliot usually slip away from. She said we'd sneak up to the cabin that's a few miles from the lodge once everyone starts to have a few drinks. Oliver handed me one on my way in. I've only been here a few minutes and my glass is already a pile of melting ice. I might be a little on edge tonight.

Elliot smiles at me from across the room, and it eases some of the tension brewing inside of me. I haven't seen Judah yet and I'm not exactly looking forward to it. I still haven't gotten around to apologizing to him for what happened. It blows my mind that he agreed to stay quiet about everything. He could destroy me and yet he chooses not to. Something seems a bit too convenient about that in my opinion.

Pushing that thought aside, I walk over and greet Elliot's mother, Claire. She has the same silky, brunette hair down her shoulders, flawless skin, and exotic hazel eyes as Elliot. The gene pool in this family runs deep.

She gives a warm smile when I stop in front of her. She reaches out and squeezes my elbow. "Hunter, we're so happy you came." She starts to guide me into the dining room. "I hope you're not missing something with your own family. They were welcome to come, too."

I hold my sarcasm inside. Maybe we can set up a Face-Time with my dad from prison? I'm sure Mason would be thrilled with that living next to his teenage daughter.

Instead, I give a polite smile. "No, they had a prior engagement. I'll see them tomorrow."

She nods to the chair directly across from Elliot. Judah appears from around the corner at the exact time our eyes meet. Elliot glances over her shoulder at him and then back to me, an apologetic smile on her lips.

I wink at her so she doesn't spend the entire meal worrying that I'm angry he's here. I spent most of the week assuring her that I wouldn't be, and I can't derail that promise in the first five minutes. I'm the one who created this drama, and I have no right making her feel like it's her fault.

I take my seat and Oliver smirks from beside me. He

already has half a dinner roll in one hand and a whiskey in the other. He's in such a good mood right now. It makes him unpredictable—and that fucking scares me.

Elliot gives a look of warning to Oliver when Judah steps up beside her. I see he ditched the punk-ass, backwards hat and has his hair gelled into messy spikes. He also appears to have just stepped out of a Polo ad. A douchey cable knit sweater and dark dress pants complete the illusion that he's anything less than a pretentious jock.

He leans down to hug Elliot and kisses her on the cheek. My eye is already twitching. He must feel safe right now with his father and Elliot's father, Mason, in attendance—and the fucker would be right. He could spend half the dinner making out with her and there's not a damn thing I can do about it. *Don't play hardball with me, Judah. I'm trying to be nice.*

The table is suddenly filled with close family and friends and the small chatter that breaks out begins to relieve some of the tension. Claire passes a bowl of potatoes my way.

"So, how's it going teaching up at Central? Do you and Ollie get to see each other much?"

I take the bowl from her and grab the spoon. After dropping a spoonful on my plate, I pass it to Oliver. "I love it," I say. "It's nice being back at our old school together."

"Yeah," Oliver chimes in. "He's a real hands-on kind of teacher. Takes extra special care of his students."

Elliot's face turns one shade redder, and she apparently kicks him, because I see him wince out of the corner of my eye. I hide my smile with my napkin.

Claire remains oblivious. "That's very nice to hear. Teachers really help mold their students into what they will become."

Elliot raises her steak knife discreetly a few inches off of the table and points it at Oliver in warning. Thankfully, he shows mercy and keeps his mouth shut, shoving another piece of bread in with a grin.

"Well, I think you chose a respectable teaching profession," Mason says between bites. He points his fork to Oliver from the head of the table. "More so than teaching kids how to play dodge ball."

Oliver scoffs. "Hey, I also teach girls how to run fast."

Mason gives a mocking look back to him. "Yeah, I'm sure you're doing it for their benefit."

I see Oliver's jaw working as he shuffles food around his plate. Serves him right for giving me so much shit. It's hard enough dealing with everything going on at this table without his twisted sense of humor.

Mason turns his attention to Judah. A look of pride spreading across his face. "How was your first season playing for Cornell, son? Had to feel good after winning State last year."

The cocky grin I expect in response to the stroke to his ego doesn't come. He glances nervously at his father before answering. "It was different. That's for sure."

Judah's father is still somewhat glaring from across the table but doesn't add anything to the conversation. Something tells me his behavior this past semester affected more than just his relationship with Elliot.

"That's okay," Mason says dismissively. He reaches for his glass and takes a drink. "I'm sure you two will figure it out."

Elliot chokes on the bite of food she was trying to swallow. Her eyebrows pull in and she reaches for her glass. After taking a drink, she directs her attention back to her dad. "Figure what out?"

Mason exchanges a look with Judah's father and laughs. "You too will be back together come Spring." He smiles at Elliot. "You know you'll be a Holloway soon enough."

Now Judah looks uncomfortable. I watch him toss back the rest of his drink and wish I could do the same. I turn to Oliver and steal his. He doesn't argue like he usually would. He just gives a knowing smile. He's clearly enjoying this.

Elliot's face remains tense. I know she wants to say something back, but the position she's in right now prevents her from doing so. It makes sense that her father would feel this way. Who wouldn't want their child to end up with someone from a nice family that has a successful life?

Mason's comments are forgotten quickly, and the conversation moves on to the game tomorrow, and I couldn't be more grateful. Anything to distract me from the picture of perfection sitting right in front of me. I think that's the biggest problem. By all accounts, they look good together. It makes sense for her to choose to be with someone like him. Why she chose me doesn't really make any sense.

I let those thoughts eat away at me until after everyone is finished with dinner. All of the guests have broken off into smaller groups, and I spot Judah standing to the side by the small bar in the corner of the room. With a sigh, I start walking toward him.

Deciding to get it over with, I reach out and nudge Judah's arm. He looks over at me with the hatred I expected. "What?"

"Can I talk to you for a minute?"

He looks back to Elliot who's standing between her father and Oliver. She gives an uneasy smile, clearly concerned with our close proximity to each other. With a sigh, he nods.

I walk out into the empty seating area just beyond the dining room. When I come to a stop, I turn back to Judah, and he shoves his hands in pockets. "Say what you need, man."

I take a deep breath. "I owe you an apology. I'm sorry for the way I handled our argument. I shouldn't have hit you."

"It's fine," he says indifferently and then turns to walk away. I grab his arm to stop him.

"Wait—it's not fine, okay?" I pull my hand back and his shoulders tense, but then he turns around to face me with a scowl. Obviously, he's going to make me work for this. I run a hand through my hair. "I shouldn't have reacted that way and what I did to you was not okay."

He laughs under his breath. "Whatever, dude. I already told Elle I'm not going to say anything. So you can save your bullshit apology."

Instead of punching him again and ruining all of the great progress we're making, I focus on breathing calmly. It doesn't help, but at least he's not knocked out on the hardwood floors right now.

"It's not bullshit," I say. "You didn't deserve that."

He stares at me for a beat, not saying anything. I can tell he's pissed, and I don't blame him. I'm pretty sure he's used to being a dick to her and then being forgiven for it with little to no effort. It must be extremely difficult to have things change so much.

His jaw hardens. "Look," he says, leaning into me. "I'm not going to pretend that I'm cool with this when I'm not—but I would never do or say anything that would hurt Elliot. So you can quit acting like you're a decent guy when all you're really doing is trying to save your own ass."

I clench my teeth so I don't say what I'm thinking right now. The last thing I need is for things to get heated and have a throw down right here in the formal sitting area—or whatever the fuck they call this room.

So, instead I take a breath and the high road. "That's fine. I get that you're feeling some type of way about all of this and I don't blame you." I pull my hand into my chest. "—but I wanted you to know that apology comes from me. I feel bad about how things went down, and I want to make it right."

Judah laughs and then rolls his eyes. "Consider our beef squashed, dude. She's all yours."

This time when he turns to walk away, I let him. It's obvious his words are bullshit. It's written all over his face how torn up he is over losing Elliot. The only problem I have now is that I have no idea what he plans to do about it.

30

I ONLY MISS YOU WHEN I'M BREATHING

Elliot

 $\mathcal{M}$ y heart drops when I see Judah storm away from Hunter. He disappears around the corner and then the side door slams shut. I'm guessing their conversation wasn't a pleasant one. Oliver squeezes my elbow and leans down to my ear.

"I'll talk to Hunter. Go check on Judah."

He walks away from me before I can reply. He swaggers into the dining room and leads Hunter toward the bar again. His eyes meet mine briefly, and I don't see the reassurance in them that I saw before. With a sigh, I turn away and walk toward the back door.

The wintery air hits me hard when I step out onto the porch that wraps around the back of the house. Judah is standing at the railing with his back to me. I wrap my arms around myself and take another step toward him.

"You okay?" I ask when I get closer.

He doesn't turn around. "I'm fine, Elle. Go inside."

"You're obviously not fine," I say back.

He laughs under his breath and his shoulders shake. He turns around, and there's no amusement on his face. "I don't know what you want from me," he says, leaning back on the railing. He shoves his hands in his pockets and shrugs. "Your boyfriend apologized, so everything's cool right? You got what you wanted. Everyone's happy."

I shake my head. "I don't want you to be upset. I hate that you're so mad at me."

He laughs again. "Mad at you?" He pushes off the railing. "Why do you keep thinking I'm mad at you like we're having some kind of fight?" He pulls his hand into his chest. "You broke my fucking heart, Elliot. I'm not mad at you." He takes a shaky breath. "I fucking miss you."

I lose my air again. Hearing him say those words hurts so much worse than I ever thought it could. "I'm sorry," I say, my voice small. It's a pathetic response, but it's all I have. I really am sorry, and there's nothing I can do to fix it. We both knew the risk we were taking at the beginning of the year. It was a 50/50 shot this would all end in heartbreak.

Judah blows out a long breath and then runs his hand roughly over his hair. "It's not your fault."

I don't have a response for that. Yes, I feel guilty that he found out about Hunter the way that he did, but what did he expect?

Even so, I still feel the need to comfort him. It's weird seeing Judah so emotional. "We are still going to be a part of each other's lives," I say, my voice softer. I place my hand on his arm, and he meets my eyes. "I know it won't be in the way we planned, but I can't lose you completely. You were my first everything. All of my best memories have you in them."

He sniffs, lowering his eyes from me. "I just feel so bad about the way I acted. I'm still acting like a dick because I'm so angry with myself."

"Hey," I say, shaking his arm. He still won't look at me, so I wrap my arms around his waist and hug him. I can't take the look on his face anymore anyway.

He hugs me back tighter than I expect. When his body starts to silently shake, I rub my hand up and down his back gently, no longer feeling the cold in the air. This kind of emotion from a guy like him is still troubling to me. Any male influence I've seen firsthand has come off stone-faced and detached. They don't discuss their feelings in a way that makes it acceptable to have them. That's why I've always tried so hard not to—until now that is. Now it's all I ever feel, and sometimes I'm so overwhelmed by it I can hardly breathe.

When the back door opens suddenly, he pulls back from me and discreetly wipes his eyes with his sleeve. Oliver strolls onto the porch in his puffer jacket and snow pants. He grins at Judah.

"You ready to take the sleds for a rip?" He motions over to the garages, and his grin widens. "The new racing motor I just had installed is sick."

Judah's face is back to being passive. All traces of his inner torment are safely hidden away from anyone who could possibly judge him for it. "Sounds cool."

Oliver clenches his fist in excitement. "Fucking right." He tosses his truck keys to me. "Take this and be prepared for search and rescue if I call."

He gives a stern look, but I just laugh. The guys do this every year after dinner and one of them always get stuck or breaks down. It usually leaves me all alone at the cabin while I wait for them to bail themselves out, but this year I have a feeling Hunter will be staying with me.

I think Judah knows because I see the muscle in his jaw

working. I'm glad Ollie is so close with him, but I can't imagine he's a comforting shoulder to lean on. That's why Judah always acts like he doesn't give a shit when he's around.

"Let's go," Ollie says, nodding to the door again. "I got a thirty-pack stuffed behind the seat."

I narrow my eyes and then grip the front of his jacket. "Be careful."

He winks at me. "Always."

Judah walks past me and nudges my shoulder on his way by. "Later, Elle."

I watch them walk off of the porch and over to the garages. It doesn't go longer than a minute before Hunter steps out behind me. When I turn to face him, it takes every-thing inside of me not to throw my arms around him and kiss him. Despite the awkward conversations I seemed to be having all night, he's been at the front of my mind the entire time.

He smiles at me and it's like all of the tension surrounding this evening starts to break away at once. His hand discreetly finds mine, and he laces our fingers together. He squeezes them and then lets them go all too soon. "You ready to get out of here?"

It's my turn to smile. "You have no idea."

∾

The cabin is modest compared to the rest of our properties. My parents rarely come up here, and Ollie only uses it when he's too drunk to drive home from the lodge. For me, it has everything we need. A large stone fireplace in the center of the room with sectional couches, two bedrooms downstairs, and spacious loft upstairs complete with its own bathroom. Personally, I'd rather live here than our main house. It's less cold and more like a home.

Hunter comes in the side door carrying a large armful of wood just as I'm pouring a glass of wine. I need a drink after the intense evening. Holidays are usually filled with some type of drama, but I've never had it directed toward me before. That's usually Ollie's job.

Even though I want to move on from all of it and enjoy the rest of the evening, I know I need to say something. I could see the look on Hunter's face when my father was talking about me and Judah.

I sit down on the couch and pull the knit blanket across my lap. Hunter was disappointed when I changed out of my dress and into a sweater and jeans, but the look he gives when he puts the wood down sets me on fire. He crosses the room toward me and kisses my lips once before lifting the blanket and sliding in beside me. His arm snakes around my waist, and he brings me as close to him as I can get. I snuggle into him and sigh. This feels perfect.

The flames flicker in front of us while his hand rubs slowly up and down my arm. I tilt my head so I can look into his eyes, unable to stand it any longer.

"I'm sorry about my dad."

He looks down and smiles before facing forward again. It's a front to cover up the look he has on his face now. "I'm fine."

I sigh again. "He's very into appearances. It had nothing to do with any type of love I have for Judah."

Hunter laughs. "I figured that." He tilts his head down to me. "Honestly, I'd be upset if he wasn't that way." He kisses the tip of my nose and then sits up straighter. "What father wouldn't want their daughter to be with someone like that? Good name, excellent career—he can take care of you."

This causes me to sit up straight. I run a hand through my hair and brush it behind my shoulders. "Hunter, you have all of those qualities, too." He scoffs, but I keep going. "No, you have a good job and despite the shitty life you were given, you rose above it. You didn't go down a shady path even though you had every right to not care about being a good person."

He tries to look away from me, but I grab his face with both of my hands. "You're a good person." I kiss him once and pull back slightly. "—and I love you so much. Nothing else matters to me."

His eyes go darker and he lifts me onto his lap to straddle him. He grips my ass hard, pulling me flush against him. My hands drape around his neck, and I press my lips to his. He swipes his tongue inside my mouth and then pulls back.

"This right now," he says and then he tucks my hair behind my ear. He kisses me once more. "Is everything."

I don't respond with words. My lips crash onto his, our tongues tangling together as he lifts me up and lays me down on my back. He climbs on top of me, pushing my sweater up under my chin and gripping my breasts firmly in his hands.

My back arches in response, and he begins to kiss a trail down my stomach, stopping at the waistband of my jeans. With deft hands, he unbuttons my pants and then pull them down my legs. I'm nearly breathless while I watch him lick and suck his way back up my legs until he reaches my panties. He slips them to the side and his warm tongue swipes up my center. It doesn't take long for me to be tugging his hair and clawing at his shoulders, begging for him to climb on top of me again.

He doesn't make me suffer. His tongue swirls once more and then he sits up and practically tears the hoodie off his back and tosses it onto the floor. His belt buckles clangs next, joining the increasing pile of clothes next to the couch.

After placing a kiss onto my stomach, he slowly slides my panties down my legs before positioning himself above me. I take a sharp breath when he pushes inside of me.

Hunter is rougher when it comes to sex than I'm used to. I'm not sure if that's due to his level of experience or the intensity that always seems to flow between us. It's like a magnet when we're alone. I want him to grab me and touch me everywhere he can get his hands on.

If it's not the looks he gives that sear me, it's the way he kisses me that feels like he can devour my entire soul. I'd gladly give it to him and all of my air if he never stopped. That's how much I love him.

He continues to rock into me slow but hard at exactly the same time. I don't hold on for long, feeling the pressure building so quickly that I can't hold it in. I lean up in search of his lips, clutching the back of his neck and moaning my release into his mouth. His movements become faster for a moment. He gives one last forceful thrust and then pulls out to lay beside me.

His lips meet the side of my head and then he reaches down and pulls the blanket from the floor. The soft fabric encloses around us and he lays his head next mine, still breathing heavy.

He gently kisses the side of my head. "Best Christmas ever."

His words make me smile, and I nuzzle further into his neck. I couldn't agree more.

31

CASE OF THE EX

Elliot

The bonfire is in full blaze as I drive along the dirt path. I used to live for nights like these, but now all I want is to be cuddled up next to Hunter on the couch watching shitty reality TV. I guess it's a small price to pay so that I can seem normal again.

Holden has a party on his parent's property every weekend. Their hundred-acre farm has several old barns that they no longer use for horses. Now they serve the purpose of housing about a hundred drunken idiots, puking and spilling beer all over the place. I'm sure his parents are thrilled about the return on their investment.

As soon as I exit my car, I hear my name being called from over by the kegs. I flash a smile and wave as if I'm totally happy to be here right now. Poppy intercepts me before I'm halfway up the winding path that leads to the barn.

She throws her arms around my neck sloppily, spilling half her drink in the process. "Oh my god, Elliot," she slurs. "I swear it's been months since I've seen you out. You're like a ghost, girl."

I take a step back when she releases her death grip on me and force a smile. Even though Poppy and I used to be fairly close, I can't remember the last time I actually had a full conversation with her. "I've been around," I say as a plastic cup is handed to me by one of the guys manning the keg.

Poppy twirls a strand of hair around her finger and leans into me. I think her intention is to whisper, but she's too lit to pull it off. "Did you see Cameron? She's completely wasted already." Her arm flings to her right, and sure enough, Cameron is stumbling around awfully close to the fire. It would be a shame if she tripped.

"It's so sad the way she follows Dylan around," she continues. "It's obvious he's still into you. I wouldn't want to be the one someone dated after you."

I laugh before taking a much needed drink. "We dated for like a month."

"I know right?" She laughs and leans into me again. "I mean, look at Judah. You guys were together for like ever, and now he can barely function."

"We're fine now. We had a good talk, and I think he finally got some closure."

Poppy snorts. "Um, have you seen him? That's not exactly what I would say closure looked like."

My eyes scan around the party until they find his. He's standing just outside the barn, surrounded by our usual group, but he's not smiling. He has that same blank, somewhat bored expression he's been sporting since we broke up. My chest seizes up again, the guilt forever consuming me.

Poppy nudges me with her elbow. "See what I mean."

I take a large sip of my drink so I don't have to answer. Cameron takes this particular time to notice my presence and starts walking toward us. She stumbles on the knee-high boots she's wearing, and I stifle an eyeroll. Why she would choose such inappropriate footwear to basically stand in a field is beyond me.

I force yet another smile when she stops beside me and flicks her hair over her shoulder. "I'm surprised you showed up."

I'm suddenly finding it hard not to laugh. If this is a show of dominance, I'm not in the mood. So I choose to remain aloof. I shrug and then tilt my plastic cup to her.

"I told you I would."

She gives a strained smile of her own. I can tell when Cameron is acting petty, and right now, she can barely stand herself.

A small circle forms around us, and the party moves in my direction. I can tell it bothers her that I'm already getting so much attention just by being here. I actually think it's funny because I'm sure it has nothing to do with me at all. They don't miss the fact I've been absent from their parties—they want the dirt on why.

Holden comes up beside me and throws his arm over my shoulder. He hugs me into his side. "You still mad at me, Elle?" He tilts his head down, sincerity in his eyes. "I really am sorry about the other day at lunch."

His shaggy brown hair is sticking out from under his beanie, and he has that infectious grin on his face. I can't help but smile back at him. We all used to be really close, and it's hard being on the outside of it for once.

I hug him back. "No, I'm not mad anymore."

"Good," he says with another squeeze. He releases me, and I catch a glare from across the dirt lot.

Judah watches us for another minute and then starts

walking over. I keep my eyes on his until Poppy nudges me. She leans into me and tucks a short strand of platinum hair behind her ear. "So, I've been meaning to ask you. Who are taking to prom now?" My eyes widen a little, and she laughs. "I know it's a couple months away, but it's like a really big deal."

Honestly, I forgot all about prom. It's a moment I've been dreaming about since I was old enough to walk around in my mother's heels. I always assumed it would be Judah, but now I have no clue. Maybe I won't go at all.

I take another drink and shrug one shoulder. "I don't know. Guess I didn't really think about it."

Judah's quiet, sipping his beer and pretending not to stare in my direction. Holden's eyes light up. "You can go with me, Elle. It would be fun."

This causes a reaction. Judah reaches over and grips Holden's shoulder—*hard*.

"Not happening," he says, leaning down to his face.

Holden shrinks back. "I was just thinking we could go as friends." He gives me an uneasy look. "You know, since you guys broke up and stuff."

The curious eyes around us are becoming overwhelming again. This is the exact reason I've avoided this for so long. The answers to their questions aren't easy and not something I can be honest about. I'm pretty sure Cameron is enjoying this. She has a smug smile on her face while clinging to Dylan off to the side.

Judah releases Holden and tilts back the rest of his beer. He throws the empty cup into the large metal can and turns back to face everyone. "She's going with me."

I work really hard to keep the stunned look off of my face. I'm about to ask him what in the hell he's talking about when he winks at me, causing my eyebrows to pull in.

Poppy looks confused. She motions between us with her cup. "I thought you guys were done?"

I open my mouth to reply, but Judah beats me to it. "It's complicated," he says, stepping closer to me. He drapes his arm over my shoulder and tucks me into his side. "We're working on it."

Judah is demonstrating a different kind of dominance, and its effect on everyone is immediate. Us being apart is unnatural to them. It disrupts some kind of balance in our world I'll never understand.

Poppy lets out a squeal and slaps Cameron in the arm. "See, bitch. I told you they would be fine." She gives me a megawatt smile and a sneer spreads across Cameron's face.

Even though I'm incredibly confused, the fact Cameron is so bothered by all of this baffles me the most. I don't get her intentions lately. It's like she wants me to be miserable.

Judah is still pressed up against me, and I lean into him and pinch his side. "Can we talk for a minute?" I whisper.

He looks down to me and then nods with a sigh. We don't offer any more explanation before turning away from them and walking down the dirt road away from the party. He holds my hand, and I wait until we're out of earshot until I pull it away.

"What are you doing?" I ask.

He shoves his hands in his pockets and glances over my shoulder and then down to me, lowering his voice. "They'll never believe your excuses for not being around anymore."

"So?" I say, my level of irritation peaking. "I don't owe them anything."

"I never said you did, but I'm trying to help you."

I laugh. "Help me?"

He nods, the sadness returning to his eyes. "They expect us to be together. If they think we are, then they won't question it."

I take an unsteady breath. "You don't have to do that."

Judah lowers his eyes and his throat bobs. "I know."

He gets that look on his face again, and I can't stand it. I step forward and place my hands on his arms. When he looks at me again, I shake my head. "You don't. I started this and now I have to deal with whatever comes. It's not your concern anymore."

His brow furrows like I said something ridiculous. "Elle, you're always my concern." His hands fall to my waist, and he pulls me closer. "I know I fucked up, and I know that no matter what I do I can't go back and make it right—but I have to try."

I squeeze my eyes shut. I can feel myself starting to lose it, and the emotions begin to hit me in waves. Just the thought of something happening to Hunter because of me makes me sick, but I can't sacrifice Judah to save him. He's barely hanging on as it is.

He clears his throat, regaining some of his composure and looking to me with determination. "Come on, Elle. We used to run this shit. Let's show them that hasn't changed."

I can tell by the look in his eyes, he has a plan. Even though teaming up with Judah seems like a bad idea, I have a feeling it may actually work.

～

*H*unter throws his arms up in frustration. "No fucking way, Elliot."

"Will you at least hear me out on this?" I say, crossing my arms.

His eyes widen. "You're joking right now." He takes a step toward me. "Because you are not standing here and asking me to let you date Judah."

"I'm not." His shoulders relax for a moment until I speak again. "He knows it's fake."

Hunter lets out a growl and turns away from me, stalking toward the bedroom. I follow him and watch as he begins to rifle through his closet like a crazy person.

"What are you doing?" I ask, my voice exasperated.

He pauses and then continues his search without looking back at me. He rips a dark blue button-down shirt from the hanger and throws it on the bed before reaching back and pulling his T-shirt off. "I'm going down to the school right now and I'm fucking quitting."

"You can't."

"Why not?" He pulls it on and begins roughly trying to fasten all the buttons. His eyes meet mine finally, and he shakes his head. "If I eliminate the problem this all goes away. Tell me how that's not a better solution than what you came up with?"

"If you quit now all it's going to do is make you look guilty. Is that what you want?" My eyes are pleading as I meet his dark stare.

He finishes the last button and reaches for a tie. "So, now you expect me to trust him?" His fingers quickly weave the fabric into place. "I'm supposed to trust someone like that?"

"No," I say moving toward him. "You're supposed to trust me."

The anger on his face doesn't subside, and I gently place my hand on his waist. He looks down at me, and I lean up and kiss him once. "Nobody is even there right now," I say softly.

For a second I think I've gotten through to him before he steps around me. "Then I'll tell them first thing tomorrow morning." He doesn't slow his pace as he exits the bedroom.

"Hunter, where are you going?" I call after him.

I manage to grab his arm before he opens the door. He fists his hands in his hair when he turns around. His hands drop to his sides again. "I'm supposed to be the one who takes care of you, not the other way around."

"You do," I say, reaching for him again. This time he lets me get my arms around him, so I squeeze him tight. His lip press against the side of my head next and then he sighs.

"I can't let you be with him, fake or not," he whispers.

My heart aches for him, but as crazy as it sounds, I trust Judah. I know our plan will work even if Hunter is opposed to it. "It's only four and half months until graduation, after that we don't have to worry about this anymore."

With my head pressed against his chest, I can hear his heart pounding. Now the thrill I once found in getting caught seems absurd to me. What started as a harmless game has turned into something I never expected.

I never expected to fall so helplessly in love with him that I would do anything to keep it, but I did. He changed the way I feel about love entirely, and I'll never be the same. I wouldn't take it back now even if I could.

He sighs. "I don't know how I let you talk me into these things."

With a smile, I lean up on my tiptoes and grab his face, kissing him deeply. "Because you love me."

That look of contentment finally returns to his face. "I really do."

32

DAMAGE CONTROL

Hunter

*B*iting my tongue when it comes to Judah is the hardest thing I've ever done. I'm at the point where I could just say fuck it and quit my job so Elliot and I can be together with nothing to worry about. I would do that for her. Honestly, I couldn't think of many things at this point that I wouldn't do for her.

In the spirit of moving on and trying to get my life together, I have decided to go and visit my father. I've lived here for almost seven years and have only been to see him once. It didn't go well.

As I pull up to the Huttonsville Correctional Institute I grip the steering wheel so tightly my knuckles blanch. He's serving a ten-year sentence for second degree felony assault.

One of the main reasons he called is because he is up for parole next year. Rehabilitation couldn't possibly happen that quick, and for him, I'm not sure it can happen at all.

If he would have been charged with attempted murder, his sentence would have been life. Unfortunately, my testimony prevented that from happening. Even after all the shit he put us through, I still couldn't be the one who put him away forever. It's not something I can explain. Saying it out loud would have made it too real.

That sick feeling returns to my stomach as I pass through the metal detectors. It's been nearly six years since I've been here, but the memory is still burned into my mind. After placing my things in the bin, a stoic guard checks the guest sheet.

"Hunter Graham," he says my name slowly as he runs his finger along the computer screen. "Yep, you're listed."

I swallow back another wave of nausea threatening to spill all over the floor. The visiting hours are only an hour, but I don't think I'll need that long. It only took three minutes to say what I needed to last time.

He hands me my license with a stiff nod. "Have a seat. We'll call you when he's ready."

I force a half smile, and I shove my ID in my pocket and take a seat on the metal chair. For as many times as I've run through the conversation in my head, I still feel nervous. What could he possibly want from me? Forgiveness? If that is a learned trait, I haven't mastered it yet.

About twenty painfully long minutes later, I'm waved back to the visitation room. I spot him immediately at a table back in the corner. His sandy blond hair is longer than I remember but the piercing blue eyes that we share remain the same. The corners of his mouth turn up slightly as I approach. The chatter of the other visitors and their loved ones starts to blur together, drowning out the incessant thoughts in my head.

My father stands as the guard and I come to a stop at his table. I'm half surprised he isn't shackled or cuffed at all. He's in his light blue uniform, with the addition of a few tattoos I haven't seen before.

"I'm so glad you came," he says. I can tell he wants to hug me, but I make it clear that isn't going to happen by taking a seat in front of him.

He runs his hand through his hair and follows suit. "Your mother said you're teaching now. That's good, son."

I grit my teeth together and narrow my eyes slightly. "That's what you want? To make small talk with me? To pretend like you give a shit how my life turned out so far?"

His eyebrows pull in and he shakes his head. He reaches for me, but I cross my arms and lean back in my seat. "Hunter, of course I care what you're doing. I'm your father."

The scoff that explodes from me is louder than I expected. "My father, huh? You wouldn't know the first thing about being a father. You were a sperm donor at best."

"That's fair. I know how terrible I was. I can't even deny that." He pats his chest, and I notice the cross around his neck. "But I've changed. I saw the error of my ways."

I roll my eyes. "Please don't fucking tell me that you found God now. Is that what you want me to believe? That you've been saved?"

"I'm serious. I have repented..."

I clench my fist on the table, speaking in a harsh whisper. "You haven't done shit! Your sorry things didn't work out the way you planned and now you want out early."

"It may take a while to regain your trust, but I think our relationship can be salvaged." The way he's sitting there so calmly while he spouts this bullshit almost makes me laugh.

I close my eyes for a moment as the unexpected tears begin to burn. "I still wake up at night drenched in sweat thinking that I'm going to die. When my eyes finally open my chest still feels so tight, I struggle to breathe. Do you have any idea what that feels like?"

His eyes drift down to the table for a moment, and if I believed he was capable of it, I would say it looked like remorse. I watch his throat bob as he swallows, looking up at me again. "I wish I could take it back. I wish I could do it all over again differently, but I can't."

"You're damn right you can't." I press my finger into the metal table. "But I tell you what you didn't do, you didn't completely ruin me. Despite everything, I'm still capable of loving someone. Of showing an emotion that was never expressed to me."

He smiles. "That's good, son. I'm happy for you."

I let out a bitter laugh. "I don't want you to be happy for me. I don't want anything from you. I only came here for one reason."

"Which is?"

I crack my neck. "To tell you I'll be at your hearing. I won't be too afraid to speak this time." He shifts uncomfortably in his seat, and I continue. "You won't get out early, not if I have anything to do with it."

"I'm sorry you feel that way."

Pushing my chair back from the table, I stand. "I'm sorry I spent so much of my life thinking I would end up like you. I finally have someone who believes in me, who loves me. She sees the good I'm capable of and that's all that matters to me."

I don't wait for a response. I've said what I needed to say. Making peace with my father is something I'll probably never have, but as I leave the prison today, I finally feel like I can breathe again.

∼

I've tried to avoid telling Elliot about most of my past. A part of me is ashamed of the life I've led up until this point. A stronger man would be able to move past the upbringing he was cursed with, but mine continues to haunt me. What type of life could I really give her if all I'm ever going to be is a violent, jealous psychopath? I was never lying when I said she deserves better. The man I just saw behind bars proves what a future could look like if she chooses to stay with me.

My thoughts are interrupted when I see Oliver and Elliot in a heated discussion outside the garage doors. I exit my truck and take tentative steps over to him. Oliver runs a hand through his messy hair when he sees me. He whispers something to Elle that I can't hear.

"What's going on?" I ask, slipping my arm around her waist.

Oliver gives me his serious look. It doesn't always mean something is actually serious, but it is to him, so it could go either way.

He sighs. "Principal Bellamy and my dad want to go skiing this weekend."

"And?"

Oliver looks at me like I'm an idiot who should be able to read his mind. "And, they want you and I to go with them."

He points between us like something should be clicking together. The only thing running through my mind is how much I hate heights.

"What's the big deal?"

Oliver's eyes widen. "The big deal? I know you're smarter than me, I've never denied that, but right now—you're very dumb." He steps forward and slaps the side of my head, and I scowl at him. "They're digging for dirt my dude."

Elliot huddles closer to my side, and I wrap my arm around her. "They don't have shit."

"You sure about that?" Oliver asks, cocking his head. "You two aren't exactly discreet all of the time. And you've been racking up the enemies, Cameron, Dylan, pretty soon Judah —I can list people all night who would love to see Miss Perfect fall from grace."

"Everyone thinks Judah and I are together," Elliot chimes in.

Oliver mock claps for us. "Excellent plan, Elle. Have the one guy in this entire world who couldn't be more in love with you as your only ally."

Elliot narrows her eyes. "You're our ally too, asshole."

"Yeah, but that only gets you so far. I'm your brother. I'm supposed to lie and shit."

I tilt my head to him. "So, what are you suggesting?"

Oliver grins and I cringe. "Well, Mrs. Barns popped that baby out six weeks early, so there is an opening for the director of the play."

"So?"

"So, that could be you." He motions to Elliot. "And you and Dylan are already in the play so you do that thing you do and get everyone off your trail."

Elliot scoffs. "That thing I do?" She crosses her arms, deepening her glare. "What? You want me to flirt with Dylan?"

Oliver shrugs. "It worked before."

I shake my head. "Fuck that. New plan."

"Aw, come on. Be a team player—"

I release my grip from Elliot and move closer to Oliver. "I am being a fucking team player. My girl is dating her ex. What more do you want from me?"

Remorse comes over Oliver's features finally and he nods. "Okay, you're right. But use this opportunity to put distance between you two. Talk about Judah, gush about prom and all that girly shit to Cameron. Don't stand there and make doe eyes at Hunter."

"I do not," Elliot protests.

"Whatever," Oliver says, holding his arms out to his sides. "You wanted to play games, now let's put on a show."

Elliot looks up at me, and I give her a smile. She looks uncertain, and the only way for us both to make it out of this intact is to put forth a united front. I turn her around in my arms.

"When this is all over, we'll look back on this and laugh at all the ridiculous things we had to do just so that we could be together."

She smiles a little, but it's still tinged in sadness. "And when that time comes, I hope it will be worth it to you."

I don't answer her question. I press my lips to hers and lift her almost off her feet. I catch a noise of revulsion from Oliver, who is still standing a few feet away. I keep it brief and set her back on the pavement. With one last peck I whisper, "It already is."

33

FOR I NEVER SAW TRUER BEAUTY
UNTIL THIS NIGHT

Hunter

It seems like a cruel joke to have to direct the school play this year. Typically, I'm all in for things like this, but the cast has already been set, and the play, that's another story. Romeo and Juliet will be played out by none other than Elliot Monroe and Dylan Andrews. *Fuck my life.*

The rest of winter break, Elliot spent a lot of her time with Judah. Oliver did his best to keep me entertained, but it didn't help much. Even though I tried to act cool when I actually did get to see her, I don't think I succeeded. Regardless of our intentions, this arrangement has already begun to put an unwelcome strain on our relationship.

The only time I get to spend alone with her is in class and

now it seems it will be more often than before. I've been reading through the script while I wait for everyone to arrive during my free period. Elliot enters first with her hair intricately braided down her back and a large bag slung over her shoulder.

"Dress rehearsal, eh?" I say over my book.

She winks at me. "No, just my first fitting, Mr. Graham."

I bite the inside of my cheek to hide my smile. I love it when she says that.

She drops her bag to the floor with a thud. "I may need your help with Dylan." She motions over to where he is currently leaned back in a chair tossing a ball in the air. "He's kind of an idiot."

I set my script down and hop off the edge of the stage. "I can try to run lines with him."

She rolls her eyes. "It's going to take a lot more than that." She lowers her voice a little. "I think he's only doing this so he could hang out with me. He's acting weird."

My eyes drift to where Dylan is sitting in front of the stage. Cameron walks down through the aisles and sits next to him—he doesn't even glance over at her.

"Are they fighting?" I whisper to Elliot.

She shrugs. "I don't think so, but I haven't really talked to her much either. She was still being a dick at Holden's party."

"But she thinks you're with Judah, right?"

"As far as I know."

I laugh lightly, picking up my script again. I tap her on the shoulder with it. "Maybe you should find out. Have a girls' night."

She gives me a tight smile. "I'll get right on that."

I shake my head as she carries her bag backstage. Cameron could be a problem for us. I catch her staring sometimes and that makes me nervous. Girls like her are always looking for the quickest way to get to the top. In her

233

case, destroying Elliot. Best friends or not—I wouldn't put it past her.

The rest of the cast begins to file in, along with Dylan Andrews, who finally decides to pick himself out of that chair. For the first time I'm thankful everyone thinks she's with Judah so I'm not forced to watch her hang all over Dylan again. I wonder what scenes they chose?

A small mousy girl comes up beside me. "Mr. Graham."

I look down at her and smile. "Hello, and you are?"

"I'm Darcy Benton. Your director's assistant."

I shake her hand. "Oh, nice to meet you. I'll be needing your help. This is my first day, and I'm not sure where we're at."

"The balcony scene, sir."

Fuck me. Of course we are. "Alright then. We will begin there."

Surprisingly, everyone moves around like a fine tuned machine. The stage transforms as the balcony is shifted out. Dozens of stage-hands carry trees and other props turning it into the Capulets back garden in a matter of minutes.

I give an appreciative nod. "Okay, that looks great. Where's Romeo?"

Dylan swaggers out with that stupid grin on his face. "Right here, Mr. G."

"Do you know your lines?"

He waves me off. "Of course. We've been working on this for weeks." He leans into me. "I'm almost to the part where I get to kiss her. Not that I already haven't or anything."

My nostrils flare, but I keep it in check. "All right, take your places."

Elliot enters the balcony and she takes my breath away. Her hair flowing down her shoulder, her dress is covering most of her body, but is fitted in all the right ways.

I take a breath. "Okay, you can start from your last line Juliet."

She smiles, but not at me. "Romeo, lose your name. Trade in your name and take all of me in exchange."

Dylan moves forward, raising his hand up the tower. "I trust your words. Just call me your love, and I will take a new name. From now on I will never be Romeo again." His deep monotone voice is already making me cringe.

"Cut!" I yell. Dylan looks at me in confusion, and Elliot huffs a frustrated sigh. She wasn't lying about him being shit.

I walk up to stand next to Dylan and place my hand on his shoulder. "You are proclaiming your love to her." I motion to Elliot. "This girl is your one true love. Forbidden to you by all accounts and yet you stand here and pledge your undying devotion. You sound like you are reading off the menu at Arbys."

A couple of snickers flow through the room and Dylan blushes. He tilts his head to me, lowering his voice. "Um, dude. I'm not good at this. I just wanted to be in a play with, Elle. You know what I mean?"

I pat him on the back with a little more force than I intend to. "Yeah, I know what you mean." I take a small lap around the stage, before moving back to Dylan. I place my hand on his shoulder. "Theater is about expressing emotions through words. You need the audience to feel what you're saying."

He still has a dumb look on his face, so I try another approach.

I motion to Elliot. "She's a pretty girl, huh?"

Dylan nods and gives Elliot a wink. "Like the hottest."

I can't help but roll my eyes. "Okay, the hottest girl is in love with you and you love her. Now, can you prove that to the audience? Pretend it's just you and her up there and no one else."

Dylan nods again, a little more appears to be sinking into that thick skull of his.

"You think you can do that?"

He smiles. "Yeah, I'll give it a try." He pops a mint into his mouth. "I get to kiss her soon."

I grit my teeth. "Okay, everyone! Places."

Dylan moves to stand at the base of the balcony, appearing more relaxed than before. He gives a thumbs up and closes his eyes for a moment. With one last deep breath, he finally speaks. "Oh, are you going to leave me so dissatisfied?"

A coy smile crosses her lips as she leans over the balcony. "What satisfaction could you possibly have tonight?"

He takes a step higher. "I would be satisfied if we made each other true promises of love."

Her chest begins to rise and fall faster, but her eyes remain locked on mine. "I pledged my love to you before you asked me to. Yet I wish I could take that promise back, so I had it to give again."

He reaches for her hand. "You would take it back? Why would you do that my love?"

Elliot's face falls, and she pulls back and plants her hands on her hips. "Is that better, Mr. Graham?"

I smile. "Much."

Dylan grins. "See, angel. I can be super romantic for you."

Elliot smiles back at him, but it's forced. I don't know what exactly happened in the last few minutes to make her seem so upset, but I can see it in her eyes. Our situation isn't easy no matter what environment we are in. We constantly have to be mindful of the way we interact with each other in public, and that's hard. I knew it was going to be difficult, but I don't think I realized how much it would affect her.

～

*I*n an attempt to make Elliot feel better, I decided to do something nice for her. Since we can't even go to the movies or anything remotely normal, I found a way to get around that—with Oliver's help of course.

I'm just packing the last of my supplies in the back of my truck when I see Elliot walking out of the back door. She smiles when she sees me, and it penetrates straight through my chest. I don't even wait until she's all the way across the driveway before I pull her to my lips. She kisses me for a moment, and then all too soon, pulls back.

"What are you up to?" she asks, still smiling.

"It's a surprise for you."

The way her eyes light up at my words already makes it the best night. I toss a few more heavy blankets into the back and motion to the passenger door. "Get in, baby. It's almost dark enough."

She raises an eyebrow, but complies, practically skipping to the door. I follow behind and make sure she gets in okay and plant another kiss to her lips before closing the door for her. When I make my way around to the drivers' side, she leans over and unlocks my door for me. I know it's a small gesture, and probably one that many people do, but for some reason it makes me smile. Everyone can form their own opinions about Elliot, but what I see is a girl who cares about everyone. She's kind and thoughtful and she does it so effortlessly some people may see it as a show, what I see—is a girl who just wants to be loved.

I pull off onto a dirt road with the directions Ollie gave me in the back of my mind. It seemed simple enough, go past the bridge, turn on the dirt road right before the orchard. So far, so good. I see the old barn in the distance and there's tracks through the worn grass where other people must come to hook-up. That's not what this is about though. I want to show Elliot we can be like normal couples—just as long as nobody sees.

When I put the truck in park, Elliot turns to me with a grin.

"Oliver told you about this place?"

I nod.

She laughs. "It doesn't seem like somewhere he would hang out."

"All Oliver said is this is the most romantic place he could think of. I didn't ask for details."

She laughs again and we both move to get out of the truck. Elliot walks around outside, taking in all the trees with snow-covered branches hanging down around us. I'll have to thank him again later. This place is pretty fucking amazing.

Elliot continues toward the largest tree in the row and runs her hand along the bark. I watch her for a moment and then lower the tailgate to spread blankets across it for us to sit on. When I turn back, her hand pauses on one of the trees for a moment and then she turns back to me with a smile.

"What?" I ask, when I see her expression.

She shakes her head, still smiling. "Nothing." She walks over and wraps her arms around my waist. "This is about us tonight." She kisses my cheek. "What do you have planned?"

I kiss her other cheek for good measure before placing a longer one on her lips. Placing my hands on her slender hips, I lift her to sit on the edge of the tailgate. "It's a little colder than I thought so I brought extra blankets."

She gives a demure smile, trailing her fingertip down my arm. "I can think of a few ways we can keep warm."

The man part of my brain—my cock—agrees with her wholeheartedly, but the smaller, more rational one, wants this to be romantic—and maybe a little kinky too.

I hoist myself up to sit beside her. After pulling her between my legs, I wrap a wool blanket around us. She snuggles into my chest as I reach in my pocket for the remote to the projector Oliver set up for us earlier. After a moment, the screen lights up on the old barn and the movie begins to play.

She sighs happily. "You brought me to a drive-in."

I kiss her ear. "I know they're your favorite."

She pushes back against me deeper and rests her head on my shoulder. I chose a movie that's cheesy as fuck, but I know she loves it. Before the opening credits even begin to roll, she places her hands over mine as they are wrapped around her and whispers, "Even if this is the only date we ever go on, it will always be my favorite."

I lean down and kiss the side of her head. "Every moment I have with you is my favorite."

If anyone could hear us now, they would call us love-sick fools. But fuck em'. I love her and she loves me, and if I had to sit in arctic temperatures and watch *Dirty Dancing* off the side of an old barn every night for the rest of my life I would. I love her that much—and that's all that matters.

34

AFTER SCHOOL SPECIAL

Hunter

Dress rehearsal is only three days away and Elliot and I have been avoiding each other for most of the week. Well, she answers me if I ask her questions at school but that's about it. Now's not the time to bring any attention to ourselves and we've been extra careful not to.

I watch Dylan stroll onto the stage with his shirt buttoned incorrectly. "How did people wear these clothes Mr. G?" He fumbles with the buttons once again. "They're so not cool."

I shake my head. "Well, I'd bet if Shakespeare saw what you wear, he may have the same opinion."

"True that," he says with a smirk.

I walk to the center stage. "Okay, if everyone's final fitting went well you are free to leave. If you still need some adjustments, see Darcy on your way out."

Most of the cast leaves quickly, throwing dresses and other random items Darcy's way. Darcy rolls her eyes at me. She's quiet, but I rather like her sarcasm. After a few minutes the chatter dies down, and it appears I'm the only one who remains. My eyes drift up on the alter, and I see someone still laying on it. I smile when Elliot's delicate frame comes into view. Her arms are splayed out to her sides, her eyes closed.

I take a few steps up so I am looking over her. "Rehearsal is over, Miss Monroe."

She peeks one eye open and then closes it again. "Well, Mr. Graham. If I had a decent acting partner, I wouldn't be so nervous about this scene."

I laugh. "All you have to do is die. Romeo has most of the lines."

She sits up and glares at me. "Exactly. It's a very pivotal scene where he professes his undying love for her. He actually *dies* for her. You can't recite lines like that without emotion. It compromises the integrity of the whole play."

I run my hand along my jaw in amusement. "I didn't realize theater meant so much to you."

Her eyes widen. "This is one of the most influential plays ever written. Love through generations is based on it. How could you not want it to be done properly?"

I watch as she throws her dress over the alter and begins to jump off. I place my hand on her waist to stop her. "What if I ran the lines with you? Maybe it would make you feel better about it, even if Dylan does suck."

She remains skeptical for a moment while she dangles her legs over the edge. A smile crosses her face. "Did everyone leave already?"

"I believe so."

She nods slowly. "Okay."

"Lay back like you were."

She hesitates but complies, resuming the position she was previously in.

"Okay, now close your eyes."

Her eyes flutter closed, and I lean myself over the alter, speaking softly. "First, I need you to relax. A dead person, or someone pretending to be dead, can't be so tense."

Elliot peeks an eye open and closes it again before taking another deep breath. "Is that better?"

"Hmm, much." I run my hand down the length of her arm, and she trembles. "The chemistry between the actors is very important. He comes to find that his one true love has taken her own life. The grief that he feels is overwhelming, it makes him desperate. Desperate to take her place. To be with her even in death."

Elliot's chest rises and falls faster as I move my hand along her face. I feather my lips against hers as I speak without touching. "He knows her kiss is literally poisonous, but the madness of his heartache makes him reckless."

Her hand grip the bottom of my jacket, and I smile. "Dead people don't move, Elliot."

She sighs, and I trail my free hand down her neck to the plunging collar of her dress. A quick breath escapes her lips as I slip my hand beneath the fabric. My lips are still just above hers, and I can feel her breathe into me as I begin to slowly palm her breast. She arches her back into my hand, and I gently push her back down.

"I don't remember this being part of the scene," she breathes.

I silence her with my mouth, running my tongue along her bottom lip. "Everyone improvises," I say harshly.

Her hand travels to my belt, and I stop her, placing my hand on top of hers. "No, baby. You don't get to move right now."

"I can't even touch you?"

I shake my head slowly. "Not unless I say so."

She lets out a huff and bites her bottom lip. I press my finger to her lips. "Do you want me to kiss you here or..." My voice trails off as I run my finger down to the top of her dress pulling it down. "Or here?"

Her breathing is reduced to short pants, but she doesn't reply. "I'm waiting," I say , twisting her nipple gently between my fingers.

"There," she whispers.

Hungrily, I take her nipple in my mouth, grazing my teeth along the firm bud. She moans softly, writhing off the table. She doesn't listen very well, and her hand travels inside of my pants and along the length of my bare skin. I bite down firmly in response and she lets out a startled moan. She liked it, but then again, she always likes to break the rules.

Her hand stills, but she doesn't pull it away. I bring my lips back to her ear. "What did I tell you about touching me?"

She turns her head and catches my mouth, plunging her tongue inside. When she moans into my mouth, my plan goes out the window, and I climb fully on top of her. She presses her hips up to grind against mine, and I'm suddenly wishing these dresses didn't have so much material.

Slowly, I run my hand up her leg and up the center of her panties. "I would say you are more than ready, but..." I glance to the stage door. "I don't think we should continue this here."

Elliot's eyes darken with desire as she firmly grips my tie pulling me back to her. "Since when were you afraid of getting caught?"

I lean forward and kiss her once before pulling back to calm my breathing. "Since the risk started to outweigh the reward." I pull her dress back into place and kiss her forehead. "Losing you is a fate worse than death."

Her eyes gloss over as she holds my stare. She brings her hands up to grip the back of my neck. "That's not going to happen."

"I know, baby." I sit up and pull her with me, placing a kiss to the side of her head. "Let's get you changed so we can go home."

She smiles as she hops down and hurries into the changing rooms. I take another lap around the stage when I hear the side door click. My heart lodges in my throat for a moment as I make my way over and open the door. I look both ways down the hall, and there is no trace of anyone. Maybe it shut all on its own?

Elliot appears at my side dressed in a hoodie and jeans. She looks just as beautiful as she did in her gown. She could wear a brown paper sack and still outshine every girl in the room.

"Ready?" she asks.

"Yeah." I shut off the last remaining light and place my hand on the small of her back guiding her out of the door.

When we make it to the parking lot, we are the only two cars remaining. My heart rate begins to slow. We've been pushing our luck lately, and the last thing we need is a scandal right now.

She leans in and kisses me quickly. "I'll see you soon."

"Drive careful. I'll be right behind you."

She waves me off with a wink, and I make my way to my truck. As I place the key in the ignition a strange feeling comes over me. Something doesn't feel quite right. I shake out my hand and crank the engine just as she pulls out.

The ride to her house is only about fifteen minutes but for some reason my heart pounds the entire time. When we pull into the driveway there's an extra car there. Elliot exits her car first and is intercepted by Cameron.

I run my hand roughly down my face. This can't be good. Tentatively, I get out of my truck and walk toward them.

"Well, well, Mr. Graham. It seems you've been offering some extra credit." She cocks her head to the side and sneers at me.

Elliot gives me an uneasy glance.

"I don't know what you're talking about," I say.

Cameron laughs and flicks her hair over her shoulder, taking a step toward Elliot. "You don't always get everything that you want. And this time, I'm going to make sure of it."

35

NEGOTIATIONS

Elliot

I cross my arms firmly over my chest and glare at my best friend. My best friend—*yeah right*. I should have seen this coming.

"What do you want Cam?"

She taps her finger against her lips and all I see is that horrible shade of nail polish she insists on wearing. "I want to be Juliet. It's not fair I'm stuck being her fucking mother who has like four lines in the entire play."

I laugh. "Done. I don't give a shit."

"Elle, do you really think it will be that easy?"

My glare deepens, and Hunter's hands circle my waist from behind me. Cameron flares her nostrils. "Don't you even care about Judah?"

"Why do *you* care so much? Judah's a dick, remember?"

Those words are actually hard to say considering how he's been acting lately, but she doesn't know that.

"Not anymore. You've completely ruined him. He used to be this tough, no nonsense player and now he's just a pussy-whipped puppy that falls at your feet every time you call."

Hunter gives my hip a squeeze, and I lean back into him. Even though I want to commit murder right now, just his presence is calming to me.

I cock my head to her. "Again, why do you care? You have Dylan like you wanted."

She scoffs. "Yeah, I have Dylan alright. All he ever talks about is that stupid fucking play and how cool it is that you two get to hang out so much." She presses her fingertips to her temples. "If I have to hear your name one more time, I'm going to fucking scream."

"Elliot!" Oliver calls from the side porch. "Is that you?"

Cameron's eyes widen, and I stifle a laugh.

Oliver strolls over to us and shoots me a look at our position in front of the enemy.

"It's okay, Ollie," I say quickly. "Cam knows."

He slings his arm over her shoulder, and I swear she blushes. "Risky, but if you trust her who am I to argue?"

Cameron's body visibly stiffens as Oliver continues to stand beside her. My mind drifts back to the comment she made about him being attractive. Oliver does owe me a favor —or twelve.

"I was just about to catch the highlights from the game." He nods to Hunter pointedly. "Care to join me?"

Hunter nods. "Yeah, sounds good." He leans into my ear. "Come get me when she leaves."

Hunter steps forward to follow Oliver as he pulls his arm from Cameron. "Later, Red."

I wait until the side door closes before I speak again. "Okay, what else do you want?"

"You were always a terrible friend," she sneers.

I pull my hands into my chest. "I was a terrible friend? I'm not the one doing the blackmailing right now."

"You don't understand because you already have everything. You're always first, never second." She angrily brushes away a tear. "It sucks always being second."

I sigh. "Cam, I don't want any of this. That guy in there," I point my finger toward the house, "that's what I want. I love him and I'm tired of fighting it. I don't care how much it terrifies me or how much trouble we could be in, he's worth it to me. You can have whatever you want as long as I get him."

She quiet for a minute, staring down at the pavement.

"You want Judah?" I offer.

She laughs once. "Please. He's madly in love with you. This is going to kill him."

I shake my head. "Don't even joke about that," I say firmly.

"I'm sorry," she says holding her hands up. A devious expression crosses her face again. "I want to be prom queen too."

"Fine, I'll withdraw my nomination."

Her eyes narrow. "You don't care about any of this do you?"

"No, I really don't. It means nothing, Cam. Next year we'll be at college and nobody will care who the fucking prom queen was."

She balls her fists at her sides. "Well, it's a big deal to me!"

My eyes widen. Cameron is known to be dramatic, but this is a bit much. "Okay, you're right. Just don't tell Judah. I don't want to hurt him."

"Are you kidding me? You think that cheating on him isn't hurting him?"

My jaw clenches, and I close my eyes, taking deep breaths through my nose. "Cameron, you don't know the whole story. Let me handle Judah, okay? You can have whatever you want, just leave him out of it."

She slings her bag roughly over her shoulder. "Fine. Opening night, you get the stomach flu or something."

I nod and give a curt smile. "It's your story."

"Your damn right it is." She opens her car door and leans against it. "And I have a feeling things are going to be a lot different from now on."

Anger surges through my veins as I watch her pull down my driveway. Of all the ways I envisioned us being caught, this wasn't one of them. I must have stood here for longer than I realized because Hunter's arms come around me again. He presses his lips to the side of my head. "You okay, baby?"

I turn around in his arms and shake my head. "No. This is completely fucked."

He smiles and I glare at him. "It's not. Cameron is a nobody."

"Well, her desire to be a somebody is going to destroy us."

His arms close me in tighter, and I bury my face into his chest. "We'll figure it out. We always do."

All I can do is sigh and pray that he's right.

∼

*A*s planned, I stage a dramatic vomit session in the ladies room an hour before curtain. I don't actually throw up, but I've heard Janie Thomas do if for real so many times after lunch it wasn't hard to imitate.

It worked perfectly, and Cameron showed off some of her acting skills by pretending to be the concerned friend. No one questioned it when she stepped in to take my place, although I could tell she was pissed they were worried about me.

Judah came to help me orchestrate my exit and is

currently driving me home. He's quiet again, and I wish I knew what he was thinking. Even though I had to convince Hunter to be on board with this, I also had to convince myself. I know the damage it's doing to both of them. I can't even imagine how I would feel if Hunter had to pretend to date his ex. I'm not typically a jealous person, but with him I think I might be.

When Judah pulls into my driveway, he puts the truck in park, but doesn't cut the ignition. He stares straight ahead with one of his hands on the steering wheel.

He bites his bottom lip, clearly choosing his words carefully. I mentally prepare myself for whatever he has to say. "I know Hunter isn't cool with this."

"Would you be?"

He laughs, shaking his head. "Nope." He looks at me, and his gaze makes my stomach flip. "I'm not even okay with it now."

I open my mouth to respond, but he keeps going. "—but I understand why this happened. I should have never left you alone and at least I can be thankful he was here for you when I should have been."

My words get caught in my throat again. I'm still struggling with the honesty I've been getting from him lately. I try not to dwell too much on the 'what ifs' in our situation. Everything happens for a reason I guess, and if I could have one wish, it would be that Judah finds someone deserving of everything he has to offer now.

He turns toward me. "I want you to know I'm not doing this so you'll take me back. I know you won't. I know you've moved on, and the only thing left for me to do is to make sure I protect what's left of us." He gives me half a smile, but it's still so sad it makes my heart ache. "I want to be friends with you and try to be supportive even if it's hard. I can't imagine my life without you in it and I hate even more when you're sad, so I want to make sure you get to be happy."

"I want you to be happy, too," I whisper.

He bites the inside of his cheek and nods. "Yeah, I'm working on that."

I take his hand, lacing my fingers through his. "I can't think of a single person that would do what you're doing. It's the opposite of selfish and if you're doing it because you feel like you need to make up for something, I want you to know you don't have to. I forgive you. We all make choices we regret, and I don't blame you for it."

Judah stays quiet for the longest time, staring down at our hands. His face is shadowed in the darkness of the cab of his truck so I can't read his expression. After another moment, he sighs.

His eyes flick up to mine. "It's hard to walk away from something you thought you'd always have, but I can see how much you love him." He laughs once. "It fucking kills me, but I would never take that away from you. You deserve to be happy, Elle." He gives my hand a squeeze and finally smiles a little. "That's why I'm doing this."

RUMOR HAS IT

Hunter

*E*lliot is wrapped into a cocoon of blankets when I enter the game room downstairs. I motion toward the TV. "Please don't tell me you and Judah were watching Netflix?"

She tosses a pillow at me. "Get over here." She pulls her blanket down and smiles at me.

It doesn't take long for me to cross the room and take the seat next to her, pulling her against me. I hug her tightly and my chest starts to ease for the first time all night. Leaving her with Judah all of the time is starting to wear on me. I still don't trust his intentions, and I probably never will, but it's something I'm going to have to deal with, I guess.

Elliot pulls back and places her hand on my face. "I missed you."

Instead of answering, I press my lips to hers and kiss her hard. I miss her every time I'm forced to be away from her. Especially since that time away now usually involves her hanging out with her ex.

She grips the back of my neck and climbs onto my lap, straddling me. She deepens our kiss, and I run my hands down her sides to grip her ass. I pull her closer and get lost in the urgency of her lips on mine. Every moment feels so fleeting I'm never sure when I'll get another one.

I curse myself for even thinking that when Oliver comes bounding into the room. He flops down on the recliner beside us with a grin. "Geez, Elle. You should have never faked sick. The play was a disaster."

Elliot readjusts her position so she is sitting next to me. "What do you mean?"

I exchange a look with Oliver. "Let's just say you were the one keeping Dylan on track. He messed up some of his lines, and Cameron had a complete meltdown on stage."

Laughter bursts out of her. "Well, you know what they say. Karma is a bitch and so is Cameron."

Oliver smiles. "That may be true my dear sister, but she's not finished with you yet."

"What do you mean?"

"Considering her plan didn't work out how she had hoped, her new plan is to destroy you in a different way."

Elliot shoots up from the couch to the floor and begins to pace. "No way. We had a deal. I can't help it if Dylan is an idiot."

Oliver grabs the bag of popcorn from the end table and shoves a handful in his mouth. "Doesn't matter. She wants the *throne*." He makes a very serious face, but ends up laughing anyway.

She crosses her arms. "Okay, so now what?"

Oliver dusts his hands off dramatically, and she glares at him. "She told everyone you got sick tonight because you're pregnant."

She rolls her eyes. "No one's going to believe that."

Oliver's expression shifts again to serious. "That's not the worst part—she said it's not Judah's."

The look of horror on Elliot's face matches the churning in my stomach. "And who's the father then?"

Oliver leans in and mock whispers to us. I fight the urge to punch him. "Rumor has it—it's a teacher."

Tears pool in her eyes. "She wouldn't." Her jaw clenches tight as she balls her hands into fists.

I stand up from the couch and hug her to me. "Don't panic yet. She didn't say who." I look to Oliver. "Right?"

He nods while still chewing obnoxiously. "For now."

Elliot clutches my T-shirt. "See, this is what I was afraid of. We are—"

I press my lips to hers to silence her. "We're going to be fine. I'll put in my resignation first thing Monday morning."

Elliot pulls away and gives me an incredulous look. "Really, Hunter? That will make you look beyond suspicious. The hottest teacher at Central suddenly resigns in the wake of a scandal."

Oliver scoffs loudly. "Hey now. I think that's up for debate. I say we declare a vote."

Elliot rolls her eyes again. "I'm surprised you're not the one in trouble."

Oliver shrugs. "Easy. I don't fall in love."

That's where Oliver's wrong. It's not easy. Falling in love with Elliot was inevitable. The feelings I had for her were simmering beneath the surface for so long it was only a matter of time before the heat was turned up and they boiled over. The despair on her face breaks me. I need to find a way to fix this.

Elliot clasps her hands together. "Okay, I have a plan."

"Um, should I be scared?" I grip the back of my neck nervously.

She plants a chaste kiss to my lips. "You're just going to have to trust me."

~

*E*lliot's idea of a plan is scaring the shit of out me. She is currently wearing an actual fucking school girl outfit. Bare mid-drift, pleated plaid skirt, and those sexy fucking knee high socks. I'm definitely getting fired today.

I can say one thing, showing off her body like this will certainly put to rest any rumors. At least I hope so. She saunters down the hallway like she always does attracting attention with every sway of her hips. Oliver comes up beside me, twirling a Twizzler around in his mouth.

"What's she doing?" he asks.

I cover my mouth with my hand. "I have no idea."

"Well, whatever she's doing, it's definitely causing a scene."

My eyes go wide as I watch the crowd forming around her. She smiles and flips her hair, saying God knows what, while everyone eats up every word. Elliot really is a force to be reckoned with. Cameron is stupid.

Something pokes me in the side of the face. I look to Oliver in irritation. "Twizzler?" he asks with a smirk. He flops it around in front of me, and I slap his hand away.

"Don't you have a class to teach?"

He looks thoughtful for a moment. "Good question."

I shake my head and continue to direct my attention to the dramatization in the hallway. Cameron shoots daggers in Elliot's direction from around the corner. I watch her grab Dylan by the shirt and drag him down the hall. The warning bell rings, and everyone scatters like rats from a sinking ship. Elliot shoots me a wink as I step into my classroom.

It's my free period, but pulling double duty teaching drama has me really behind. I get lost in my notes and don't even hear my door shut. Elliot props herself up on the edge of my desk, crossing her legs toward me.

My eyes travel slowly up her body until I reach the glimmering in her eyes. She's going to get me in so much trouble today.

"You like my outfit?" She casually fluffs her skirt, and I bite the inside of my cheek.

I swallow hard, running a finger up her bare leg. "Yes, I do."

She tilts her head and twirls a strand of hair around her finger. "You don't think my skirt is too short?" My eyes go dark as she lifts the hem of her skirt up right below her panties.

"I think I warned you about the dress code before." My voice is thick as my finger travels just outside the lacy thong she is killing me with.

She pulls my finger from between her legs and slides it into her mouth. I take in a sharp breath through my teeth as she sucks on my finger with a skill that I don't want to think about. Before I can stop her, she slowly releases it from her mouth and places it back between her legs, pushing it all the way inside with her hand.

Her head tilts back as I add a second and slowly guide them in and out. "This is starting to seem like a pretty dangerous plan, baby." She licks her lips, and for first the time in my life premature ejaculation seems like a possibility.

When she starts to rocks her hips against my hand I can't take it anymore. I stand up and lean into her ear. "Did you lock the door?"

She nods, but it doesn't ease the pounding in my chest. The whole purpose of today was so that she could dispel any rumors about her sex life, not get caught red-handed in my classroom. I place a kiss on her neck and slowly pull my hand away. She gives me a look of protest, but I smile and kiss her lips quickly.

"Go to class before my new uniform becomes an orange jumpsuit."

She grabs the front of my shirt, keeping me close to her lips. "I think you'd look sexy in orange."

I laugh because I know she's kidding, but the thought still makes me shudder. She kisses me once before standing and readjusting her skirt. She tilts her head and hold her arms out to her sides. "Better?"

I nod. "Much." She turns to walk away, but I grab her arm and pull her back to me before she can take a step. "You can't wear this to school ever again."

Elliot smiles. "See you after school, Mr. Graham." With the same level of stealth she used to get in here, she leaves my classroom.

My heart is still pounding when I slump down in my chair. Elliot is out of her mind, but I have to hand it to her, her plan works. By the end of the day, the pregnancy rumors are long forgotten. All anyone can talk about is how hot Elliot looks after getting back together with Judah.

Cameron goes home early.

All hail the queen.

37

CATCHING AN EDGE

Hunter

"*A*re you afraid of heights?" Oliver asks, readjusting his grip on his poles.

I swallow hard as I take a long look at the ground below us. "No, why?"

Oliver laughs, shaking the already precarious lift. "Because you have a death grip on the handrail and you look like you're going to puke." He pulls a flask out of his puffy coat and hands it to me. "Here, this might take the edge off."

Although falling to my death still feels like a real possibility, I take it from him. The scarier part of this outing is what's on the lift in front of us. Somehow Oliver got us raked into a fun evening hitting the slopes with their dad Mason and the principal Mr. Bellamy. He actually insists I call him Trevor, which is weird all things considered.

I take a large swing and the liquor burns its way down my throat. My chest is on fire and I let out a cough, handing it back. "Geez, what the fuck is in there?"

Oliver winks at me. "Some shine I confiscated from some kid in my fourth period class. Dumbass kept it in his locker."

I pat him on the shoulder. "I'm glad your students have someone they can look up to."

He smiles. "Thanks, man." Oliver's deluded sense of self never ceases to amaze me.

My anxiety decreases minimally as we begin to ascend the top of the slope. I manage to make it off the lift without falling, which is a victory in itself. My eyes widen as I take in the sign next to the peak. I punch Oliver in the arm. "Hey, dick. This is a black diamond slope. I'm going to seriously die." I risk a glance over the crest of the hill. "It's like straight fucking down."

"Relax. Just do what I do, and you'll be fine." He pulls his hat down further and gives me a thumbs up.

"Ollie, that is not how skiing works," I say through my teeth.

He smirks. "Just avoid the trees."

I'm about to argue his logic when Mason comes up behind me and clasps his hand on my shoulder. "Let's take one last run and head into the lodge for a drink."

Oliver's grin widens. "Dad, you read my mind."

Mason just shakes his head as he and Trevor make their way to the edge of the slope. I grab Oliver by his jacket to hold him back for a minute. He laughs. "You're not going to die, Hunter."

"No, that's not it." I lower my voice even though the slopes are fairly crowded today. "What if they start asking a lot of questions? Like, ask us if we know anything?"

He shrugs, planting his poles into the snow. "Be cool. My family is pretty tight with several members of the board so that's helpful." He makes a face. "It's also why Elliot is so concerned about you two getting ousted. I would try to avoid any mention of the dirty sex you two have been having all over the school."

"Good advice, genius," I remark dryly.

"I try," he says before shoving off down the slope. I take a deep breath and follow.

~

*S*omeone above was definitely looking out for me as I glide not so gracefully to the bottom of the hill. Oliver gives me a nod. "See, easy."

I withhold my urge to punch him as I amble up the stairs to the patio that leads into the bar. Usually there isn't a sight that makes me happier than Elliot's face, but right now, I really wish she wasn't bartending.

She doesn't notice us walk in right away, and I can't help but stare at her. Her smile glows on her face as she greets customers and exchanges pleasantries. I also like the way she has her hair twisted intricately on top of her head. It'll give me something to grab onto later.

Oliver nudges me from behind. "Being cool would include not fucking staring at Elliot," he whispers.

Her curious eyes meet mine as we all take seats at a table off to the side of the bar. The connection is brief, but it is still enough to make my heart beat a little faster.

Mason circles his hand above his head and Elliot immediately begins filling pitchers of beer. He looks to us. "You guys hungry?"

Oliver cocks his head. "Seriously?"

"Elle, bring menus too," Mason calls to her.

Elliot is already on her way over with a tray of frosted mugs and pitcher in her hand. She sets it down and pulls the menus out from under her arm handing them to Oliver. "I already grabbed them before you asked." She nods to Oliver. "You think you'd have that thing memorized by now."

Oliver dramatically opens his menu. "I like to be spontaneous sometimes. Nobody likes to eat the same thing every day." He smirks at me, and I stifle a laugh.

"Elliot, I was sorry to see that you were ill during the play last week. It wasn't the same without you," Trevor says to her as he takes a menu.

Elliot gives a small smile. "Yeah, it was unexpected."

"I noticed Judah Holloway was there as well. I'll bet he's tearing up the field at Cornell. He surely is missed."

"I'll be sure to pass that along," Elliot replies. She's using her polite voice, but I detect the tension in her tone.

Mason raises an eyebrow. "You two seeing each other again?"

Elliot nods. "Yep." She avoids his eyes and begins to turn away.

This makes her father smile. "Hopefully he keeps it together this time. I would hate for him to try and drown himself in our pool."

Oliver spits out a mouthful of beer. "Dad, you are so brutal."

He shrugs. "I'm just honest. People can't handle honesty." He directs his eyes at me with his last statement, and I take a drink. Something tells me he's not as unobservant as he seems.

Elliot manages to escape, and the conversation moves forward onto more desirable topics. That is until, Trevor speaks again. He turns to Oliver. "I've been meaning to ask you a favor."

"Sure."

Trevor laughs once. "I didn't tell you what it was yet." He crosses his hands in front of him. "The locker room is a good place for gossip. I need you to keep an ear out for any rumors about teachers acting inappropriately with students. I have some anonymous tips, but no names yet."

I suddenly realize I wasn't actually breathing the entire time he was speaking. The fact that no names were given is a good thing, but I'm wondering why Cameron didn't just come right out and say what happened? Unless it wasn't actually her that said anything?

Oliver leans back in his chair and crosses his arms casually. "Yeah, I could do that. You know how guys talk, I'm sure if there's something going on, I'll be able to find out."

Trevor nods. "I was thinking more along the lines of a girl. The impression given to me is it's a male teacher involved."

This meeting doesn't feel so spontaneous anymore. Oliver and I are by far the youngest members of the faculty. There are a few in their early to late thirties, but no one you would really suspect of luring a young girl into their classroom.

Mason points his finger at Oliver. "This is your chance to set a good example." He nods to me as well. "You too. I'm sure between the two of you, you can prevent this nonsense from continuing further."

We nod both in unison. I decide to make it a permanent rule that Elliot is never allowed to wear a skirt to school again.

~

*A*fter the tense evening, I go straight to the guest house when we get back. What I don't expect is to see Elliot sprawled on my bed. I shrug off my coat and raise an eyebrow to her.

"Do you really think you should be here right now?"

Her eyes are mischievous as she leans back on her elbows. The outline of her black bra showing brazenly through her tight white sweater. "That depends on what you want to do with me?"

I bite my lip as I make my way over to her, positioning myself between her legs. I kiss her slowly. "All the things I want to do to you will get me in trouble."

She sucks my bottom lip with her teeth, and I instantly harden. "I promise I'll be good."

I release a chuckle as I roll myself to lay next to her. "I don't doubt that, baby. Tonight is probably not the best night for a sleepover though."

Ignoring my words, she crawls on top of me and leans down to kiss my neck. "Who said anything about sleeping?"

The larger part of my brain lets her continue for a moment because it feels good, but the smaller, more rational part, pushes her back by her shoulders. "I'm serious. We can't tonight. I think your dad knows."

She leans back on her heels and brushes her hair out of her face with a huff. "How?"

"I have no fucking clue. But there was something about the way he was looking at me."

Elliot rolls her eyes. "He looks at everyone like that. He likes to intimidate people."

I shake my head. "No, he's smarter than you think. We haven't exactly been careful." I motion to the main house. "Any random night he could've been glancing out a window and saw you sneaking over here."

She shrugs. "So, we're friends."

I let out a humorless laugh. "That's cute, but nobody would believe that."

Elliot smiles and begins to crawl her way back up to my mouth again. "Fine. I'll sleep in my bed tonight," she says against my lips. Her mouth moves to my ear. "But first I

263

want to leave you with something to think about while I'm gone."

Even though this girl may very well get me thrown in prison at some point, I couldn't think of a better way to go down.

38

HURDLES

Hunter

$\mathcal{M}$y grip tightens on my phone when I come across Elliot's new Instagram post. It's a picture of her and Judah. He has his arms around her, and she's kissing his cheek—six hundred and twenty-seven likes. *Really?* That many people felt the need to click like on this bullshit? I toss my phone to my bed and let out a groan. I get the need to put on airs for everyone, but it doesn't make it any easier when I have to look at it.

Elliot comes walking into my room carrying coffee. "Good morning." She gives me a quick kiss and hands me the cup. Her eyebrows pull in when she takes in my face. "What's your problem?"

"Nothing," I mutter before taking a sip and setting it

down on the side table. "Thank you," I say over my shoulder as I continue to get dressed for work.

Her fingers graze my stomach as she comes up behind me and places a kiss to my shoulder. "It doesn't sound like nothing."

The unease in her voice makes me feel like a dick. I agreed to this. My eyes squeeze shut, and I attempt to reign in my anger. "Should I double-tap on your picture too, or would that be weird?"

She bites my shoulder in response to my sarcasm, and I laugh. Turning around, I pull her against me. "I'm sorry, it just pisses me off."

"It's not real." Her hands travel behind me and she grips me tight. "*This* is real."

The sincerity in her words melts away at my irritation, and I begin to relax. I kiss her softly. "I know, baby. I can't wait for the day you and I can actually do things like that."

"Do what?"

I laugh. "Declare our love for each other on social media, hold hands in public—do basically anything in public."

She frowns and leans her head on my chest. "It won't be much longer, I promise."

My hand rubs up and down her back reassuringly. "I hope so."

~

*S*ince Judah has been busy trying to get his grades up he hasn't made the trip home as much. Officially Elliot and Judah have been back on for three weeks and this weekend is the first time he's been here since the play.

Thankfully, Elliot has a track meet and I can at least be there for that. The after party is another story. Although she promised to keep their public displays of affection minimal, it still sucks. Having to see her with him for so long, you would think I would be used to it. The truth is, you never get used to seeing the girl that you love with another man, especially when he loves her too.

My knee bounces nervously as I sit behind Oliver on the bleachers. He's actually pacing back and forth blowing his whistle and screaming profanities at the girls below. Evidently this is a big meet. They are competing against North Ridge and have been rivals since the dawn of time. At the last meet, they only narrowly edged them out and that was in part due to Elliot's ability to run faster than basically anyone.

Oliver turns back to me and shakes his head. "Where is she?"

I glance down at my phone again. "She said two minutes."

The scowl on his face deepens. "You know, it's really fucking cute and all that you two have yet another elaborate charade going on, but I have a meet to fucking win."

I laugh. "Relax, man. She'll be here and she will perform like the champion that she is."

He grits his teeth. "She better. Or I'm punching you *and* Judah."

It's pretty amusing when he gets all pissed off. I'm about to attempt to diffuse the situation further when I see Elliot round the corner of the field house hand in hand with Judah. That's cute he's walking her to the field. *Motherfucker.*

Oliver chuckles as he spots them too. "Second thought, I take that back." He turns to me with a wide grin. "You're about to suffer plenty I'm sure."

My fist clenches when he grabs her face and kisses her passionately, eliciting some whoops from the crowd. I really want to break his jaw right now, but I can't exactly blame him for taking advantage of the situation. I'm not convinced his motives are pure even though Elliot assures me they are.

Oliver waves his arms in air to get her attention. "Elle, get your ass on the field already!" he yells to her. He points to

Judah and then motions behind him. "You, get your ass on the bleachers. You can grope each other later."

Elliot gives him a glare, and Oliver puts his whistle in his mouth in warning. With one final peck, Judah reluctantly leaves her side, and she jogs toward the rest of the team. As he's ascending the bleachers, he gives me a nod. I give one back in return as he keeps on toward a group of guys at the top.

Oliver shakes his head in disbelief as he looks back and forth between us. "My mind is fucking blown. You two are completely ridiculous."

"Me and Elliot?"

He laughs. "No, you and Judah. Elliot is a genius. I've taught her well." The look of pride is evident on his face as he pats me on the shoulder before stalking down to his team.

I lean forward and rest my elbows on my knees, contemplating what he said. He's pretty much right. If you asked me eight months ago if I would ever let a girl manipulate me into breaking every rule I've ever had, I would say you were crazy. Now, it almost feels normal.

Her eyes meet mine as the announcements begin, and I smile. I can't help it. It's almost an intrinsic reaction when she looks at me no matter what the situation is. Three more months and this will all be over.

The crowd goes crazy when her event is called, and she saunters to the starting line. That's one of the sexiest things about her, the confidence she portrays without even trying. Perhaps a major misconception about girls like Elliot is that they're insecure. With her, that's not the case, at least not in the way you would expect. The way she acts is a product of the life she's led, not of the heart inside her.

When the shot sounds, I take a breath as she surges from the starting line. This is an event she typically doesn't do, but after Ollie made her run hurdles for being late to practice, she managed to master it.

She's still edging everyone out as they round the last corner and the crowd rises to their feet. An audible gasp escalates through the air when she unexpectedly trips and stumbles to the track. My hand flies up to grip my chest when she doesn't bounce right back up. After only a split second hesitation I leap over the railing and down to the field. I sprint toward her, beating Oliver for probably the first time in my life.

Her face is twisted in pain when I drop to her side. "Something's wrong," she gasps, clutching her knee. "I can't...move it."

I immediately scoop her into my arms and carry her off the track toward the bench. Several paramedics are standing by off to the side and come rushing over as I approach.

"She needs help," I spit at them.

They scramble to a stretcher, and her eyes widen. "No," she says, gripping my shirt. "I can't leave now. Let me walk it off."

I lean down to her ear. "Baby, you can't even walk right now. You have to go."

Oliver comes rushing to us and stands on the other side. "Give her here," he says quickly, reaching toward her. Elliot slowly lifts her arm and wraps it around his neck as I gently hand her to him.

"Meet us at the hospital," he says over his shoulder as he carries her off toward the ambulance.

Nodding, I run both my hands through my hair and take a deep breath. I reacted so quickly without even thinking. Before I can fully process what is happening, Judah comes up beside me and grips my shoulder. I narrow my eyes at him. "Not now."

"Dude, he says calmly. "Take me with you, dumbass. You're not making this look too good right now."

He shoots me a look, and I grit my teeth. The douchebag's

right, I need to play along if I have any hope of salvaging the damage I've probably already done.

~

Oliver noisily chomps on his gum beside me as we wait not-so-patiently in the waiting room. I glare over at him. "Could you chew that like a normal human person, or would that be too much to ask right now?"

"Geez, sorry," he says with a laugh. "I'm fucking hungry. This is taking a really long time."

I roll my eyes and continue to focus them toward the door where they took Elliot. Judah leans nonchalantly against the wall beside us, scrolling through his phone. "You're still ahead," he says to Oliver without looking up.

Oliver holds his hands together in an exaggerated prayer. "Thank fuck someone is looking out for me today. I hated leaving my team in the hands of my sorry excuse for an assistant coach." He nudges me with his shoulder. "It was for good reason though."

A bitter laugh passes my lips. I find it incredibly hard to believe that anyone could think of anything other than Elliot right now. This is her passion. What if something is seriously wrong and she can never run again? The thought alone makes me nauseous.

After what feels like an eternity, the door finally opens, and a woman in scrubs motions us back. "She's ready for visitors now," she says with a smile.

I practically jump up from my chair and follow her back the hallway. When we reach the end, she pulls back a curtain and Elliot's smile nearly takes my breath away. I lean down and kiss her once, taking her hand in mine. "Are you okay?"

She pats the brace on her knee gently. "I'm going to be fine. Nothing's torn, it's just a mild sprain."

I release a quick breath and press my forehead to hers. "Oh, thank God. I was so worried."

Her hand cups the side of my face. "Thank you for saving me," she says softly, stroking her fingers down my cheek.

Oliver clears his throat loudly behind us, interrupting the moment we're having.

"Um, my parents are on their way back. Unless you want to unleash that load on them, I suggest you take a step back."

I kiss her once more as Judah moves to her other side, and I take my place next to Oliver. My eyes burn into his hand as he moves it over hers. "I'm glad you're okay, babe."

Elliot laughs, and it makes me viciously jealous. "Thank you, Judah."

Mason steps up behind us and clasps his hand on *my* shoulder as he speaks. "Your mother is taking care of the rest of the paperwork. It shouldn't be too much longer until we can go."

"Thanks, Dad," she says with a smile.

His hand is still clutching onto me, and I can already feel the sweat trickling down the back of my neck. "Let's go get some coffee, huh?" he asks.

I swallow hard. "Sure. Coffee sounds great."

He releases me with a very firm pat on the back, and I turn to follow.

"I'll come too," Oliver says with a smirk.

"No," Mason says and points to the chair beside the bed. "You stay here."

We exchange uneasy glances, and Ollie tugs at my sleeve. At first, I think he's about to wish me good luck, and then he opens his mouth.

"Hey," he whispers. "Get me one of those cookies." He holds his hands up to demonstrate the size. "You know the great big ones with the tiny chocolate chips."

I shake my head as I turn away from him. "Yeah, I'll be sure to do that."

He grins, leaning into me again. "If my father looks like he's going to kill you, give it to him first." He gives me a wink as I reluctantly follow his father out to the cafeteria.

It's only a two minute walk, but it feels like a lifetime. He never says a word until we have a carrier full of coffee and that damn cookie for Oliver.

He sets the carrier down on the table and lifts the lid, shaking a sugar packet in his hand. "So, it seems you've gotten yourself in a bit of trouble."

Straight to the point I see. Okay, so maybe lying is out of the question? "Um…"

He laughs and turns his eyes directly to me. "There's no point in lying, Hunter. I may be a busy man, but I know what my daughter is doing." He pours the packet into his coffee and stirs it before looking back to me with a fury I've never seen before. "And who she's doing it with."

I hold my hands up. "Sir, I promise you my intentions when it comes to Elliot are pure. I would never…"

"Let me stop you right there," he says, cutting me off. He takes a step toward me, and I almost flinch. "Let me tell you what you would never do."

His eyes hold me captive as I stand there helplessly. We knew this would eventually happen, I can only hope he's more forgiving than he looks.

39

DISTANCE

Elliot

"Should we be worried?" I ask, glancing at the clock for the tenth time in the last fifteen minutes.

Oliver shrugs and leans back in his chair. "We're in a hospital. If Dad really does hurt him he won't be far from medical treatment."

Judah begins to laugh beside me, and I slap him with the back of my hand. "It's not funny." Carefully, I readjust my position on the bed and reach for my phone. Still nothing. "I'm seriously worried."

Oliver clasps his hands together. "Well, Elliot," he begins with a solemn expression. "You've been having a torrid affair with your high school English teacher that lives in our guest house. How do you think Dad's going to respond to that?"

I bite my lip. "Reasonably?"

He laughs loudly and wipes fake tears from his eyes. "Oh, you really are about to get a dose of reality." After composing himself, he stands and pats Judah on the shoulder. "You guys may need to have a team meeting after this. I have a feeling things are going to change."

Judah's face falls, and I feel guilty for dragging him into this. I know he tries to be okay with everything when he's really not. I'm about to respond to Oliver's unwanted commentary when my father walks back into the room, sans Hunter.

He hands me a coffee. "Your mother's getting the car." He turns to Oliver. "Did you drive here?"

Oliver nods slowly.

My father smiles. "Good. You can take Judah home." He casually takes a sip of his coffee. "Hunter had to leave. He has some packing to do."

My heart drops into the pit of my stomach so fast I almost throw up. I struggle to keep my voice even as I open my mouth to speak. "I'll ride with Oliver. I left my things at the field house."

My father's eyes are hard as he looks between us. Oliver gives an unconvincing smirk, and I consider punching him. "Okay," he says curtly. His eyes narrow slightly. "Come straight home afterwards."

I don't have to try to decipher the meaning behind his words. The fact that Hunter is gone, and currently packing, speaks volumes for how well their talk went and what's going to happen now.

After getting discharged, and trying to nail down the art of walking with crutches, we finally make it to Oliver's truck. Judah helps me inside and takes a seat in the back. I can tell he wants to say something, but for some reason he remains very quiet. Oliver, however, almost can't contain himself as he slips behind the driver's wheel.

"You've really done it this time, Elle," he says as he pulls out of the parking lot. "Dad is extremely pissed and the fact we haven't seen Hunter doesn't rule out his body being stuffed in a trashcan somewhere."

My typical sarcastic remark back is replaced by unexpected tears. A small sob escapes my lips, and I cover my mouth quickly. Oliver looks over at me in shock.

"Elliot, I'm sorry. I'm just messing with you." He pats my leg gently. "I'm sure Hunter's fine."

"No, I know he is," I choke out. "But I just feel so terrible."

"It's not your fault. Hunter's a big boy, he knew the risk he was taking."

"Yes, but I'm the one who started it."

It goes silent for a moment and Oliver's face turns thoughtful. "So, after I told you not to, you basically just went and did it anyway." He shakes his head. "I should have never said anything in the first place. Maybe we wouldn't be here now."

I let out an incredulous laugh and tilt my head to him. "You think I'm only dating him out of spite?"

"No, Elliot. I think you *started* dating him out of spite. What you are now is exactly what I was afraid of."

His words linger heavily in the truck as I turn my head away from him and stare out the window. I don't want to continue this conversation with Judah in the vehicle. Regardless of our history, he's been through enough without adding all the details of what's happened while he was gone.

Nobody speaks again until we arrive at the school. Oliver pulls in next to Judah's truck behind the field house.

Judah leans up in between the seats. "I'll get your stuff for you, Elle." He squeezes my shoulder and exits the truck before Oliver turns to me.

"I'm sorry if I sounded like a dick. I just know him, Elliot." His eyes are pleading when I catch his stare. "He's all the way in with you. If this is some kind of game…"

"It's not," I say forcefully. My eyes begin to burn with a fresh set of tears as I glare back at him. "I *love* him, Ollie."

He just nods and leans back in his seat. "Okay. I really hope so."

It says a lot that my own brother doesn't even believe I am capable of having an actual meaningful relationship with someone. But my words are true. My love for Hunter is the only thing keeping me sane right now while everything feels like it's completely falling apart.

～

*W*hen Oliver and I enter the kitchen, my father is waiting for us. Although I saw this coming, it's never a good sign.

I hobble over to the barstool with my crutches and sit down. He glares at Oliver and points to the chair beside me. "You sit too. I know you're somehow involved in all of this."

Oliver pulls his hands into his chest in disbelief. "Me? You think I could possibly be involved in such things?"

My father rolls his eyes. "Don't bullshit me, Ollie. Sit down."

Oliver just nods. "You're right. I'm an accomplice." He holds up a finger after taking the seat next to me. "I want to let the record show I have only recently become privy to all the details." He looks at me and shakes his head in admonishment. "They lied to me too."

I kick him with my good leg, and he winces.

"Alright. I'm not going to pretend to understand why you have the Holloway boy involved as well, and to be honest, I don't want to know." My father's voice is relatively calm, which surprises me. I wait in trepidation as he folds his hands in front of him. "What I do want to know, is why you thought something like this was a good idea?"

I take breath. "Honestly dad, Hunter wasn't a teacher when we started seeing each other. Well, not one at Central."

He raises an eyebrow. "So, that makes it okay? Since you are a high school student and all, as long as he's not *your* teacher, it's perfectly fine?"

Oliver opens his mouth and I punch him in the ribs before he can speak. "God, Elle. You are super violent today," he whispers, grabbing his side.

"I know it's not fine, but I... I mean we lo..."

My father holds his hands up. "Don't tell me that you love him. He already made it very clear how deep you two think your relationship is."

I smile involuntarily at the thought of Hunter professing his love for me, and my father's eyes narrow again. "Okay, don't get too excited. I told him he has to leave."

"You can't do that! He has nowhere to go." I am very aware I sound like a whiny teenage girl, but that's basically what I am.

"Listen, I'm not heartless. I gave him a week to find a place, but I can't exactly have him living essentially in the same house with you anymore. If this really gets out, how will that make me look? Like I'm okay with this?"

I lower my eyes and begin to pull a string from the edge of my placemat. He has a point, but the thought of Hunter leaving kills me. When I glance up again, he's leaned back against the counter with his arms crossed. His expression softens, minimally.

"Elliot, you're an adult, and I can't tell you what to do. I'll be honest, I actually like the kid, but you have no idea what something like this can do to your future. It is my responsibility to protect you from things like that." He motions to Oliver. "I haven't exactly left you with a good role model."

Oliver scoffs. "Hey, I tried my best. She does what she wants."

"Sounds a lot like someone else I know," he responds

bitterly. My father shakes his head and lets out a long sigh. "Look, all I want is for both my children to have a nice life and be successful. Is that too much to ask?"

Oliver and I shake our heads in unison.

"Okay, then." He turns to me. "Elle, I can't make you stop seeing him. In fact, I'm sure it will only make you want to do it more."

I give a warning glare to Oliver, but he remains stoic beside me.

"Just keep it under the radar for the next three months," he continues. "After that you can do whatever you want. I can't let you make a mistake now that could affect the rest of your life."

As much as I hate to admit it, my father's right. Hunter and I have been less than careful when it came to our relationship. Half of the problems we have right now are because of that. I'm sure we can find a way to make it work, *discreetly*, until graduation. I just hope that this newfound space between us doesn't cause us to fall apart.

40

SACRIFICE

Hunter

*E*lliot's father is a surprisingly reasonable man. I was fully prepared for him to murder me, but he didn't. His major concern is for her, and I agree one hundred percent. That's why I know what I need to do. I can't let this relationship ruin her future. No matter how much I love her —how much I've always loved her, in order to prove that I need to let her go. I just haven't quite worked up the courage to do it yet.

Ollie texted me and said he was coming over to help me pack. That was a couple hours ago and due to the lack of things I actually had, I'm almost finished. I crack open another beer just as a knock comes at my door. Before I can take a step to answer it, Oliver finally peeks his head in.

"Oh, good," he says with a smirk. "You're still alive."

My eyes narrow. "Ha-ha, asshole. You're very funny."

He shrugs, closing the door behind him. "I'd like to think so." He walks over to the kitchen and sets a six pack on the counter. "Sorry I'm late. Family meeting ran over."

I take another drink. "You have those often?"

Oliver laughs, cracking a beer open for himself. "Yeah, like never. I've haven't seen my dad that pissed since he caught me drag racing his mustang across Cherry Bridge."

I smile. I remember that night. Cooper Thomas bet Ollie his car was faster—and the prize? The heart of Farrah Briggs, resident lover of all things dangerous and a smoking body to go with it. Long story short; Ollie won, they dated for a magical two weeks.

Oliver takes a seat on the barstool and twirls his bottle between his hands. "I don't necessarily think this will be a bad thing. A little distance is good for a relationship."

I scoff, almost spitting out a mouthful of beer. "How would you know what is good for a relationship? I think your longest one lasted about a month."

"It was six weeks and that wasn't my fault," he argues pointing his finger at me.

"Uh huh, I'm sure it wasn't." I set my beer down and continue shoving random items into a box. "I really don't want your father to hate me."

Oliver smirks. "He doesn't hate you, but you have to admit he took the whole situation rather well. I've done a lot of shady shit over the years, but Elliot is like his pride and joy. The one who was supposed to do great things." His smile fades as he takes another drink. "He's pretty much given up on that dream when it comes to me."

"Come on, man. You're not that bad."

Oliver raises an eyebrow, and I laugh.

"I'm serious. Sure, you like to dick off a lot, but you get shit done when you need to."

He ignores my comment and takes another drink, staring over my shoulder. "Elliot's really upset."

My heart sinks when he says that. The last thing I want to do is hurt her more when she's already so messed up over this. Oliver senses the weirdness in my mood and smirks at me.

"Don't worry, brother. My dad's cool. This whole thing will blow over in no time."

I drop a box to the floor with a thud and lean against the counter. "I'm going to break up with her."

Oliver's eyes widen. "I'm sorry, I don't think I heard you correctly." He stands up from the stool. "You mean to tell me that after everything you two put me through over these past couple months, you're just done?"

I nod. I also kind of want to laugh. Leave it to Ollie to somehow take my tragic break-up personal.

"You don't have an explanation for that?"

I sigh heavily. "You were right. She's young and she needs to be with someone her own age. Someone who can give her what she needs."

Oliver rolls his eyes. "What? Like Judah?" He laughs, reaching for his beer again. "You nearly killed the guy and now you want her to be with him?"

"It doesn't have to be Judah. It can be anyone, but you have to admit he has changed, and he really, truly loves her. That's what she needs."

Oliver's face falls. "You love her, too."

I give him a sad smile. "That's why I have to let her go."

～

*L*ater that night, I tilt back my third shot of whiskey. As soon as it slides past my teeth, I can feel the burn all the way down. It doesn't numb my heart though. That's a pain that may never go away.

I started looking for jobs far away before this all started. I didn't give it much thought until I got a call last week. At the time Elliot and I were in a good place, but something told me to take the phone interview when they offered it to me. I still didn't accept the position, but I'm planning on it. After talking to Elliot's dad, I realized that maybe I am bad for her. She's about to go off to college and start living her life for the first time. I've already experienced all of those things. I don't want her to worry about what she's doing and how it might affect me. As much as I love her, I can't be the one to take that away from her.

The sun is just starting to set when I see Elliot hobbling over to the guest house in her knee brace. She's supposed to be on crutches for at least a week, but as usual, she's too stubborn to listen. I move from my seat on the couch and open the door for her, reaching my arm out for her to balance on.

She smiles and kisses me instead. "I'm fine, Hunter. This isn't the first time I sprained something." She hops over to the barstool and sits down. "See, all by myself."

I frown. "You need to listen to the doctors."

She rolls her eyes before looking around the room. "It's so empty in here. I'm sure it won't be long before Ollie fills it with beer posters and sorority girls again."

When I don't laugh, her eyebrows pull in. "It won't be so bad. You'll still see me all the time."

She can see it in my face, because she braces her hand on the counter and stands. "Hunter, what is going on?"

I cringe as she balances on one leg. "Maybe you should sit back down."

Defiantly, she crosses her arms and stands perfectly straight. Her eyes narrow. "Tell me."

I shake my head, my words already getting caught in my throat. "I don't know how."

She slowly walks over to me and places her hand on my

chest. "I think you know by now that you can tell me anything. Whatever it is, we'll get through it—together."

She smiles on the last word, and all I want to do is break down. My heart starts to pound and my stomach knots tighter. After I say what I need to say, we won't be together. There won't be an 'us' anymore. I'm not even sure if we can be friends after this. It's almost impossible to love someone that much and then go back to being platonic. Judah can attest to that I'm sure.

Gently, I take her hand and lead her toward the couch. She sits next to me without objection. I continue to hold onto her hand for dear life. At any moment she's going to pull it away from me and I may never get to it back again.

I take a deep breath. "Elle, I'm leaving at the end of the semester."

Her face remains stoic, but I can see the wheels turning in her head.

"Leaving? Where are you going?"

I squeeze her hand a little tighter. "I got a job offer in Florida and I think—or I know, it's something I should do."

My attempt at keeping my tone light is already faltering, even I can hear the shakiness in my voice.

She pulls her hand back, and my heart beats double time. Her arms cross over her chest, her expression dumbfounded. "So, you're leaving me?"

"I'll never be able to leave you if I stay here."

Her eyes widen. "Are you being serious? You're breaking up with me now?"

She stands up before I can stop her. I try to pull her back down beside me, but she yanks away.

With a sigh, I motion back to the couch. "Will you sit down baby, please. You'll hurt yourself."

Her dark eyes glare, and she points her finger toward me. "Don't speak to me like that. Don't be cute with me if you don't even give a shit about how I'm feeling."

"Elliot—"

She puts her hand up. "Just stop talking for a minute." She closes her eyes, and when she opens them again, there's wetness in the corners. "This past year has been hard, I won't deny that, but I think that's what made us stronger. We never let anyone tell us what we could or couldn't be. We loved each other, and we didn't care about anything else." She pauses and looks over at me as a tear falls. "I don't care about anything else."

"But you should. You need to think about your future. You're so young—"

Elliot wipes under her eye and laughs bitterly. "Oh, we're back to me being too immature to handle a relationship with you." She steps closer, almost leaning over me. "Haven't I proven that I'm in this as much as you are, if not more?"

"Yes, but—"

"But, what?" she interrupts again, throwing her arms up.

I stand to face her and place my hands on her shoulders. "Will you let me explain, please?"

She sniffs, hardening her expression. "What is there to explain? You don't love me anymore."

I shake my head immediately. "That's not true. Of course I love you, I just…" my voice trails off, and I run my hand through my hair. The only way I'm going to get her to walk away is to lie. "I just can't do this anymore. The secrets, the lies. It's not what I want, and you shouldn't either."

"What I want is you." Her voice is almost as broken as my heart right now.

Every part of me is screaming to tell her I want her too. Seeing the hurt in her eyes is ripping every bit of my heart out of my chest. It seems so wrong to be doing this to her, but I have hope that one day she'll understand. I want Elliot more than anything but holding onto her is selfish.

"I'm sorry, Elliot." I reach for her again, and she shoves me back. I choke down another wave of emotion. "Maybe in a couple years when you're done with college, things could be different. You'll know what you want to do—what you want to be."

I'm stuttering, but I can't stand the way she's looking at me right now. This already feels like a mistake, and she's close enough I can pull her to me. I can still tell her I love her more than anything and I'll never leave her. But I don't do that.

Her sadness turns to anger. "I'm not stupid enough to believe you actually mean that. You and I both know if we break up now that will be it. We won't come back to each other after spending years apart and pick up where we left off." Her eyes lock on mine. "If you really loved me, you wouldn't be able to leave no matter what the circumstance."

This time when I reach for her hand, she lets me hold it. I close both of my hands around hers, feeling the softness of her skin for potentially the last time. That thought alone guts me. It tears me open from the inside out. I don't want to ever let go.

"I'm doing this *because* I love you."

Elliot sniffs and slowly pulls her hand from mine. She runs a hand through her hair, brushing the long waves behind her shoulder with a bitter laugh. "Well, excuse me if that doesn't make me feel any better. You made it very clear before this all started what the risks were—we both knew." She shakes her head again. "I guess I was the only one who was willing to make that sacrifice."

When she turns to walk away from me, it takes everything inside of me not to run after her, to tell her she's wrong —but I can't. If I take one step outside that door, I'll hold onto something I never should have gone after in the first place.

~

onday at school everyone swarms Elliot as she limps down the hallway. She still insists on walking without her crutches even though the doctor said she may need them for a couple of days. The girl is determined, and if it's something she wants it's almost impossible to talk her out of it.

I do my best not to stare at her for too long, but I can't help it. Not only is she the only person I want to look at but with her injury I worry for her. The last thing I want is for her to cause further damage by doing too much too soon.

Even though I'm not looking directly at her anymore, I can still feel her eyes on me as she walks past me into my classroom. I cast mine down to my desk, unable to see the pain in hers.

As I take my spot at the front of the room, she dips her head and pretends to be engrossed in her notes. I clear my throat as the chatter begins to die down. "Okay everyone, I know it's getting close to the end of the year and you all are very excited to get out of here." I pause for a few excited cheers. It makes me smile too. "Yeah, I know how you feel. It wasn't too long ago I was here myself, but we still have work to do." A series of groans echo, and I laugh.

"It's not too bad I promise." I reach behind me and pull out a stack of papers. "For our last big assignment, we'll do a group project. You can work with a couple of people or in pairs, it doesn't matter to me."

Holden Parker immediately nudges Elliot from behind. "Hey girl, we got this?"

He holds his fist out, and she bumps hers against it with a smile. "Yeah, we got this."

The casual way she interacts with him gets under my skin. I clench my teeth at the stupidity I must have for suggesting partners. Of course she would pair up with a football player. I always see him paling around with the group of guys that Judah hangs with when he comes home.

"Alright," I say almost too loudly as I begin to pass the papers back the rows. "Here is the assignment. Put your names at the top." My eyes meet hers briefly before I force myself to tear them away. "You can have the rest of the period to start on it."

Casually, I stroll through the rows like I'm being observant, but I'm actually just trying to hear what they're saying. Elliot gives me a sideways glance when I linger too long next to her desk.

"Okay," Holden says. "I have baseball now, but after practice I can stop by later this week, and I'm sure we can bang this out real quick." He gives her a crooked smile, and I clench my fist. *Bang this out?* I don't like his choice of words.

Elliot flips her hair over her shoulder and continues to write on the paper. "Sure, sounds good. I'm not allowed to run until next week at the earliest, so I should have my evenings open." She says the last part loud enough to make a point, and my jaw ticks.

I walk back up to the front of the classroom before I unexpectedly cause a scene. My ability to control myself when it comes to her hasn't proven to be too reliable. I have to find a way to fight through this. There's only three months left until graduation, and I already want to throw the flag. Three months and I won't have to see her smile in the hallways, or hear her laughter travel all the way to my desk. No amount of distance can erase my memories of her. Those will haunt me until my last breath.

41

WAITING GAME

Elliot

$\mathcal{W}$alking around the track feels weird to me. I want so badly to run I can barely stand it. Taking things slow has never been my thing. I've always wanted to find the fastest way possible to get to the end of something, and my current situation, is no different.

The music blaring through my iPod is barely drowning out the incessant yelling coming from Ollie over by the bleachers. I shake my head as I scroll through my playlist. I'm about to round the corner when I see Judah walking toward the track. He smiles over at me as he approaches.

"Hey, babe." He pulls me into him and kisses me before I have a chance to fully register his presence.

I kiss him back and barely think twice about it. Hunter

was right, this does almost feel normal to me. "What are you doing here?" I ask, taking a step back.

"It's the end of the semester. Not a lot going on right now."

I nod forward. "You can walk with me." I take my earbuds out and wrap them around my hand as he falls into step beside me. "I have to talk to you anyway."

He laces his hand with mine. "Sure, what's up?"

It's hard to feel so desolate inside when Judah is walking around like everything is roses. I know I'm slowly torturing him by allowing him to go along with this charade and he does it with a smile on his face.

I lower my eyes to the track. "Hunter and I broke up."

His hand squeezes mine, but he doesn't miss a step. He's quiet for a moment and then he tilts his head to me. "Are you fucking with me?"

I shake my head slowly. "Nope."

He pulls me to a stop and places his hands on my shoulders. "Elle, are you okay?" His eyes darken after a moment. "Did he hurt you?" He removes his hands from me, his nostrils flaring as he looks around the field. "Is he here?"

I laugh a little and tug on his arm. "No, Judah. He's not here." He looks down at me, his chest still heaving slightly in anger. "And no to all of your other questions too."

His face falls. "So, you're not okay?"

I smile. "That's the only part you're worried about?"

"Of course, babe. That last thing I want is for you to be sad." He grabs my hand again and kisses the back of it. "That's what I'm here for. To make you smile."

For some reason his words have the opposite effect, and I start to cry. He pulls me against his chest, and I wrap my arms around his waist. "It's really over this time."

Judah continues to console me while I cry into his T-shirt. I find it incredibly strange that neither of us finds it odd I'm crying over the guy who basically tried to kill him and is most of the reason we aren't together in the first place.

He pulls back and wipes a tear from my cheek. "What can I do?" he whispers.

I shrug. "Walk with me?"

Instead of answering, he takes my hand again and continues to walk slowly around the perimeter of the track. We're both quiet for the longest time until he finally speaks.

"Elle, I know there's nothing I can say to make you feel better right now." I look up at him and the sincerity in his eyes almost brings me to tears again. "But I want you to know that this doesn't change anything. I'm here for you no matter what. If you still want to go to prom, we'll go to prom. If you don't, then we'll do something else. None of that stuff matters to me. I just want you to be happy."

That unending guilt I constantly feel intensifies. Judah came into this knowing he would eventually get hurt, and he's still here. The person I thought I knew so well continues to surprise even me.

"Why are you even doing this? I mean, I'm very grateful, but you didn't have to."

He sighs, looking over at me and then focusing forward. "For you, Elle. If I would've treated you better, maybe you wouldn't be in this situation in the first place."

"You deserve better than me," I say simply.

He winks. "No, you do. You just can't see it yet."

Although his words confuse me, I don't respond. What hurt the most about Hunter's break-up speech, is that he was always preaching how I deserved better and he couldn't give me that, and now Judah is saying the same thing. Maybe I'm the one who isn't good enough for anyone.

"Hey, Judah!" Oliver calls over to us from the bleachers. "Unless you grew a vagina I'm not aware of, get off my field!"

Judah looks over at him and laughs, and Oliver plants his hands on his hips with a stern expression.

"He likes to act like a dick at practice," I say.

Judah gives my hand a squeeze. "It's okay, I'll stop over later." He gives me a smirk. "I heard Holden is coming by to work on a project."

"Please don't tell me that you're jealous?"

He smiles again, but it doesn't reach his eyes. "What do I have to be jealous about? This wasn't real, right?"

~

I need a new word for awkward. I'm currently seated at my kitchen table with Holden and Judah while Oliver and Hunter watch the game in the living room. I'm actually doing all the work as Holden and Judah talk about the baseball game they'd rather be watching.

Oliver comes strolling into the kitchen with a large grin plastered on his face. I glare at him while he rummages through the fridge.

"Judah," he says before taking a large drink of orange juice straight from the container. "Did you have fun interrupting my practice today?"

Judah laughs and throws his arm over my shoulder. "Sorry about that." He plants a kiss to the side of my head. "I had to make sure my girl was okay."

Oliver shoots me a look, which I pretend to ignore. "Does she need your help with her English assignment as well?"

I shift uncomfortably in my chair, but Judah just smiles. "I like to help her in any way that I can." He gives me a wink and all it does is make me feel worse.

The tension in the room continues to build as they stare back at each other. For the life of me I can't figure out why Ollie feels the need to get involved, but I'm about to put a stop to it. I glance over at Holden, who thankfully, is oblivious to the whole situation.

"I'll be right back," I say to Judah as I get up from my chair.

I tug Oliver by the sleeve. "I need to talk to you," I say through my teeth on the way past.

He follows me into the hallway, and I cross my arms. "Care to explain to me what you are trying to do?"

He leans into me. "I thought I should remind you that you have someone in the other room about to blow a gasket."

I press my fingertips to my temples. "What's with you? You act like you're so loyal to me, but I get my fucking heart broken and you side with the enemy."

Oliver lowers his eyes to the ground before looking back up at me, speaking softer, "I'm sorry. This is the whole reason I never wanted you two to date in the first place. It sucks being in the middle of this situation."

I throw my arms up. "How do you think I feel? Can't you watch the game at a bar or something?"

He shakes his head. "He won't talk about it. I've asked him a dozen times why you really broke up and he won't give me any solid answers. What happened?"

"It doesn't matter."

Oliver glances back to the kitchen before giving me a skeptical look. "It must matter a little bit, or you wouldn't still have Judah hanging around."

"Judah is…" my voice trails off, and I sigh. "I don't know what Judah is, but he's my friend and I'm not going to ask him to leave."

"Are you going to get back together?"

I cross my arms. "Why do you want to know? So you can run to Hunter and tell him he was right?"

Oliver shakes his head. "Elle, I know you're upset right now, but I'm still on your side." He meets my eyes. "I mean it. My loyalty lies with you first."

He hugs me to him, and I reluctantly wrap my arms around his waist. Ollie may be a dick most of the time, but I know he loves me. He would never do anything that would intentionally hurt me. When I pull back, Hunter is standing in the corner of the hallway.

"I can leave if you want me to." He glances to Ollie and then locks his eyes on me.

"No," I say, forcing a smile. "It's totally fine. As you know, I have work to do."

He smiles a little, but when I don't return it back, his face falls again. "Okay."

We stare at each other for a moment until Oliver claps his hands together loudly.

"Well, this isn't awkward or anything." He pats Hunter on the back on his way to the living room. "You know where I'll be."

Hunter nods to him and then shoves his hands in his pockets. He doesn't make an attempt to move closer to me, and I'm grateful. It's barely been a week since we broke up, and I already want to beg him to take me back. I would never do that though—Oliver taught me better.

"I don't want to make this any harder on you," he says. His deep voice resonates through me, and I take an unsteady breath.

Swallowing the lump in my throat, I force another smile. "You don't have to worry about that. I'm perfectly fine." I turn and walk back into the kitchen before I can see his reaction. It's either that or I'll start to cry and then Judah will see. The last thing I want is for them to get into another fight when there's nothing left to fight about. For the first time in my life—I lost. Not only that, but I lost something that meant more to me than anything ever has. I don't like this feeling, and I'm afraid it will never go away.

42

CLEARING THE AIR

Hunter

$\mathcal{I}$'ve been marking off the days until prom on my calendar like I'm awaiting parole. It's not really a far stretch. This definitely feels like slow torture. As of now, I've only seen Elliot and Judah together in passing, spending an entire night watching them together might actually kill me.

Oliver grins at me from beside the coffee pot in the teacher's lounge. "What's so funny?" I ask.

He takes a sip from his cup. "Nothing. I just signed us up for something."

I narrow my eyes at him, and he laughs. "What did you do, Ollie?"

"Me and you are going to chaperone the prom." His smile

turns smug like he did something good. I kind of feel like punching him.

"And why would I want to do that?"

He shoots me a look. "Come on, you know you want to be there."

I let out a humorless laugh. "I actually don't. Seeing Elliot and Judah prance around all night is probably the last thing I want to do."

He walks over a puts his hand on my shoulder. "If you're not there you'll just sit at home thinking about it anyway. You know I'm right."

An angry sigh escapes my lips. "You're right."

Oliver gives me a firm pat on the back. "I never get tired of hearing that."

I roll my eyes before pouring another cup. Sleeping has been difficult to say the least. I run my hand down my face in frustration. "Two more weeks and this can all be over."

The look on Oliver's face strikes me as odd. "What now?"

He shakes his head quickly. "Nothing, man."

"Seriously, what?"

Oliver's face shifts into anger. "Are you breaking up with me too? You act like once the school year ends you're just going to leave and never come back."

My eyebrows pull in. "I didn't really think it all the way through yet, but I probably won't come back."

He takes another sip of his coffee, eyeing me carefully. "That's a lot of distance to put between you and someone you don't want to be with anymore?"

I sigh. "It's not like that..."

"Then what's it like?" he growls, cutting me off. He slams his cup down on the counter and takes an aggressive step toward me. "I warned you from the beginning I didn't want to be involved in something like this and you did it anyway. Now I have to choose sides and guess who I'm going to choose?"

"I'm sorry."

He laughs. "You're sorry?" He shakes his head. "That's not good enough. She may seem strong and confident to you, but she's not. She worked really hard to make you happy and now you're just going to throw her away when things get the slightest bit difficult."

I grit my teeth. "I fucking love her, Ollie. I wouldn't be doing this if I didn't."

His jaw starts to tick as he continues to glare at me. Without another word he turns and grabs his cup before storming out of the break room, slamming the door on his way out.

～

*S*itting in my classroom during my free period is usually a decent time to catch up on my work. I've been behind lately and with the end of the semester rapidly approaching I really need to get my shit together.

I hear a small knock at my door, and my heart skips a beat. When I look up at the red-haired traitor that feeling is replaced by anger.

"What can I do for you, Miss Gray?"

"Oh, cut the shit Hunter. You and I both know you're the furthest thing from professional," Cameron retorts with a sneer.

I take a deep breath and fold my hands on top of my desk. "You obviously have something to say so would you mind getting to the point? I'm very busy."

She rolls her eyes. "I'm sure you are." She folds her arms across her chest. "You really look like a fool, you know that?"

My teeth clench as I work to maintain a calm demeanor. Cameron would love for me to freak out and lose my shit. I'm not about to give her the satisfaction. "I don't know what you are referring to, but unless you have

296

a question about an assignment, I would advise you to go to class."

She takes a step toward me defiantly. "She'll never really leave him. You know that don't you?" Her eyes almost sparkle as she studies my face for a reaction. I've never seen someone take so much pleasure in being a spiteful bitch. "I feel sorry for you actually. She does this to everyone. Makes you feel so special, like she really cares, but I know how she really is."

I shake my head. "Cameron, I really think you should go to class." My voice is clipped, and I swear I see a hint of a smile on her face.

"It's okay," she says causally. "She's about to get everything she ever wanted. Her and Judah at prom. It's all she's talked about since the beginning of the year."

"You're lying," I grit out. At this point, I actually don't know if she's lying or not. Her and Elliot aren't on any kind of speaking terms, so I'm sure she has no idea that we broke up.

She pouts her lips at me. "Oh, I wish I was. They may have somehow convinced you this benefits you, but you really are an idiot if you believe that. Elliot's the most selfish, vindictive person I've ever met."

I stand up from my desk and lean forward with my palms flat. "I'm not going to ask you again. Go to class, Cameron."

She smiles again, challenging me. "Or you'll what? Give me detention?" She takes a step toward the door. "You don't want to do that. We both know how you wouldn't want your extracurricular activities to get out, now would we?"

She holds my stare as I glare over at her. Her smile turns wider before she brings her hand up and blows me a kiss. "See you at prom, Mr. Graham."

I watch her strut out of the door like she owns the place. It took everything inside of me not to put her in her place, but I know that would only make things worse. I decide that

I will go to prom. I want to be the one to smile when Elliot takes that bitch down.

⟲

For the rest of the day I let her words build up inside of me. By the time I get home, the sight of Judah's truck parked in the lot next to my building makes my blood boil. He leans against the side of his vehicle with his hands shoved in his pockets. He gives me a nod as I exit my truck and walk toward him.

I hold my hand up when he opens his mouth. "Listen, I'm really not in the mood for this right now. I suggest you leave."

He shakes his head. "I can't do that."

My fist clenches in response at my side. I crack my neck. "I would really, really hate for this to end up like the last time."

The unamused expression on his face only makes me angrier. He pushes off from the side of his truck. "Hunter, I'm not here to fight with you. I want to call a truce."

I let out a laugh. "A truce? For what exactly?"

He shrugs. "I don't want to fight with you anymore."

"I'm leaving in three weeks. Problem solved." I step around him and start walking toward my building.

"So, that's it?" he asks loudly, making me stop in my tracks. "You're going to leave her after you fought so hard to be together."

Ollie giving me shit is one thing, taking it from Judah is not going to happen. I grit my teeth before turning around. "Are you kidding me right now?" I keep talking while closing the distance between us. "You're going to show up at my fucking apartment and tell me what I should be doing?" I narrow my eyes at him. "I suggest you leave before you miss next season too."

298

Judah doesn't budge and cocks his head to me. "Well, this isn't about you. It's about her."

I nod, still pointing my finger at him. "That's what I'm talking about right there. She is no longer a concern of yours."

"As much as you hate it, Elliot will always be a concern of mine. I love her too, and regardless of how you feel about it that's not going to change."

My nostrils flare at his words. I take unsteady breaths through my nose. "What do you want, Judah?"

His eyebrows pull in. "She loves you, and you're acting like an asshole."

"You don't know what you're talking about."

"I think you do. If you're jealous of the arrangement we had, don't take it out on her," he says harshly. "People expect us to be there together. It's the only way to put these rumors to rest. Don't you want that?"

I scoff. "Of course I do."

"Then stop making her feel so bad about it. She's completely miserable right now and it's because of you." His tone is forceful as he throws his arms up.

I take a breath. "Judah, it's not about that. I didn't break up with Elliot because I was jealous."

"Then why?"

"Why do you want to know so badly?" I laugh bitterly. "You should be fucking happy right now. There's nothing left to stand in your way."

A sad smile crosses his face. I can see the knot in his throat as he swallows. "I know —but the problem is, she isn't. She's miserable, and I can't take that away for her because I'm not the one she wants." He runs his hands through his hair. "All I want is for her to be happy. I don't have a hidden agenda or anything." He shrugs. "I just love her." The thickness in his voice almost makes me feel bad for him.

Seeing Judah this way is weird. At one point he was just

an arrogant, entitled prick who only cared about himself, but now, he seems different. The sincerity in his words seems genuine for probably the first time in his life.

I take a deep breath. "It's complicated. I'm not trying to hurt her; I just want her to be happy too."

Judah laughs. "You know, I thought leaving would make it easier." He opens the door of his truck before turning back to face me. "The funny thing is, it made it worse. I thought about her more because I wasn't there to make sure she was okay." His eyes harden a little. "Someone else was and it killed me. I'll never know what might have happened if I stayed and that's the thought keeping me up at night. I wouldn't wish it on anyone—not even you."

When he turns to get back in his truck, I get the sudden urge to stop him. "Hey, Judah."

He turns back to me with an emotionless expression.

"For what it's worth, I'm grateful for everything you're doing for her." I run my hand through my hair. "If it were me, I'm not sure I could. You're a good dude."

The corner of his mouth turns up. "I appreciate that."

Even though it pains me to admit, I know Elliot loves him too. She sees something redeeming in him, so he can't be all that bad. Even the purest of hearts get tainted sometimes, and I can't blame him for not being able to let go. That's something I'm not sure I'll be able to do myself—but I'm going to try.

43

FEARLESS

Elliot

Sitting across the counter from Oliver, I watch as he smears an obscene amount of peanut butter on a piece of bread. My face scrunches up in disgust when he tops it with an equally thick layer of marshmallow fluff.

"That's gross."

He takes an extra-large bite and speaks with his mouth full. "I'm sorry, I didn't hear you. Did you say delicious?"

I roll my eyes. "If I ate like that, I'd have an ass the size of a barn."

He pats his perfectly toned stomach. "I guess I got the good genes." He motions between us. "Obviously."

When I don't smile, he sighs. "You're going to have to tell me what happened between you and Hunter. If I don't have a

301

good enough reason for murder my defense will be shit." He pats his face this time. "With looks like this, I wouldn't last long in prison."

"I can't argue there." I continue to mindlessly pull my paper napkin into tiny pieces. "I don't want to talk to you about Hunter either."

He shoots me a look, causing a large drop of peanut butter to fall out of his sandwich. He swipes his finger across the counter and places it in his mouth.

"Okay, I'm seriously going to puke."

He scoffs. "Come on, you know Mom cleans really well." He takes another bite. "Any way, do you really expect me to believe you want to go to Cornell with Judah?"

He gives a pointed look to the stuffed bear wearing a Cornell sweatshirt I'm holding. I found it when I was cleaning out my closet earlier. Judah bought it for me when he went for his college visit last year. He held out hope I would eventually go with him until the very end.

I shrug. "Why not?"

"You don't even love him."

"Of course I do," I say defensively, sitting up straighter.

He cocks his head to me. "You're not *in* love with him."

"Love is overrated. What does it mean anyway? Two people go out of their way to constantly declare their undying devotion to one another while in the end all they manage to accomplish is destroying each other."

Oliver shoves the rest of his sandwich into his mouth. "You're preaching to the choir sister."

"I don't want to be sad anymore. Judah doesn't make me sad."

Oliver's face softens, and he mirrors my position. "That's because you don't care what he does. If you did, he would make you sad too."

"I applied to Cornell before he left. I guess I thought I

would end up there anyway. My relationship with Judah defined me in a way. Without him, I'm not sure who I am."

Oliver laughs. "That relationship didn't define you. You like how it felt to be his girlfriend. It's comfortable for you."

I cross my arms, suddenly angry. "What are you trying to do?"

He sighs, dusting his hands off on a towel. "Elliot, don't you think it's kind of strange both of you are going out your way to be as far away from each other as possible?"

I shake my head, and he rolls his eyes.

"You can fool a lot of people, but you can't fool me. Running away from this won't bring it to an end. It will just make both of you regret what you could have had."

I stand up from my stool and set the bear in my place. "It was never my choice." I shrug. "I'm just giving him what he wants."

He mutters something under his breath when I turn to walk away causing me to turn back to him. I arch an eyebrow. "What did you say?"

Ollie sighs and then walks over and slides the barstool out next to mine. He takes a seat, and motions to the one in front of him. "Sit down."

My initial reaction is to say no, but the expression on his face is strange. He looks—well, he looks serious. I begrudgingly comply and take the seat in front of him.

His chest rises as he takes a deep breath and then rests his hands on his knees. "Elle, I'm going to tell you something that might be a little shocking."

My stomach tenses. "What?"

He takes another dramatic breath and blows it out. "I'm not perfect."

I stare at him silently. Is he for real right now? When I don't respond, he keeps going.

"I know you probably need a moment to process that, but it's true."

I can't help but laugh, covering my mouth with my hand. "You're joking." I move to stand, and he grabs my arm, causing me to look down at him and narrow my eyes. "Ollie, I don't have time for this."

"Just sit," he says, his eyes pleading. "I'm actually being serious, and I want you to hear me out on this."

Color me skeptical, but I do as he asks. I retake my seat across from him and fold my arms. "Go on then."

His hazel eyes appear distant for a moment, not focusing on anything in particular. When he looks back to me, the sincerity in them strikes me hard. "I've done some things I'm not proud of." He laughs once. "Maybe that *will* be hard for you to believe because I act like I don't give a shit."

He swallows and for the first time he appears to struggle to find the words to say. Internally, I start to panic. Ollie is never at a loss for words.

I sit still as he takes a long, faltering breath. "I know what the weight of those words feels like. When you tell a girl, 'I love you'—that's it, it's end game. If you're promising a girl your heart now belongs to her, you better make damn sure you can protect it." He clenches his fist and the conviction pours out of him in a way I never imagined he could be capable of. "You want to give her everything. You want to shield her from anything that could possibly harm her even if it means yourself."

My breath hitches in my throat at the rawness in his voice. This is a rare look for him, and I'm suddenly nervous for what he'll say next.

He leans back a little. "Any guy who says those words and doesn't feel that way isn't worth a shit." His jaw ticks. "You hear me, Elle."

I jump a little at the change in his tone of voice and then nod.

"That's not the guy you end up with. You want the one

who would literally stop the Earth for you if that's what you needed." His throat bobs. "That's a fucking scary thing."

Now I'm confused. My eyebrows pull in. "Ollie, did you love someone?"

He runs his hand back and forth across the hair on his jawline, clearly contemplating his answer. If you have to think about it, then the answer is no.

Another moment passes before he laughs under his breath. He leans forward again to rest his elbows on his knees. "I don't talk about this. Not with Hunter, not with anyone." He lowers his head into hands and takes another breath. His shoulders tense and then he picks his head up and stares straight into my eyes. "That's not because I didn't want to, it's because I've never spoken those words out loud. I fucking can't."

The tightness in my chest doubles hearing the anguish in his voice. "What happened?" I whisper.

"I can't tell you everything, but I feel like I need to tell you something. You need to know that these feelings that you have…" his voice trails off, and he clutches his chest with one hand, "…are normal. It's okay if you're afraid."

He's right. I'm terrified what I had with Hunter was too perfect. That it was too special to ever feel it with anyone else again. That's what scares me.

"I've never said those words to anyone. That doesn't mean I didn't feel that way, but I knew I couldn't handle the gravity of what they meant." He takes a shaky breath. "I stood in front of the girl who owned every ounce of my soul and I couldn't say it back."

He gets quiet, and his eyes lose focus again, and then they close. "I knew I wouldn't be enough for her. I couldn't make those promises knowing I couldn't give her what she needed."

A tear slips down his cheek, and my eyes begin to burn. I can't remember the last time I saw Ollie cry. Seeing someone so strong and so confident be vulnerable like this takes my breath away. It's hard to watch someone you love struggle, especially when you have no idea they're hurting in the first place.

He quickly brushes a hand across his cheek and sits up straighter. "In a lot of ways, I was worse than I am now. What could I possibly give her when all I did was walk around like some entitled, arrogant prick?"

"That's not true," I cut in, and he laughs.

"I appreciate your need to defend me, but trust me," he says, locking eyes with me. "I was an asshole."

"But you were young, right?" I ask, trying my hardest to take away some of the guilt on his face.

He nods. "Seventeen. I was seventeen and madly in love with a girl I knew I'd never be good enough for. That's why I didn't say it back when she told me, and that's why she left." He laughs again. "Well, most of the reason."

I want so desperately to ask him to tell me everything, but I respect the fact he's shared this much. Ollie never talks about girls in the long-term, especially not with words like love.

My fingers absently pick at the frayed hole in the knee of my jeans. I look up at him and sigh. "I guess we both know what it feels like to have the person you love leave you." I sniff and hold back another onslaught of tears threatening to overflow. "It sucks."

Ollie shakes his head. "But Hunter doesn't want to leave."

"You're just saying that," I scoff.

"No," he says, more determined. "If he wanted to leave, he would be gone by now. He wouldn't be waiting around for you to graduate, chaperoning a dance you're about to be crowned at."

I'm not convinced. "He's obligated to do those things, Ollie."

He shoots me a look. "You really think he gives a shit

about finishing out his contract?" He pulls a hand into his chest. "I know him. He didn't break up with you because he doesn't love you—he broke up with you because he thinks he's protecting you. Maybe he and I were both afraid of different things, but our reasons for the doing the things we did are the same."

"So what am I supposed to do?"

Ollie smiles and it breaks the tension filling the air around us. "You have to forget about all that Monroe pride I instilled in you and convince him to stay."

I laugh once. "How am I supposed to do that?"

He nudges my knee. "Come on now. I've watched you love someone fearlessly without even giving it a second thought. You were willing to risk everything to be with him and now's your chance to show him you're not giving up without a fight."

His optimism is usually contagious, but right now I'm not so sure. It's been weeks since Hunter told me it was over, and I haven't so much as gotten a text from him. He's either really good at hiding his emotions, or he's already given up.

"I'll think about it, okay," I say, standing up from my stool.

Ollie gets up too and pulls me in for a hug. I wrap my arms around his waist, and he squeezes me a little tighter than usual. "I love you, Elle. I want you to have everything you ever wanted."

I hug him and sigh against his chest, letting all my pent-up tears finally fall. "I love you, too."

44
BLOOM

Elliot

 stared at my reflection in the mirror for the longest time before I got the strength to walk downstairs. This is the day I looked forward to for as long as I can remember. It doesn't feel that way anymore, not for the reason it should. I have the perfect dress, the perfect date, and I know without a doubt I'm about to be queen. Keeping my nomination was the last nail in Cameron's coffin. She doesn't get to win this battle. I've been fighting it for far longer than anyone even realized.

Sitting in the cab of Judah's truck, the air feels almost stifling. When Ollie told me he and Hunter were chaperoning, I was livid. Why would he want to be in the same place as me when he doesn't care anymore?

Judah's eyes shift from the road to me. "You okay, babe?"

I nod quickly. "Yeah, why?"

"You look like you're headed to death row," he remarks with a smirk.

I twist an errant curl of hair around my finger as I stare out the window. "Aren't I? I mean, Cameron is just waiting to ruin my evening. It's all anyone can talk about. If I were smart, I would just skip this night all together."

He reaches over and pats my knee to get my attention. "Elliot, look at me." When my eyes meet his he continues. "Cameron won't win tonight."

He holds my gaze for several moments before looking back to the road. "And I'm not just talking prom queen. She's not going to win period." The determination in his voice almost makes me emotional for some reason. "The Elliot I know would never be afraid—of anything. You're confident and beautiful and that is what attracts people to you."

"Well, I'm scared now. I've never been more afraid of anything my life." I look down to my hands clasped in my lap as I speak. I'm not really talking about prom, and I think he knows that. "I don't think it's fair talking to you about this."

He shakes his head. "You can talk to me about anything, Elle." I look over at him, and he winks. "That's what I'm here for, babe."

All I can do is give a small smile back as we pull into the parking lot of the venue for prom. It's being held at one of the fancier golf courses just outside of town in their ballroom. I think my father was upset they didn't have it at the lodge, but this is tradition, and most people don't like to stray from that.

Judah gives me a reassuring smile when we exit the vehicle and takes my hand in his. All eyes are on us as we make our entrance, including a pair of blue ones I see standing next to my brother in the corner. The sight of him dressed in a tuxedo makes my chest ache. It takes everything inside of me to pry my eyes away as I greet our friends.

We are immediately swarmed by groups of people commenting on how nice my dress is, how happy they are we're here together, and most importantly, how much of bitch they think Cameron is. I never wanted to start a war with her. She was my best friend for almost my entire life. If anything, what she did hurt me deeply. How could anyone sacrifice their friendship just so they could be noticed? Well, she got her wish, just not in the way she planned on.

I lean into Judah's ear. "I'm going to ladies' room. I'll be right back."

"The last time you said that you were gone for over twenty minutes."

My cheeks flush as the memory of Fall Festival flashes in my mind. We would be insane to pull a stunt like that again so close to the end. I give his arm a squeeze. "I promise I'll be right back this time."

His eyes drift to Hunter and then back to me. "Okay." The uncertainty lacing his voice brings on a new wave of guilt I attempt to push down as I make my way through the crowd. I do my best to avoid Hunter's glare as I pass him.

When I'm safely in front of the mirror in the restroom I pull my lip-gloss out of my bag. I see Cameron coming out of the stall behind me in the reflection, and I glare at her.

She washes her hands beside me. "Well, well. I see you and Judah finally decided to grace the little people with your presence." Her eyes are narrowed to practically slits as she leers over at me. "I'll bet one person is less than happy about it."

I close my eyes and take a breath before speaking. There are still a few girls lingering around us. "It's good to see you too, Cam." My voice is clipped as I turn to her. "After all, everyone loves a little competition."

She laughs once. "If you are referring to prom queen, I

would advise you not to jump to conclusions. You haven't been crowned yet."

I stand my ground. "*Yet.*" I emphasize. She turns several shades of red.

"You think you're so smart, don't you? Bringing Judah here trying to recreate your former glory." She leans into me, and I fight the urge to break her newly reconstructed nose. "I've got news for you, Elliot. You're not as hot as you think you are."

I let out an incredulous laugh. "That's cute coming from you. I think you know it's the other way around."

Her hands ball into fists, and she lets out a scream. The misplaced hatred toward me is palpable as her body begins to shake with rage. "Oh wouldn't it be tragic if little miss perfect didn't win something? All you do is use people, and they worship you for it!"

"That's not true."

She rolls her eyes. "Oh, really? What about Judah? You're willing to destroy him to prove a point. What kind of a person does that?"

My eyes scan around the small restroom as the last person reluctantly makes their way out. Girls love drama, especially mine.

"You don't know anything about me and Judah," I say through my teeth. I take a step toward her, and she backs against the wall. "And furthermore, you don't know shit about me either. If you were any kind of friend, you would have seen how miserable I was and tried to help me through it." I laugh once. "Instead you chose to use it as ammunition to try and get one up on me."

She shrugs and her indifference pisses me off even more. "Everyone has to fall sometimes. You can always be perfect."

Her level of insecurity is so unbelievable I actually feel bad for her. Not bad enough to let her win. If there's one lesson to be learned, it's that actions always have consequences. If you go into a situation maliciously, you deserve everything you get.

Tired of arguing with her, I clasp my clutch shut and tuck it under my arm. "I'm done fighting with you. I don't care what you think about me."

She cocks an eyebrow. "If you don't care then why go to so much trouble to make sure I lose?"

A smile crosses my face. "You think I had to do anything? I showed up. That's it. You were always going to lose." I lean in closer. "But I think you knew that."

Her nostrils flare as I step back and turn to walk out of the room. If she was going to say something, she would have done it by now. That's the thing about followers like her, they can't think for themselves.

The look of relief on Judah's face is almost amusing when I walk back. He pulls me against his side and whispers close to my ear. "I was worried about you. There was talk of a catfight in the bathroom."

I brush it off with a shrug. "I was just reminding Cameron of a few things she may have forgotten."

He smiles before planting a kiss to the side of my head. "That's my girl."

Involuntarily, I smile back. Out of the corner of my eye I catch a glare from Hunter and Oliver shakes his head. There will be no winning tonight with the two of them here. No matter what I do my every move with be thoroughly scrutinized.

∼

*A*fter dinner and pictures, the first slow song begins to play. I take Judah's hand, and he leads me out onto the dance floor. When I wrap my arms around his neck, his eyes meet mine as we start to sway gently to the music.

"You don't know how much it means to me that you

brought me here, Elle. I know I wasn't your first choice, but I always saw us ending up here together."

I smile. "Me too, and that's not true." He arches an eyebrow, but I continue. "I mean, I always saw myself being at my prom with you. I'm really glad you came with me."

"Really?"

The sadness clouding his eyes almost breaks me. I don't want Cameron to be right; I don't want to the one that destroys him.

"Of course," I say softly, rubbing the back of his neck with my hand. "You'll always be important to me."

He bites his lip, spinning us around, away from the crowd as much as he can. He lowers his voice. "I wish I would have realized how important you are to me."

When I open my mouth to speak, he smiles. "Let me say this, okay?"

I nod, smiling back.

He takes a breath. "I wish I would have fought harder for you before I left, but I can't change that now. All I can do now is make sure you don't make the same mistake I did."

My eyebrows pull in. "Judah, what are you saying?"

"I'm saying, I don't think you should give up. You clearly feel strongly for him, and I would hate for you to settle for something that isn't what you really want."

I grab both side of his face so he has to look directly in my eyes. "Being with you is not settling."

He smiles again. "I know that, babe." He glances over his shoulder and then back to me. "But, I also know what you really want—and I think he knows that, too."

I laugh once. "I can't believe you're the one telling me this."

"I love you, Elle. If that means I have to let you go so you can be happy, then that's what I have to do."

Hugging him closer, I press my lips just below his ear. "I love you, too. You know that, right?"

He nods quickly, swallowing back the emotion he tries so desperately to hide from everyone except me. Without thinking, I pull back and kiss him once. "Thank you, Judah. For everything."

He gives me a genuine smile. "Always, babe. Always."

I take comfort in the friendship that was able to bloom between us from the love we've always had but were too afraid to show each other. All of the pain wasn't for nothing. It made us stronger. Now that we're able to love ourselves, hopefully we can love others as well. I know I can, and I have faith he'll be able to do the same.

When I cast a glance over my shoulder at Hunter, he's visibly struggling to keep it together. I watch him hand something to Oliver before walking brusquely toward the exit.

My heart begins to pound, and I consider running after him. Oliver's words play over and over in my mind, and the moment to bring this all to an end feels like it's slipping away. Those thoughts are interrupted when Poppy Lincoln takes the stage in front of us. She grips the microphone with a smile while holding a small silver envelope.

The music fades out and all the attention shifts to her. "Hey guys, I'm sure you're all just as excited as I am for this. It's time to announce this year's queen."

I exchange a heated glance with Cameron right before Judah wraps his arms around me from behind. "You got this, babe," he says in my ear.

I bring my hands up to grip his arms and take a breath. After all, this is the moment we've all been waiting for.

Poppy's crimson lips curl into a wicked smile as she peels back the envelope. Her eyes light up as she reads. "Well, it should come as no surprise," she says enthusiastically. "This year's prom queen will be—"

SAVE THE LAST DANCE FOR ME

Hunter

J can't watch them anymore. It doesn't matter if we aren't together, there's only one person Elliot is supposed to be with, and it isn't him. Reaching into the pocket of my jacket, I pull out the flask Oliver gave me earlier. He said I would need it and he was right—again.

After taking a long pull, I twist the cap back on. Oliver nudges my shoulder with his. "You cool?"

I shake my head. "Not really." I hold the flask up so he can see before tucking it back in my jacket.

His eyes drift to the dance floor where Elliot and Judah appear to be in an intimate embrace. "It's almost over, man. They're about to announce the queen."

My teeth clench as I continue to stare at what should be

mine. I want all of her moments, not just the ones nobody sees. "I don't care," I say suddenly.

He raises an eyebrow as I hand the flask to him. "I have to get out of here." I look back to the dance floor again, and her eyes meet mine before I turn back to Oliver. "Cover for me, okay?"

Oliver grips the flask in his hand, his eyes narrowing. "You're really going to leave?"

I glance at Elliot and then back to him. "Please, Oliver."

"Okay," he says, uncertainty in his tone.

I shoulder past him before I can change my mind. It feels like I hold my breath until I reach the hallway right outside of the ballroom. I take deep breaths and pace around with my hands clasped on top of my head.

Is it wrong for me to want to leave before it's over? I know I told her it was over and she should move on, but it doesn't mean I have to watch it anymore. My hand reaches in my pocket, and I grip my keys. With one last glance at the doors I turn around and walk straight to the parking lot.

$\sim$

J drive to my apartment in silence. After all the music blaring from the dance, a little quiet is in order. Before getting out of my truck, I lean over and grab the six pack I got at the convenience store on the way here.

Sitting on the tailgate, I crack the first bottle. The way this night is going I'm sure there will be many. No matter how hard I try, my thoughts keep going back to her. Oliver was right yet again, whether I'm there or not, I'm still going to think about it.

I'm working on the second bottle when Oliver's truck pulls into the lot. I laugh because he must have bailed too. I smile as I wait for him to get out of the truck. All the air escapes my lungs when Elliot does instead.

She walks over to me with her dress bunched in her left hand, her crown still on top of her head.

I nod to it as she stops in front of me. "Congratulations." I tip my beer to her before tilting it back. "But the dance isn't over yet."

"I know," she says softly.

"Then what are you doing here?" The sarcasm lacing my voice is unintentional, but I keep going anyway. Seeing her with Judah is something I'll never get used to and maybe I carried some of that bitterness with me. "This is your prom. You only get one of them."

She smiles, but it's so painfully sad my own heart twitches. "I had to tell you something."

My stomach begins to twist up again. "And what's that?"

She takes a breath, stepping closer. "I came to tell you I don't care anymore."

That's when my heart completely stops. I clutch my chest to make sure it's still in there and am surprised to find it beating erratically against my palm. I swallow hard. "I get that."

She shakes her head, smiling a little more. I raise an eyebrow when she walks even closer. "I don't care if you think you're not good for me, because I know you are. I know I've spent every moment since you've been gone thinking of ways to change to your mind about us."

The heaviness increases with each word to the point where it's crushing me from the inside out. "Elle—"

She steps in front of me and places her hand on my knee. "Just let me say this first, okay?"

I nod.

"All I could think about since this day began was how important everyone thinks it is. It's like all of your high school memories come down to this one night and everyone wants to hear your story." She takes a breath and then smiles a little. "Do you want to know what I want my story to be?"

I shake my head slowly.

"One day when someone asks me how my prom was I want to be able to tell them I had the perfect dress, the perfect date, and at the end of the night I had my last dance with the person I love."

I swallow the lump in my throat. "But that won't be true, will it? You basically sacrificed everything you've been looking forward to just to be with me, and I've been acting like a jerk the entire time."

"That's not true." She moves between my legs and pulls the bottle from my hand and sets it down beside me. "For the first time in my life I listened to my heart, and I'll never regret that." She laces her hand with mine and pulls me off the tailgate. "So, what do you say—will you dance with me?"

Elliot nods her head to the empty parking space between our vehicles, and I laugh. "Right here?"

"Yeah, there's still time. It's not over yet."

She bites down on her bottom lip while she waits for my answer. I hold up a finger before reaching inside my truck to switch on the radio. I flip through the stations until I find a slow one and turn the volume up enough to hear it. Neither of us even know the song, but I don't think that's what matters.

As we move together in small circles on the pavement, I think about my future and how I can't picture it without her. She remains quiet in my arms and then she presses her head into the crook of my neck.

"Don't leave," she whispers.

When I don't reply, she lifts her head and searches my face. I gently place my hand on the side of hers. "I wanted to do the right thing for once, but I don't think that I can. I can't leave here knowing I left behind the one person in this world I can't live without." I lean down and kiss her once. "I love you, Elliot. I'm not going anywhere."

The smile that breaks across her face melts away all of the

rest of the doubt still lingering inside of me. How can something that is supposedly so wrong feel so amazing? She doesn't give me an answer and she doesn't have to. Being apart was never the solution, and I think we both knew that. I'm just lucky she was strong enough to show me.

~

Graduation day holds a much deeper meaning for me than prom did. This actually signifies we can finally be together, and nobody can hold it over our heads anymore. When I watched Elliot walk across the stage earlier today, I felt relief. There were so many times over the past year I thought we weren't going to make it, and somehow, we remained strong. The bond we have is stronger than all of the obstacles that stood in our way and now we get to just —*live*.

I watch her load the last bag into my truck and it makes me smile. Although I insisted she attend the graduation party this evening, she convinced me to spend it at her family's lake house instead. To be honest, it didn't take much convincing.

"I think that's everything," she says with a smile, walking over to me. Her arms wrap around my neck, and she kisses me once. "We have the whole weekend to ourselves."

I run my hands up and down her sides before kissing her again. "You have no idea how good that sounds."

"Oh, I think I do," she says against my lips.

"Hey lovebirds," Oliver calls from the side door as he steps outside. "Don't leave yet."

He jogs over to us, and I let out a sigh causing Elliot to pinch my side.

"Ollie, we're kind of busy right now," I say in frustration.

His face scrunches up as he takes in our current position. "I can see that." He gives a shrug. "I guess it's something I'll have to get used to. I could think of worse things than being able to spend more time with the two people I love the most in this world."

Elliot's mouth drops open, and I pull my hand up to my heart. "Ollie, you love me?"

He scoffs and shoves me in the arm. "You know what I mean, asshole. I'm just saying it makes me happy you both are so happy."

Elliot narrows her eyes at him. "Oliver, are you on drugs?"

He laughs loudly, tossing his head back. "Um, no, actually. Over the past few months I've unwillingly been a part of this whole charade and it made me realize how much you two actually love each other." He pauses and runs a hand through his hair, a smile hinting on his lips. "It made me think that maybe that's not so bad."

"Love?" Elliot asks skeptically.

Oliver shrugs, but then he winks at her. "Yeah, well—you know for other people."

She gives him a knowing smile. "You'll never change."

He winks back at her. "And I have the testimony of countless women who thank me for it."

His insistence on playing the field can't last forever. I'm willing to bet one day soon he really will change his mind, and I'll be more than willing to help him through it.

~

*A*fter spending the majority of the evening in the bedroom, Elliot and I decide it's time for the fresh air. We grab a blanket and share a lounge chair down by the dock. I wrap my arms tighter around her from behind. "You cold, baby?"

She turns her head and presses her lips to mine. "No, I feel perfect."

Perfect. I couldn't think of a better word to describe how I feel right now. I smile and then lean down to speak close to her ear. "You know, I was thinking about what I want my story to be, too."

Elliot twists herself around so she is facing me. "Oh yeah? I'd love to hear it."

"Well," I begin, tucking a strand of hair behind her ear. "I would want to tell them when I was at the lowest point of my life I fell in love with a girl who gave me her whole heart even though I'm not sure I deserved it."

Her face scrunches up, and I put my finger to her lips. "Let me finish," I say with a laugh.

She gives me a look to continue, so I do. "And I would want to tell them despite all our attempts to destroy each other, it only made us stronger."

There's a tear in the corner of her eye, so I brush it away and kiss her softly. I pull back and hold her eyes with mine. "But most of all, I would want to tell them that even though the journey we had to take to get here wasn't always pretty—in the end, it was beautiful."

THE END

ACKNOWLEDGMENTS

I wrote this book in under a month—and then proceeded to rewrite it fifty times over the past two years. There was a point (many if I'm being honest) where I wanted to light it on fire and be done with it. I'm glad I didn't. I'm so excited to share this series with everyone. It was a long time coming and I think it got to a place I can be proud of. There's so many people I want to thank, so I apologize if I miss anyone.

T.J. – You will never read this, but your unconditional love and support is what gets me through basically everything.

Amy and Lauren- Unfortunately I made you guys read every rough draft and you claimed to love every minute of it. You're amazing friends and I don't know what I'd do with you.

Sarah Hay- For nearly fifteen years you've shown me unwavering support no matter what I decide to do. And I know I change my mind a lot, so thank you for continuing on this journey with me. Your friendship means so much to me.

Wendy Million- I don't even know what to thank you for first. You're my editor/proofreader/English teacher, my voice of reason, writing bestie—so many things. I'm sure you've wanted to strangle me a time or two over the past three years, but I think that's what you love most about me. I'm so excited to enter this world of publishing with you. This is only the beginning. #texasforever

Sarah Hansen- (Okay Creations) Thank you for the amazing cover. I'm so in love with your work.

My Beta team- Melissa Rivera (Rogue Readers), Amy Halter (Obsessive Book Whore), Kirsten Moore (Beta Bitch), and Stephanie Howes. This book wouldn't be what it is today without you guys. Your insight and guidance is priceless to me and I look forward to working with all of you on the rest of the series.

Dawn and Rachel (Yours Truly Book Services)- Thank you for all your help. It was a pleasure working with you for the final (and most important) steps of this book. Looking forward to many more.

My Wattpad readers-I can't thank you enough for all of your comments and inspiring words. This was never something I planned on doing, and without all of your support I'm not sure I would have. You're the best readers!

ALSO BY COLE LEPLEY:

Cherry Grove Series:

Tragic

Tamed

Torn (Feb. 2020)

Tortured (March 2020)

Did you enjoy Tragic? Why not leave a review and tell others how much you liked it?

A NOTE FROM THE AUTHOR:

Did you enjoy Tragic? Want to read more? Follow me on social media for updates.

Did you like Ollie? Want to read the first chapter of his story?

Here is the first chapter of Tamed, Coming January 2020.

TAMED: CHAPTER 1

REMEMBER THIS

*O*liver -**Present Day**
Another season, another group of girls ready to be molded by yours truly. I have to admit I'm a little bit nervous with Elle not leading the team but my general awesomeness should be enough to pull us through.

I twirl my whistle around my finger as I pace along the bleachers and watch my mediocre crop of senior girls run sprints. It's only three weeks until our first meet so I better see a drastic improvement if I have any shot at ranking this year.

"Relax," Hunter says from behind me. "It's only the first week. They'll find their rhythm."

I turn back to him with an incredulous look. "Rhythm? Elliot could run laps around these girls without even breaking a sweat."

Hunter laughs. "Well, not everyone can be like your sister. She's one of a kind."

The look of admiration on his face when he speaks her name almost makes me nauseous. That's what love does to you. It makes you weak. Once you submit to them it's all over. You slowly turn into a shell of your former self and are somehow convinced you're happy about it. Well, not me—at least not ever again.

I turn back around to face my team. "Okay, that's enough for today. Take a lap and you can be done. Practice resumes tomorrow at four o'clock sharp. Don't be fucking late!"

A serious of nods and grunts echoes from the field and I smile. I turn back to Hunter. "So, what do you say? You up for some wings and drinks at The Roost?"

Hunter looks thoughtful for a moment. I know he wants to come but I have feeling he's thinking of a way not to disappoint me.

"Elliot has…"

I hold my hands up. "No, dude. You can't keep bailing on me now that your dirty little secret with my sister no longer comes with a stint in the slammer."

He runs his hand through his hair and sighs. "I'm sorry. She's been really busy with track at WVU. This will be the first night all week we get to spend together." He stands and clasps his hand on my shoulder. "You understand, right?"

I nod. "Yeah, yeah. I hear ya."

He smiles and turns to walk away. "Rain check," he calls over his shoulder.

At this point I'm not sure there is enough days in the year to cash them all in. I start shoving my equipment into my bags and the girls begin to slowly make their way off the field. I catch Principal Bellamy walking toward me out of the corner of my eye.

"Mr. Monroe," he says with a grin. "It looks like you have quite the team this year." He gives a pointed look to the athletes jogging off the field. Truth be told, they look more like cheerleaders than serious runners, but who am I to say what a track star looks like?

I sling the bag over my shoulder as I stand. "Yeah, I'm seeing a lot of potential, sir."

He scoffs. "I bet you are." He flips his sunglasses on top of his head before he meets my eyes. "That's not why I'm here. It seems our little problem from last year resolved itself without any major complications. I would like to think we won't be having any repeats if you catch my drift."

I swallow hard. "No, sir. Absolutely not."

He laughs once. "I like you son, but you and I both know you're full of shit."

"Mr. Bellamy, I assure you, everything will be by the books this year. No drama for me."

He laughs louder this time. "One step at a time, Oliver." He pushes his sunglasses back down and pauses. "There is a faculty meeting tomorrow morning at seven-thirty before homeroom. I expect you to be there. We have several new additions that I would like to introduce, shouldn't take longer than fifteen minutes."

"Sounds good."

He gives me a wave before walking back toward the field house. It's no secret Hunter and Elliot were the reason for the scandal last year. With the help of myself and a few unlikely sources, we were able to keep it under wraps until after graduation—*barely*. Even though they could never prove what happened, they've taken an extra special watch on the younger staff, which most definitely includes myself. No more one on one practices for me I guess.

It's not like I would ever take advantage of my position as an educator. I know I'm attractive, that's obvious—but it doesn't mean that I would allow myself to fall for one of these girls. I'm smarter than that.

~

*A*s I'm driving down my road, there's several cars lining the driveway of the Reed house across the street. This wouldn't usually catch my attention, but the house has been vacant since Mrs. Reed passed away several months ago. A part of me still feels guilty for skipping that funeral, but I had more than one reason to avoid it.

I do my best to brush it off and pull up my winding driveway. The houses on the street are far apart enough that even your closest neighbors can't be seen very well from your own property. Ours is the largest. The crown jewel of Cherry Grove if you will. I'm sure a lot people think it's easy to live a life like mine. They would be wrong. It's not easy always falling short of your families expectations. That's why I don't even try anymore.

The sight of Elliot's car in the driveway makes me smile. Even though she's only twenty minutes away at WVU, it's weird not to have her around all the time.

When I enter the house through the side door, she's seated on the floor in the living room with stacks of clothes piled around her. I pause in the archway and lean along the wall.

"What are you doing?"

She looks up at me with a confused expression. "Laundry. What does it look like I'm doing." She continues folding her jeans and I nod.

"Yeah, but someone does that for me. They fold it and everything."

Elliot throws her head back and laughs. "That someone— is mom." Her eyes roll. "You seriously need to learn how to do things for yourself."

I shrug and then walk over to take a seat in the large chair beside her. "Nah, I think she enjoys it." I smirk at her, but she's clearly not amused.

"What are you doing tonight?"

"A whole lot of nothing. I asked Hunter to go out and he said he already had plans." I give her an irritated look and she laughs again.

"You can come, too. We're just going to dinner."

I scoff. "Oliver Monroe is not a third wheel."

She finishes folding her last pair of jeans and adjusts herself to face me. "You're not a third wheel, Ollie. We can all hang out together. We always did before."

"Yeah, but it's different now." I scrunch my face in disgust. "You didn't kiss each other and call each other gross fucking pet names before."

She smiles wistfully and I almost throw up in my mouth. They've been really laying it on thick now that they don't have to hide anymore. I guess nine months of pent up public displays of affection are all coming out at once.

"You know," she says, her lips curling into a more sinister smile. "It would be nice if you found someone to settle down with. Then we could have a double date and you wouldn't feel like you were intruding."

It's my turn to laugh. "Now you're just talking crazy."

"Come on. I've never seen you give anyone even half a chance." She stands up from the floor, picking up one of the baskets with her. Her eyes lock back on mine. "How will you know if you never even try?"

Her words penetrate to the deepest part of my chest. The part that I ignore completely. I have tried before, maybe not enough, but I gave it my best shot and it still wasn't good enough. So, instead of showing her that I actually do have a heart buried in there, I press my lips together and remain oblivious.

Elliot rolls her eyes at me and then nods to the other basket on the floor. "Well, could you make yourself useful and help me carry these out to my car. Hunter is waiting for me."

I do as she asks and follow her back out into driveway. My eyes remained fixed on the fence that lines the property. I can't see the house from here, but it doesn't stop me from trying.

Elliot pops her trunk and I set the basket inside. I nudge her arm. "Hey, did you see all the people at the Reed house today?"

She tosses her long, brown hair over her shoulder with a small laugh. "I don't make it a habit to spy on the neighbors. Why?"

I shrug. "No reason. It's just I haven't seen people there in a while and I wondering what was going on."

"Maybe they're selling it."

I shove my hands in pockets and take a few steps down the driveway. "Maybe."

"Why do you care?" she asks from behind me.

I don't turn around. I can see their driveway from here and my heart picks up a few notches. "Curious I guess."

When she comes up beside me I'm so caught up in my thoughts I almost jump. She raises an eyebrow. "You seem awfully concerned." She crosses her arms and gives me a quizzical look when I glance down to her.

"Charlie might be there," I say without thinking.

"Do you still talk to her?"

My stomach knots, twisting my insides into a familiar lump. Elliot has no idea what she's asking. Not a lot of people do and I'd like to keep it that way.

"Nope," I say casually and then turn back to the house. "Tell Hunter to give me a call when he stops being a little bitch."

She laughs and then calls after me, "Will do."

I don't break stride until I'm all the way in the house. I pause in the kitchen and lean over the island with my palms flat on the granite. The coldness of the stone does nothing to calm the fire that starts to burn inside of me.

I still remember the way she tastes and the breathy way she used to say my name. Every time I close my eyes I can picture every smile she ever gave me and how I would give anything to have just one more.

This time when I close my eyes, that's not what I see. What I remember the most is the last time I ever saw her. That's the face that haunts me now and I'd do anything to never see it again.

Printed in Poland
by Amazon Fulfillment
Poland Sp. z o.o., Wrocław

50523839R00190